SPELLBOUND EMPIRE

Poppy Rose Solomon

First published by Poppy's Pages in 2024

www.poppyspagesediting.com

©Poppy Rose Solomon 2024

All rights reserved. No part of this publication may be reproduced in any form or by any means without the written permission of the publisher. The moral right of Poppy Rose Solomon to be identified as the author of this work has been asserted in accordance with the Copyright Act 1968.

Written by Poppy Rose Solomon

Edited by Pauline Menchavez and Ellyssa Paik

Cover art by Robert Ixer

Cover design by Haylee Buswell (HB Pencil Designs)

Paperback ISBN: 978-0-6456986-6-4

eBook ISBN: 978-0-6456986-8-8

A catalogue record of this book is available from the National Library of Australia

The author acknowledges the Gubbi Gubbi and Palawa/Pakana peoples, the traditional owners of the lands this book was written and published on. Respect and gratitude are extended to elders past and present.

For Angie, Zeus's first fangirl and the greatest creative
friend I could ask for.

MAP

The World of Woken Kingdom

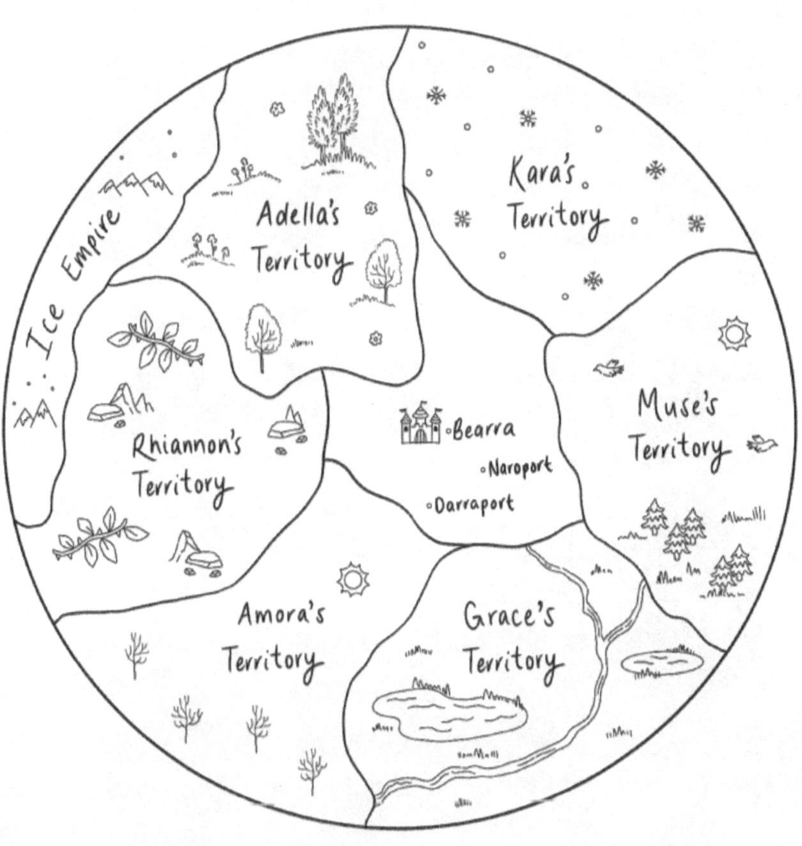

PROLOGUE

SOMEWHERE, SOMETIME...

The compass exploded in Elm's hands and the two children leapt back as it hit and singed the workshop's wooden wall – already scattered with burns from failed attempts.

Isla panted, mouth agape as her best friend hastily flicked a wave of golden Adellan magic to put out the fire. 'Is that normal?'

Elm's eyebrows knotted in frustration. 'It's a compass,' they replied. 'It's supposed to *point*. Exploding wasn't an option. Enchanted or not.'

Isla slumped at the workshop table. 'Then why did that happen?'

Elm paused, with a scholarly, thoughtful expression on their face that didn't match their eleven-year-old features. 'I can only think of one explanation,' they whispered. Isla gave them a hopeful stare, but

Elm only shook their head, not meeting her gaze. 'Your parents are . . . nowhere.'

'Hm?'

'There's a reason the magic couldn't work. You can't find someone that doesn't—'

'Are you *certain*?' Isla bit her lip to scare back her tears, but as her adrenaline from the exploding compass wore off, the reality of what it meant came crashing down. Her chest tightened like her heart was crushing itself. Wilting. Flickering out like a weak candle. The blood drained from her face, and the milky skin of her hands turned blue despite the warmth of the workshop's fireplace.

'I used all the magic I had,' said Elm. 'Your parents . . . Isla, I'm sorry, but I don't think they exist. At least, not anymore.'

Elm sat beside her at the wide, messy workshop table. Though people called Isla and Elm prodigies, Isla was quickly realising how ill-prepared the two were to deal with the reality of her parents' whereabouts. It certainly shouldn't be Elm's responsibility to tell her they were *gone*.

The inventor had only moved to the Ice Empire two years ago, scouted by a royal advisor and brought here from Adella's Territory to work for the queen and king. Isla wondered if Elm missed their family, but those people didn't seem to care about their child. They'd given Elm up, after all, and now Elm was more than happy in their Imperial workshop.

And thank goodness, because the young toymaker was Isla's best – and only – friend.

Elm's dark fingers brushed back their tight curls, eyes now focused on a doll in their other hand. They watched as it swung its arm up and down on its own – traces of magic evident in every stroke. Enchanted toys were Elm's specialty, and their works were favoured greatly by the children of the empire. In fact, people of all ages loved Elm, paying the inventor with money and magic to make yet more brilliant toys. Elm didn't only create trinkets – they created joy. And between their sweet looks and their high standing with the royals, no one could resist Elm's charm.

Unfortunately, Isla did not have the same effect. She was sharp-featured and sharp-tongued, an unlikable young woman with dubious heritage. While she was merely tolerated and respected by the masses, only Elm and Candace loved her. It didn't matter, though; just as Elm was renowned for their toymaking, she would one day be renowned for her strength in politics and war. She, alongside Candace, would lead the empire into a new age of success.

She tightened the ribbon in her dark-blonde hair. 'What if my parents had magic to protect themselves? Something to hide themselves, so even another spell can't find them?'

Elm gave her a sad look. 'Then they don't want to be found.'

'Not even by their daughter?' She swallowed to fight the persistent prickling behind her eyes. Leaders did not cry. Candace never cried. Isla stared at the red bricks of the workshop instead, and let her eyes wander the masses of half-made inventions strewn on the stone floor. Counted them. Ten, eleven . . .

But the walls betrayed her, pressing in and drawing the fireplace dangerously closer, waves of pressure radiating on her pale skin. And though the workshop was dotted with the most whimsical objects, straight out of a fairy tale, the sheer amount of stuff was cramming her mind so deeply she couldn't make sense of her own thoughts.

How could she be a good leader if she couldn't even control what was happening in her head? Why couldn't anything at all be simple and clear, the way she liked it? Clean as fresh, white snow?

'Just ask her,' Elm said. 'Your mother— I mean, Candace. I know she hasn't told you much about how she found you, or if there were even any clues. But she might if you show her you're ready.' They winced, as if knowing their next words wouldn't land on happy ears. '*Or* you could ask Zeus. He'd help you, if only to show off his connections. But that's exactly what you need. Otherwise it's time we assume your parents are—'

'No.' Isla placed her hands on the table and looked at Elm seriously until they met her gaze. 'I told you, we can't tell anyone. I can't . . . People can't know that I'm . . . That I feel—' Isla took a sharp breath. 'I can't let Zeus have something else over me.' She pressed her nails into the wood, grounding herself. 'And Candace would be devastated if she found out I was searching for my birth parents after all she's done for me.'

Elm shrugged, but Isla could sense the doubt in her friend as they said, 'I'll help you either way.'

'Great.' Isla sighed. She straightened her back and shook out her hands, prying them from the table. 'Then we think of something else. The next step. There must be something we haven't tried. A different enchantment . . .'

'Or, for now, can we take a break?'

Isla stopped, and, unable to take their pitying gaze any longer, changed the subject. 'You could be doing greater things with your skills. More than just making toys.'

This was their *other* regular topic of discussion.

Elm sighed, turning away to observe the mess on the floor. 'I care for you and your mother,' they mumbled, their words scripted from previous arguments, 'but I won't ever agree to make weapons. I make toys. I help people. Candace wants to take things from people. I can't be part of that. Not violence.'

'What violence? With your inventions, the things you could enchant – imagine it, Elm. There wouldn't even be a war. We'd be ruling the world within a year.' *And I'd have so much more reach to search for my parents.*

'Hold this,' they said, ignoring her words and passing her a small stuffed bear. She bit her lip and held it for them. Rather than turn back to their work, however, Elm watched her. With a pinched brows, they mumbled, 'Doesn't work.'

'What?'

'The bear's enchanted to heat up when you hold it. For children in the winter. It should be warm by now.'

Elm was clearly over her attempted persuasion of getting them to work for Candace, but she was happy as long as they were done talking about her parents. She was about to respond with some affirming words about the bear when—

'*Fairies!*' Isla shouted as Zeus burst through the door. She threw the bear at the tall, light-haired prince.

He caught it in confusion before yelling, 'Ow!' and hurling it at the wall. 'Did you pull that thing out of a fire?'

'What are you doing here?' Isla demanded, now more irritated than shocked. Though she was a little proud of how fast she threw the toy – her fighting reflexes were getting even faster.

'I came to visit my two best friends, but I was attacked by a bear!'

Best friends. She scoffed. The two of them didn't like the prince very much, and he surely didn't like them very much either. But to Zeus, that was the allure of spending time together. Unlike everyone else in the empire – who was either soldier-like and devoted to the prince, or adoring and obsessive, or utterly fake and seeking some gain from him – Isla and Elm barely tolerated him. Isla, because of the disdain between her mother and the royals, and Elm because they were Isla's best friend.

Unfortunately, due to their positions, the three of them were regularly forced together regardless of how annoying Zeus was. Their 'friendship' was more out of desperation for company in this icy empire than any similarities or compatibility.

Elm picked the bear off the floor curiously. 'It *is* hot. Isla, try holding it again – see what happens.'

She stepped back. 'Don't burn me!'

'If it gets too hot, put it down right away. I already need to adjust the enchantment if even our strong, brave prince couldn't handle it.'

'Now—' started Zeus.

'Okay.' Isla took the bear again. It was warm – anything was warm in the Ice Empire if it wasn't frozen – but not hot. And the longer she held it, the cooler it turned in her hands. 'I see,' said Zeus. 'It only wanted to burn me. Thank you, Elm.'

'No,' replied Elm as Isla passed them back the toy. 'It only doesn't work on Isla.'

Isla turned to hide her face. This again?

'Do you know if Candace has put any wards on you to block magic?' asked Elm.

She shrugged. It was difficult enough feeling so different from others – not knowing who she really was, having to live up to Candace's expectations and the expectations others put on her *because* of Candace. If Candace had done something to her, to make her impervious to magic . . .

Isla could be icy, but she was no snowflake. She didn't want to be protected like that, and she certainly didn't want others thinking she couldn't handle herself.

Unless, unless.

This wasn't the first time magic acted strangely around her. Not the first time an enchantment didn't work. It must be Candace protecting her . . .

Unless it had something to do with her real parents.

CHAPTER ONE

'There's been another assault.'

'I— Excuse me?' I nearly choke on my mouthful of pie. 'Where?'

'Oh, my apologies,' says the young pirate girl on the other side of the table. 'Your Royal Generalness, Saviour of Bearra and Queen of Some Empire Somewhere. *Isla Khirina.* Would you please be so generous as to *pass the salt?*'

I swallow. 'Right.'

Of course Wren has mistaken my confusion for arrogance. Everyone loves to think the worst of me. When will I stop embarrassing myself?

Candace gives the orange-haired girl a reproaching look but says nothing, and I blink, passing the porcelain shaker hastily as I pull myself back to reality. I'm supposed to be a leader, not some *idiot.*

It's all been getting to be too much lately. I can't hear a word without expecting something terrible to have happened. I can't get a moment's sleep without nightmares about Lire destroying the Ice Empire. And I can't get through a second of the day without the Bearrans making it as clear as they possibly can that they absolutely *hate* me.

It isn't that I care; I've never been liked. What I care about is being respected and obeyed. Yet they don't give Zeus the same attitude, despite us being in extremely similar situations. A power-hungry prince is acceptable, lovable if he's good-looking enough, charming enough. But a powerful woman with no title or history to her name? Oh, she needs to be humbled.

'Isla,' Queen Dawn says at the head of the table. Her partner, Relia, is by her side as always. The two are like a woven flame: the golden curls and the scarlet cascade. It's awfully dramatic. 'Tell us, have we done an adequate job of celebrating your Ice Festival? Or is this an embarrassingly tacky imitation?'

Tacky doesn't begin to describe it, I think, glancing at the paper snowflakes hung from the ceiling in one of the castle's dining rooms, and the spindly pine tree stuffed in the corner. The sconces around the room give off flickering candlelight that bounces back off the windows, only making the room feel hotter. To rub salt in the wound, the measly dinner the Bearrans have put on barely has any cake, let alone the sweet delicacies of the empire.

Our uneasy alliance makes the evening all the more awkward. But I have to admit this gesture was a step in the right direction.

I give Dawn a small, politically unassuming smile. 'All of us from the Ice Empire are simply grateful for your hospitality.'

The Ice Festival is a weeklong celebration of our culture and achievements thrown throughout the grounds of the castle and beyond, a grand party bursting with magic and warmth. But Bearra is always *too* warm, the cursed place. The dinner party Dawn has thrown hardly scratches the surface of the festivities currently happening at home. Although, a small aspect of home is more comforting than none at all – something I'm sure the Bearrans and their friends must understand too.

In Bearra's castle, with its high windows and half-crumbling exteriors, everything is a hundred years old or broken from the battle held here only two months ago. It was once lovely, I can imagine, but now it has a haunted air that's stale on the lungs and surfaces grimy with blood. No matter how much they clean, those red stains won't come out of the cracks in the brick.

Despite the archaic architecture, the castle's inhabitants reflect youth: lost young people who have, like me, found themselves at the forefront of a war.

Once, Zeus and Elm were the only people my age that I knew. At dinner tables, or the parties of leaders, or galas where we were on display, it would be us and a hundred adults. Bearra, meanwhile, is full of the young. Including pirates, the last type of people I'd expect to be leading a kingdom.

Though one of the Neptune's crew members – Ebony, if I'm remembering correctly – is off on a mission to save the fairy Amora, along with the half-fairy boy and that girl he protects with his life – Maya.

I don't know these people well, but they're all anyone in the castle wants to talk about. Whispering about how Maya's mother was killed in the last battle – and that's why her family no longer spends time at the castle – or how the pirate, Lark, is always moping because he doesn't get to see Maya's sister, Briar, all that much, even though they're *clearly* in love. It's impossible to escape the gossip, the heartbreaks and stories.

Oh, and one of the pirates, Levi, is Zeus's *cousin*. Because my luck isn't bad enough – there has to be another one.

The drama of this place, honestly. They're all so focused on their own problems, I don't know how they get anything done. If not for me and my army, and if not for my mother, Bearra would have next to no protection. Next to no leadership. And they still treat me like an outsider in this place that should be, in a fair world, *mine*. That was the deal we made.

'Speaking of gratitude,' says Candace, her eyes sparkling but her lips straight with politeness. 'We must exchange presents soon.'

The usual excitement of Ice Festival gift giving – arrays of sweet treats, new faux furs, and charmingly shiny things – is very much dulled here. The best present I could receive would be a trip home after my two torturous months in this summer kingdom, trying to wrangle Bearra into Candace's control. *Or* a messenger coming to tell me Lire is dead.

Across the table, Zeus nudges Relia playfully, giving her a glimpse at a box he has hidden in his sleeve with a pink bow on top. The muscular prince and the delicate lady make a funny pair. Suddenly close friends – something about a quest for a mirror. I'm certainly not jealous, but it does bother me that he, the only other person from the Ice Empire here, is very publicly not on my side.

Not that we were ever on the same side, for anything.

He hands Relia the little giftbox and I can't help but remember the three shimmering white horses he gave me last Ice Festival. I don't even like horses. That man is all show. Which is why, when I donated those horses to the army, he couldn't say a word against it.

All that to say, I doubt he got me anything this year, now he's so distracted by his new friends and this horrendous kingdom and his big plan to completely stomp all over me and everything I've built for my—

'Well then,' Dawn says, with a small grin at Relia, and I realise I've been tearing apart the seams of my napkin. 'Let us commence the giftings!'

As the table explodes into excitement – particularly the raucous pirates – Candace turns to me, and we swivel our chairs to face each other. Even in the most formal, crowded Ice Festival dinners, we have always exchanged our gifts this way. In our own little world.

My mother's softly curled strawberry-blonde hair and green dress display her likeness to a real fairy. But it's the smile lines around her mouth and the creases by her eyes that I see. The reminders that this woman raised me, has always loved me; that this is the person who taught me to be strong.

She hands me a doll-shaped gift wrapped in soft green cloth, her fingers lingering as I accept it. 'This might be a lot for you to understand,' she says, a little awkwardly, 'so take your time.'

'You're not sure I'll like it?' I softly tease. She always gets me wonderful gifts; no one knows me like she does.

'That's one way of putting it.' She doesn't meet my eyes. 'Sugar, this was with you when I found you in the snow. I . . . thought it was time you have it.'

'*What?*' I whisper, our bubble bursting as I feel like every eye in the room whips to me. Could this be from my real parents?

I should have a thousand questions, but I'm too shocked to register any of them. There are too many people in the room for me to have an outburst of emotion. I swallow back rising nausea.

She nods. 'It's true. I'm a few months late; I was going to give it to you for your eighteenth, but I didn't have the courage. Now I can see you're ready – more ready than me – to take life into your own hands.'

I take it from her gently, wanting to cradle the object, protect it. The room goes silent around me, and in my mind, we're in our bubble again, but now there's three of us: myself, Candace, and this present. The cloth falls through my fingers as I gently unwrap it.

My entire life I've searched for any clues of who I might really be. I've worked to prove myself in the Ice Empire, prove myself to be worthy of being Candace's daughter because I had nothing else. And now there's . . . this.

A *nutcracker?* I run my thumb across the red paint of its wooden arm. It's a soldier, with a tall scarlet hat and white gloves. Its soft face gazes up at me through kind blue eyes.

'It's enchanted, I think,' Candace says. 'Like something Elm would make.'

'But how? What does it do? Does it—'

'Lead to your origins?' She smiles sadly. 'I investigated it, Isla, but no. There has never been anything I could find about you. And that's part of why I kept the nutcracker to myself. I was afraid it would only add to your hurt and confusion.'

'But what does it mean?' I'm distantly aware I'm shaking my head, both mesmerised and frantic. 'Why would I be left with this?' The noise of the dining room comes crashing upon me again, shaking me from the outside in. 'Candace, where – what – how— What does it mean?'

'It means,' she says gently, 'that whoever left you for me to find didn't want you to be entirely alone.' There's a flicker in her eyes. Uncertainty. The most she would ever show of it, at least. 'Sugar, it's only a cheap plaything. Nothing special. I haven't even worked out what the enchantment on it is – I can just sense something in it. Your parents may have picked it out as something small to leave with you. You were so tiny, so vulnerable. They must have wanted you to have something to occupy you, maybe to protect you in some way. But it's lasted all this time. When I found you in the borders, it was clutched in your fingers.'

'My family,' I mumble, almost choking on the word. 'But if they didn't want me to die, why leave me out in the snow? If they didn't want me, why not give me to an orphanage? And if they were hoping I would die, why leave me with a toy?'

Her hand touches my shoulder. Warm. As always. 'I know as much as you do. I wish I could do more to help.'

But you always used to tell me that, while you were hiding this, I want to say. As if my heartbeat can protect it, I hold the nutcracker close to my chest.

'What's *that*?' Zeus says. I make the mistake of turning to tell him to go away – he whips around and snatches the nutcracker from my arms.

'No!' I scream at him. Horrendous behaviour for someone in my position. He holds it up by its arm, dangling far higher than I can reach. '*Zeus*!'

He gives me a playful expression. 'Darling. It's just a toy! Wait – is this one of Elm's? What does it do? Run around on its own?' He plays with the lever on the nutcracker's back, opening and closing its mouth. 'Does it *magically* crack the nuts?'

'Excuse me!' A flash of red hair appears at his side. 'What have I told you about teasing people?' Relia demands, glaring sternly at the prince.

He pouts. 'I'm only allowed to grab things on weekends and my birthday. And certainly not on special occasions.'

His arm lowers, but the nutcracker is whisked away by the tall, dark-haired girl. Sierra. She observes it like a scientist. 'Now why is everyone fighting over a little toy?' Her smirk is deadly. Of course it is – she's a Reed.

My hands tremor. 'Give it back.'

Zeus rolls his eyes and snatches it from Sierra. He smirks at me. 'You can have it if you say please.'

I look to Candace – like a child wanting its mother's help – and she only stares back. *Fight your own battles.* But I'm at my wit's end with these Bearrans. They're killing me! Making my life more than difficult.

And Zeus has been pestering me my *entire* life. Never mind that I was the only person he could turn to – who saved his life – when he got himself cursed to turn into a bird by Sierra Reed.

Why can't anything be simple?

Tears prick at my eyes. They were already threatening me, and now in my anger, they're pressing at my head like a flood against a dam. I *won't* let him win. 'Zeus. Give it to me. Now.'

'Or what?' he says, grinning again. It's only a game to him. How could he know what this toy means to me? How could he know what anything means to me when he can have anything he wants, whenever he wants?

I take a breath and stand straight. Put on my deadliest nonchalant face, channelling Candace. 'This is my kingdom,' I say flatly, with my eyebrows just slightly raised. 'The disrespect is over. *All* of you best hear this final warning. If Bearra wants the Ice Empire's protection, it will work to deserve it. I will be shown appropriate behaviour, and if not, I won't hesitate to use more forceful methods. I'm here in peace because I don't want to make an enemy of Bearra or you, Zeus. But I could take this kingdom by force – I *will* – if I must.'

He swallows and deflates. The tension in the dining room is horrendously thick, snappable. But I'm in control.

'Thank you,' I say with a small smile.

He obliges defeatedly as I reach out my hand. I curl my fingers around it, my breath loosening with a deep exhale. But a butler walks past with a tray of tea and bumps Zeus.

The prince jerks and the nutcracker falls. A spray of steaming liquid. The butler stumbling. Tea leaves splatting to the floor.

My nutcracker lands on the tiles.

Crack.

I cry out but Zeus drops to his knees even before I do. 'Sorry – I'm so sorry – I was only joking – I didn't mean to—' His pants become damp with the spilled tea, and it must be burning him, but I don't care, I'm not here anymore. All their words, their bumbling, becomes background noise.

A traitorous tear rolls down my cheek as I pick up my nutcracker. All I have of myself, my family. Its arm is broken, all the way down, two of its fingers dangling halfway off. I cradle it in my hands and step out of the room wordlessly, shamefully, unable to meet anyone's eyes. Least of all Candace's.

◆♡◆ ♣ 🪆 ♣ ◆♡◆

Although I know I'll take the nutcracker to Elm to repair it as soon as I can, I feel as if something has been irreparably damaged – the toy, my past, my parents, my *soul*. My place in Bearra, which I deserve but have never been truly given.

I'm here fighting a war against Lire, fighting for the Ice Empire, for Candace, doing everything I wanted to do, everything I've spent my life training for. Why does it not feel . . . good? I'm stressed, but shouldn't there be at least some level of satisfaction?

I bathe, and cry, feeling completely unlike the feared general I am, and then climb into bed – though not without a notebook and pen, ready to continue writing plans until I fall asleep. It's too hot for any blankets, so I nestle amongst the hard pillows and pull only a single, thin sheet over my legs. I wipe my eyes one last time, then resolve that it's time to stop being emotional.

I could handle everything before tonight, and I'll handle it again now. To do that, I need to simplify things. The nutcracker – which at first I thought could be an important piece of the puzzle – is a new puzzle in itself. And in the middle of this war? I don't have time for *games*. So I'll do my best to put it out of my mind.

A knock on the door makes my gut clench – *no more people, please* – and a guard announces the queen, barely keeping the trepidation out of their voice. Maybe they heard me banging my head against the wall earlier.

'Hello, Isla?' Dawn clears her throat. '*General* Isla? I would like to speak with you for a moment, if you're awake.'

I bury my head in my hands for a second and groan. 'One moment,' I call, hopping out of bed and closing my notebook. I wrap the thin Bearran robe they lent me around my body; I'm so used to heavy faux furs and layers that sometimes here I feel naked. 'Come in.'

The door creaks open. Dawn is, naturally, glowing and kind-looking and sweet and lovely and perfect.

Meanwhile I have a face freshly blotchy and red. I straighten and try to look brave. 'How can I help you, Your Majesty?'

Her skirt swishes as she enters, her golden hair shining as if we were in sunlight, not moonlight. 'I'm sorry to bother you now, but it felt important to talk to you after tonight's dinner.'

'Did it.' I catch myself in the mirror, hazel hair out of its typical neat braid, swept into a bun barely holding together. My eyes are cut through with crimson. At least I'm taller than the queen. By a little. And I'm willing to bet, far stronger. I'd never beat her in beauty or lovability, but at least I could win in a physical fight. *That's what really matters.* I'll tell myself that. Though she does have a Strength blessing from Rhiannon . . .

I sit at the end of my bed, and she takes a seat at my desk by the window. She watches the moon for a while – because of course she can sit there and watch the moon. Who has ever cared about *her* wasting their time?

'So?' I say.

'So, sharing power with you has been an adjustment.'

'I wouldn't say that, since you've barely adjusted.'

She shifts. 'What I did, letting you in, agreeing to your terms . . . It was a decision made out of desperation, and one that most of my people did not agree to. Don't believe I've come out of this unscathed.'

'Sure, but I don't hold any empathy for you. This is war.'

Her kind face drops slightly. 'Do you ever wonder if this sort of attitude is why people don't like you very much, Isla?'

Blood rushes to my face. 'Do you think people would worry about *liking me* if I were a royal like you? If I was Zeus?' My fists clench the bedsheets. 'Did you come in here to insult me, or to tell me something important? I would like to get on with my work so I can get some sleep for once.'

'My apologies,' she says, blinking slowly. 'Truly. I shouldn't have . . . It isn't like me to be cruel.'

'No, it's like you to be Generous, and Passionate, and Wise, and—'

'A lot of pressure for a young woman to be under, don't you think?'

Well, yes, but I have just as much pressure without any of her privileges. 'Is that your apology? An excuse?'

She takes a moment before responding, sitting perfectly still. 'I dislike being at odds with you,' she says. 'It doesn't help either of us. There are people far less like me that I've had to learn to tolerate – even love. Maya, Sierra. Even Relia. In another life, you and I could have been friends. So why don't we try?'

'And I suppose this would be on *your* terms. *Your* idea of friend-ship.'

There's nearly a flash of irritation in her eyes, and I take that as a slight win. She continues, 'I want to come to a better agreement about how we can work together. The Ice Empire may own Bearra, but I'm still its queen. I'll tell my people to be kinder and try to work with you, and in return, I wonder if you could be a little . . . warmer. Ask your troops to relax and make Bearrans feel less afraid of the Ice Empire's influence here. Win them over by appealing to them, not by force. Be our friend, Isla. It will make everything much easier.'

I bristle. I *hate* this stigma. That all my hardships stem from my personality – not the world I live in. That if I was just more amenable, more gentle, more quiet and less brash, all my problems would go away. No, they wouldn't – I'd just stop being everyone else's problem. 'I don't owe you anything. Nor do my soldiers.'

'Which means you won't take my suggestion, even if it would help you, too?'

'It won't help me, because it won't work. On your end, at least. You think you can simply tell everyone to be more welcoming? You think I haven't *tried* to be friendly? You think you'll get Zeus to stop being a hyperactive puppy? If you can guarantee things will run more smoothly, and that my power will be taken seriously, then I'll give Bearra more leniency. But until then, I won't stop being *cold* just to let your circle walk all over me. I meant what I said at dinner. The childish behaviour is over.'

Dawn keeps a straight face, but I'm *sure* I detect her lashes twitching slightly. 'Like I said, if this is our situation, I would rather work with you than against you. My friends want to punish you, despite how you saved us, and despite me asking you to. I recognise that and I'm trying to apologise. I'm inviting you to move forward with me. General, I am sorry.'

I lean back. I thought she was here to manipulate me, but maybe she really does empathise with my situation. The genuine apology has caught me off guard.

How much more powerful would we be together – how much more powerful would Bearra be – if the two most powerful young women in the world could just get along?

Could I give this friendship a try? If it turns out she has bad intentions, if it turns sour, I'll know soon enough and put a stop to it.

And even if her circle doesn't follow, her support alone would benefit me greatly.

'Your apology is accepted,' I say, but I don't give her the satisfaction of appearing kind or accepting. Instead I lace my words with scepticism. 'And you have a deal. Try not resisting this one.'

Dawn grins. I wonder if she ever *hasn't* gotten something she wants. 'See you tomorrow for a strategy session,' she says. 'I've already had a room set up for us. Sierra and Arden might join.'

Typical. 'And Relia and Zeus?'

'Now, what do you think?'

'Put my chair on the other side. I can't concentrate over constant giggling.'

When she leaves, I admittedly feel lighter. Like the tension has dropped and my head has cleared. I leave my notebook closed for the night and crawl back into bed.

Before I blow out my last candle, I observe the nutcracker again. Laying flat on my desk, broken and miserable.

With a pang of guilt, I get up and stand it upright on the windowsill. I kiss it on the forehead and face it towards the moon. Maybe it can see my parents, sense them out there somewhere.

I follow its gaze and hope, wish.

My bed engulfs me once more and I fall asleep watching my nutcracker, allowing my mind to wander, allowing myself to feel, and imagine, and pretend my family really do exist. Elm believes they don't, but this nutcracker is a sign, isn't it?

Somewhere is someone who gave me up.

And someday, I'll find them.

CHAPTER TWO

It's still dark when I wake, and I'm as restless as the twinkling stars. Moonlight sparkles through the window along with a cool breeze that protects me from the relentless Bearran heat. The nutcracker, standing on the windowsill, casts a long soldier's shadow across the room.

I curl into the comfort the shadow offers, but it isn't much use. Thoughts of my parents stir within the darkness, cutting through any potential for peace. My limbs itch to get up and move.

In what short sleep I did manage, the nutcracker flooded my anxious dreams. It came to life, fighting by my side in battles. Then it led me to a house made of children's building blocks. They kept shifting, all of indeterminable size and shape; there were no paintings on the walls, or cushions on the chairs. An echo of a life. Light-haired people warmed themselves around a fireplace lit with grey fire.

The nutcracker held my hand with its unbroken arm and pushed me forward to meet the family, but they wouldn't turn around. They wouldn't respond to my calls. The dream was hazy and numb, but every time I spoke and they ignored me, I became more and more frantic, my panic sharp and vivid.

Who are you? Who are you? Who am I?

I rolled awake before they could turn.

Now unable to resist, I slide out of bed to observe the nutcracker again. My shoulders tense as I approach it, though the tightness between my brows softens as I take a deep breath and stretch my neck. In the soldier's silhouette I see my mother and father. I see that grey fire. When I pick up the toy, it's warm to the touch, the paint soft and smooth.

Guilt and heartache rush back in as I remember how it was so stupidly broken. At once I want to collapse into tears again, or punch Zeus in the face. I turn the nutcracker so I can inspect its wounds, and

. . .

What in the seven fairies?

It *was* broken, wasn't it? I suck in a breath and nearly drop it. The nutcracker's paint seems to have a fresh brightness, glossy in the moonlight, and the joints are perfectly intact. Good as new, no sign of any break.

I reason with myself, tamping down my shock. How many magical toys have I seen in Elm's workshop? This is nothing unusual.

But of course, this isn't one of their inventions – it's something of my parents'. Why would my family leave me with a toy enchanted to repair itself?

I slip on a robe and take the little soldier out into the hall, hoping to find somewhere with fresher air and better light. I know I told myself I wouldn't go down this path, that I have no time, that I need to keep my emotions controlled – but if I can spend a few moments inspecting the nutcracker, isn't it worth trying to unlock its secrets? I can't sleep anyway.

The hallways are lit with candles that servants must keep an eye on through the night. They aren't bright enough, though; I'll have to find somewhere else. I pad my damp forehead with my sleeve and return to my room to put my boots on. I hate walking around here without shoes. The unfamiliar, gritty stone flooring makes me shiver with discomfort.

Once I'm laced-up, I step quietly past the other rooms, many still in a state of half-repair. Candace sleeps in the suite next to mine when she's here overnight, which isn't often, and as for most of the Imperial soldiers, they choose to stay out in the encampment. I would rather be with them, but to not reside in the castle would be to admit it isn't *mine.*

Since Dawn and Relia sleep in the royals' quarters on the other side of the castle, I'm left lumped in with the array of foreigners – including, once again, the *pirates* – who have made this their home.

I note each door: the one that houses the famous Teddy and Maya, the one for Sierra and Arden, then Zeus, then Levi and Ebony, then Lark, then Wren. There are no other leaders, no highly-regarded Bearrans or advisors, because no one else is in Queen Dawn's exclusive circle of young companions.

Her offer of friendship was genuine, I believe, but how I'll ever be accepted by – or hope to wrangle – this group she's created, I have no idea. Especially if Zeus is determined to continue being so—

There's a crash, and *of course* his face appears around the corner.

I groan, pressing my fingers against my temple.

'Ah!' he says, and a bucket rolls along the shadowy floor. 'Kicked it. It's dark.'

I have no words. I shake my head.

He glances at my nutcracker and his face pinches up shamefully. 'My dear Isla, I'm very sorry about that.'

'*Zeus.* What are you doing, causing trouble at this hour?'

'I'd ask what *you're* doing wandering around, but I'm well aware you're a bad sleeper. Should've known I'd see you out here.'

'Then you should have known to stay away and not bother me.'

'*Then you should have known*—' He stops himself. 'I'm sorry. I've heard enough lectures today about my behaviour. You, Relia, Dawn. *Fairies.* Everyone seems to forget I'm a prince.'

'Because you don't act like one, and I've usurped all your power.'

'Well, you're *trying* to.'

'You're an imbecile.'

'And yet we're best friends.'

'Good night, Zeus.' I turn on my heel and strut towards my room.

'Wait!' He hurries up to me, his feet thumping. 'I've already sent for someone to find you a replacement, uh, nutcracker. Really, I am sorry.'

My breath catches, but I try to stay impassive. 'Oh – you didn't have to. It's . . . already mended.' I show him the soldier's arm. 'See?'

'Elm's here?' He grins widely, and for a second the image of him in front of me wavers, and all I see is a panting dog that's just heard the word 'walk'.

'No. They are not.'

He slumps. 'Why let me get all excited, then?'

I want to hit him, but then again, don't I always? If only Elm really were here, they might take some of Zeus's attention off me. I could use my best friend right now.

'That reminds me,' I say, deciding to utilise my now ironic advantage over the prince to shut him up. 'Remember when *you* broke your arm?'

He makes a sour face. 'Don't be cruel, my sweet Isla.'

'Well, everyone here seems to know your secret anyway. Love turned you into a bird, and who had to pick up the pieces of your mistake? Me, of course, as always. Is it really too much to ask for five minutes without babysitting you?'

'Yes?'

'*Zeus.* Please, will you simply let me enjoy a nice walk on my own?'

'No. I don't want to.'

I huff, hurrying past him and his kicked-over bucket, hoping to leave him in my wake. He trails at my ankles anyway.

'How about we get a drink?' His fingers brush my arm, and I slap him away.

'Do you seriously think—'

He's about to argue when I hold up a hand. His mouth clamps shut as my expression goes from furious to serious. *Fairies,* what is that?

A soft red light filters through a window, turning the silvery moonlight scarlet. My breathing stops. Goosebumps rise over my arms and shoulders. I step back as the light intensifies. Zeus's eyes follow it too. He inhales sharply.

Before I can decide on my next move, he pulls me from behind into a far wall of the hallway. His hands grip around me – one on my waist, the other over my mouth – and I'm trying to shrug him off when a whirl of magic shoots through the window.

Glass sprays like falling rubies as the blast hits the wall opposite us. The brick crumbles – not that it was particularly *un*crumbled, since the previous attacks. I loose a breath, turning to look at Zeus; he's still gripping me tightly, my skin burning where his hands touch me. We share a glance.

Did he just . . . save me? No. There's no way. I would've moved in time on my own. Besides, magic has never affected me the way it does others. Whatever wards Candace placed upon me as a child, I doubt even a magical blast as powerful as that could *really* hurt me. The debris, however?

I shake away from the prince, regaining my composure, and inspect the damage. It would be stupid to look out the window knowing whoever attacked us could be readying their next attack, but I want to know what we're working with. I inch closer, trying to understand their purpose.

How did they get past the lines of Ice Empire soldiers outside Bearra, and the castle's guards? Is it just one person, or a group, an army? And why attack us here? Are they after Zeus? Me? The queen?

Their magic is Rhiannon-red, but that could mean anything with this war's complex loyalties. Plenty of Lire's followers have accumulated power from afar.

I sneak towards the smashed-in window. Zeus motions for me to come back, but I shake my head. This is my job. I'm brave, while he hides away. That's how it's always been.

He harshly whispers, 'We need to call for help! Get back!'

Because he thinks I'll take orders from *him*? I can deal with this on my own, and if I do, it might prove to the Bearrans how capable I am. If I call for help, they'll see me as weak. Under no circumstances can I let that happen, regardless of whether Dawn wants us to be friends.

The magical light increases again, like blood soaking through white fabric. I peek my head around slightly to get a look, and . . .

Catch a glimpse of a beating wing. Scaled and glistening.

I jump back. Oh, *fairies.*

'Um . . .' I try to tell Zeus, unable to form my mouth around the fearsome truth. The fairy of strength is here. *What on earth is the fairy of strength doing here?*

I resist the urge to scream for Candace. She'll hear me, and she'll come. But I can't be seen relying on my magical mother every time there's trouble.

Still, I'm not used to dealing with actual fairies. They leave us alone in the empire. That is, except for Kara, who we had a flimsy alliance with, and Candace is still cleaning up the mess we left saving Bearra without consulting her first. People are intimidated by Kara. That's how she retains her power. But even with all the stories my mother told me about the fairy, I've never met her, let alone *fought* her.

So, Rhiannon, here, attacking . . . *me*? Tonight?

My nutcracker is still warm in my cold hands, and I place it in a safe corner. There's no time to hide it in my room, but if anything happens to it . . . Well, I suppose it'll repair itself again, won't it? But I can't be distracted by the toy. I need to be ready to fight.

Fairies. All I wanted was a moment to myself to contemplate the nutcracker. Couldn't I have had a minute or two before disaster? This simply wouldn't happen in the Ice Empire!

A dragon's silhouette forms in the glowing red light and I widen my stance so my legs don't fail me. Zeus dives behind me. I whip my iron dagger out of my boot.

A gust of wind blows fresh remnants of glass through the hallway as Rhiannon soars inside and lands in a ball of searing fire.

I gulp, awed – as is natural when it comes to meeting fairies. I'm stopped dead for a few moments.

Her bare feet bear no signs of injury as she steps across the glass shards towards me, her ankles wrapped in thin, thorny vines that bloom with red roses at her knees. Her dress is woven around her in maroon threads; scrappy but elegant, tight but breathable. It reaches up to her neck, where a fountain of thin braids fall, her hair the same raven shade as her glistening skin. Within each braid are woven strings of rubies, which are mirrored under her eyes; a spattering like freckles, as if she's been splattered with blood.

The fairy is dressed for war.

And the dragon wings? Where do I even *begin* with the dragon wings?

I draw in a shaking breath, losing my composure as the tall fairy looms over me. Despite her territory being closest to the Ice Empire, her jungle like a thick border between us and the rest of the world, I've never seen her in person.

Where our values are order and ambition, hers are rooted in chaos. Where our landscapes are ice cold and colourless, hers are thick with heat and vibrancy. She, our opposite, is a key reason the empire hasn't been able to expand south-east. We're enemies, only one of our empires fated to win.

With that deadly scowl on her face, I know she feels the same.

'Away!' shouts Zeus. 'Back, fairy!' He waves his arms frantically. 'Whatever you want with me – the prince of the Ice Empire – you have offended us by breaking this . . . This . . .' He points to the gaping opening bordered by jagged glass.

I blink at him. 'Did you forget the word *window*?'

'I'm in shock!' He lifts his hands.

Rhiannon seethes. 'If you think I'm here for that joke of a prince, you'd be very wrong.' Her voice is deep and raspy; it slithers into my ears like hissing snakes. 'Child of the false fairy.' She eyes me, and it's as if an invisible force is reaching into my gut, turning me to stone. 'You shall accompany me to my territory. I will hold you as insurance against Candace until she and the empire are taken care of. *Do* feel free to fight me before I take you. It'll be far more fun that way.'

My shoulders relax. This is hardly my first attempted kidnapping for ransom. That's far easier to handle than if she were outright attacking the kingdom.

Zeus scoffs. 'If you're taking Isla, you're taking *me*. We come as a pair. And we are very much equal in ransomability, except that I am more powerful in almost every way, making me the far superior target.'

'If I might make a humble request,' I say to the fairy, folding my hands neatly, my dagger still gripped in one, 'please leave the prince behind.'

Her eyes blaze with magic. 'This is no negotiation, children. I am not here to talk. I am here to fight, and to leave with my prize.'

My nutcracker remains hidden in its shadowed corner. Candace would want me to face Rhiannon, but what would my parents want me to do? Would they ever have expected their daughter to be leading an empire and a kingdom? To be going up against fairies? Would they have wanted me to fight, or to surrender, or to run, or call for help?

None of them are here. It's just me, and who I've become. A woman who has become so cold she can command the Ice Empire's armies. A woman who makes her own decisions – and is never wrong. For better or worse, I *am* ice. I'm in control.

'I'll remind you Kara is my ally,' I tell Rhiannon. 'She won't be . . .' I trail off for a second as the Gracian pirates sneak into the hallway. Sierra and Arden momentarily blanch with confusion at the sight of Rhiannon and the chaos in the hallway. '. . . happy with your decision.' I blather on about alliances and other political drivel so I don't give the pirates away.

Sierra suits being bathed in red; teeth bared excitedly at the prospect of a fight. She's killed a fairy once – what would stop her from trying again? But she and Arden are still weak from the coma they ended up in after the last battle, only two months ago.

Zeus opens his mouth, relieved to see the warriors, but I reach out and dig my nails into the skin on his wrist. *Don't give them away.* He topples, groaning. Rhiannon cringes at him.

'So are you not concerned,' I say to Rhiannon, still trying to keep her distracted while Sierra and Arden have the element of surprise and can *hopefully* think of something to do, 'that taking me will set off a larger reaction than you're hoping for? Or is that exactly what you want?'

The fairy licks her wine-coloured lips. 'It's been many weeks since Lire attacked Bearra, and what has come of it? The war has begun, and still people stand afraid to make a move. Afraid of the Ice Empire, who I have warded off from the rest of the world for a very, very long time. Remember that I wrapped *this* kingdom in vines, sealing it away. That magic remembers me still, and I could strangle Bearra again.' Her fists clench. 'I will fight you, General Isla, if no one else will. I will defeat Candace. I will show the world that it is not you, and it is not Lire, who is in charge. I will always be the fairy of strength. I will win every war.'

'Then you've shown up a bit late,' says Zeus. 'Like you said, the big battle happened months ago.'

Her gaze flashes with venom. 'That squabble will seem like child's play by the end of *my* war.'

No one else has appeared yet. We're in a deep corner of the castle, and there aren't guards hanging around since we can all protect ourselves. Candace hasn't come to save me. Rhiannon doesn't seem to have brought any backup.

We aren't outnumbered, but our chances here aren't perfect.

Sierra, dead still behind the fairy's scales, gives me a sly expression that says she's itching for a battle. Her partner doesn't seem to think the same; he's gripping her arm, holding her back.

Didn't Muse kill his friend? Of course doesn't want to lose Sierra to a fairy too.

'Rhiannon,' I say, resolving to get this over with. 'I see we aren't getting through this without a brawl, then?'

She grins. 'Unless you choose to surrender. But please, don't. And Reed?' She whips around. 'I've been waiting to see you again. You owe me a story.'

Sierra doesn't flinch. With thrilled eyes, she cocks her head. 'Here's the thing. I meant to—'

The fairy lobs a ball of magic her way. Sierra ducks, expecting it, while Arden catches the beaming red in his own Gracian-blue power, rerouting it into another wall that *shockingly* crumbles.

I let out a sigh. Everything with these fairies, with these Bearrans, with the pirates, with all this magic, is so *dramatic.* And for what? Why can't we just talk like *normal* leaders? Why can't we battle like regular soldiers?

I hold up my iron dagger and stand in front of Zeus, the prince a shivering mess. 'Rhiannon,' I command, 'ignore the pirates. I fight my own battles. Let's do this like real warriors.'

Her wings stretch, deathly-sharp, horned tips scratching the bricks as they extend too wide for the hallway. 'That dagger isn't going to do much. I'm at my most powerful in Bearra.'

The *triarue.* Well, that's fantastic.

I lean into a fighting stance – but Sierra beats me to it and tackles the fairy from behind. A nasty cut thrashes open on her cheek as her face slides across the edge of a scale. Rhiannon hits the stone floor and bursts with red energy, throwing the Reed off her with a dome of magic that rips the paintings off the walls.

How are there still any walls left?

With Sierra in the action, my strength returns. All that talk about fighting my own battles *was* just talk. I was really hoping Sierra would help. A general needs soldiers, after all. Together we've got a chance.

I roll down and stab my dagger at Rhiannon's neck – but two steps ahead, she laughs wildly and tosses me to the side. I hit my shoulder on a loose brick and groan. I go at her again and try to land a hit, but she flicks me away with a wing, pinning me against the wall. A scale pokes into my sternum, and I struggle to breathe, kicking to find a foothold. My toes barely touch the floor as she scrapes me up the wall, choking me.

Rhiannon, with a hungry smile, raises one fiery hand at Sierra and Arden and another at Zeus, who is, well . . .

The prince is pressed against the wall all on his own.

'*Stop,*' he wheezes weakly at Rhiannon, but the fairy doesn't even notice. I roll my eyes, even as I clutch at my chest trying to let in more oxygen. He whines to me, 'Well what am *I* supposed to do?'

'Now that I'm winning, where shall I begin?' Rhiannon muses, continuing to ignore him. 'Should I let you all go? Give you another chance so we can keep fighting? Or do I kill you all now . . .'

'Let us go?' suggests Arden, flinching as Rhiannon's magic glows brighter in his direction.

She flicks her eyes to Zeus. 'Do I start with the meddling pirates, or the babbling prince?'

'You're just going to leave me out?' I choke. My fingers are turning numb. Is that a bad sign?

Her wing presses harder against me, and I nearly cough up an entire lung. 'You know I can't kill *you*,' she says. 'You know what you're worth.'

'More than *me*? Really?' says Zeus. 'I mean, she's perfect, beautiful, strong . . . But so am I! Why does no one want me?'

'Shut up, Zeus,' Sierra and I say in unison. Despite our situation, we share a small smirk. *Are we finally bonding?*

Levi appears behind Sierra and Arden, rubbing his eyes with his large, pale hands. 'Do you mind keeping it down? You woke m—' He notices the fairy holding us at the brink of defeat. 'Oh. Never mind.' He raises his hands.

Zeus waves at Levi. 'Cousin! I had the most shocking dream I wanted to tell you about. There was th—'

'Yes,' Rhiannon seethes, eyes narrowing. 'I'll start with the prince.'

'No!' he shouts, dropping to his knees. 'My people need me!'

Her magic becomes a blinding dagger of fire, glistening so bright it could be the middle of the day. She pulls her arm back, steadying herself to strike, the rest of us threatened and frozen.

I feel the *slightest* amount of anticipatory grief. I won't miss Zeus, but that doesn't mean I want him dead. That said, my focus is mostly taken up by the fact that I, myself, am slowly choking to death.

'No! No!' Zeus dives behind my nutcracker and holds it out like a shield.

Coward! I want to scream at him – better he gets hurt than the only gift I have from my parents.

He's still screaming as Rhiannon throws her gleaming-red dagger. I cry out as it explodes through the nutcracker and blows Zeus's perfectly sculpted skull in, blood spattering—

Except it *doesn't*. It's as if lightning strikes. Rhiannon's magic flickers and she flinches as it bursts back to her, sparking like a firework. The nutcracker glows, then the entire hallway goes dark. Zeus's hands shake as they grip the toy, still held in front of him, his last-ditch shield.

'Is this the afterlife?' he breathes raggedly. 'My psychic told me there'd be more gold.'

Rhiannon heaves, her grip on me loosening slightly as her nostrils flare, her face contorted in confusion and anger. I let in a flood of air, panting in relief.

Zeus and I glance at each other, then at the nutcracker.

Not a scratch on it.

CHAPTER THREE

The city was . . . unfathomable. Maya Nova's eyes blurred, the image of the place she once knew flickering out against the now lifeless grey streets.

The caved-in buildings that were once vibrant pink and red, now dusty and colourless. The plentiful flower beds that had given the air a sweet aroma and decorated the city in patterns Maya dreamed of painting – gone. Even the territory's signature calming haze was no longer.

When their enchanted carriage stopped at the outskirts of Amora's Capital, Ebony – who came to find her parents – fell to the burnt grass, clutching charcoal beneath her fingers. It stained the Amoran pirate's knees, ash imprinting on her tan skin, in her clothes.

The city looked as if it had been abandoned centuries ago, not destroyed within the last week.

Teddy, his auburn hair and pink cheeks the only remnant of the city's colour, clasped a hand over his mouth. He reached for Maya, grasping for her comfort. With grief weighing her bones, she lifted his arm and pressed herself beneath his shoulder.

The weather was warm, and together they were stifling, but there was no way she'd be apart from him. Not when the closest place he had to a home was rising in smoke before his eyes. Not when he must've known, based on the damage done here, something terrible must have become of Amora.

Amora. The lovely rainbow-winged fairy of love, of passion, of adoration. She was the fairy of all things beautiful. And she was . . . gone?

Maya was running away from the memories of her mother, following Teddy as he strove to defeat *his* mother. And in their search for Amora, the person closest to an actual parent to Teddy, their hope was dwindling faster than they could keep up with, suppressed under insurmountable heaviness.

When they found out Amora's Territory had been ransacked, the fairy missing, Maya and Teddy couldn't stay put in Bearra. Not while Amora was in trouble. Not after all she'd done for them. Barely weeks before, Amora had begged them to go with her, to stay in her palace, where they might be safe before the last battle.

If they had, would they have met the same fate as her, or would they have been able to protect her? Lire did this out of spite, and so much of her spite was because of Maya and Teddy. *Was* all this destruction their fault? Had they left this city in ruins because they refused to surrender?

Maya, like the rest of the world, once believed fairies were invincible. But since Sierra killed Muse, any such rules had been thrown out the window. There was no more balance, no more certainty. Now, with all of Amora's magic removed from this city, it felt like she could be dead too.

'They're somewhere,' Teddy said. He looked to Ebony, who pressed her forehead to the ground, her shoulders wracking with sobs. 'Ebony, they're somewhere. They can't all be gone. Amora would've had a plan. She would've protected her people. They've escaped. That's what happened.'

Maya worked her jaw. She hoped it was true, she really did, but it was so difficult to have any faith when she couldn't tear her eyes away from the ruins of Amora's Palace.

It was now a few weeks since Bearra's castle was half destroyed by another attack from Lire – the attack that killed Maya's mother. Since then, Maya had tried, tried so very hard, to turn cold. To be clear-sighted and decisive, to focus on winning and nothing else. Focus on what she could do, practically, to get through each day. She could grieve after the war, couldn't she? And if they lost, if Maya died too . . . then at least she'd never have to deal with it at all.

In that first week after it happened, she shed her tears alone, crying at night once Teddy was asleep. She held her father's hand, and her sisters'. It was her father she worried most about. Maya had Teddy. Prima had Matthew. Briar had Lark. Who could the bookmaker turn to now, with his girls all grown up and his wife gone?

For a few days, Maya stayed with Briar and their father in their family home, but both the girls found it difficult to be there; their mother was everywhere. In the smell of flour in the kitchen, in the fingerprints stamped in the paint on the walls, in the cushions she'd sewn.

Unable to take it, Maya moved back to the castle to be with Teddy and help Dawn. Prima and Matthew had taken residence in Aunt Olivia's old house. Briar spent her time between home and the castle, she and Lark going between.

At least if nothing else was going well, those two seemed to be. The pair had known each other barely a couple of months. Love at first sight wasn't real to Maya, but to them, it seemed right.

And if she'd thought Wren, Lark's little sister, would be a problem, jealously keeping the pair apart to protect her little family, it was the opposite. Wren was their biggest supporter. Maya could tell she was thrilled for her brother, particularly that Lark had someone else to focus on so he wasn't always worrying over her. Plus, Wren adored Briar, and often travelled with Lark when they went home to spend time with Maya and Briar's father.

In fact, Wren had all but moved into Prima's old bedroom. She loved being in the bookmakers' house, whether Lark was there or not, and spent days on end there, enraptured as Maya's father told her stories and showed her how he worked with cloth and paper and leather.

Once, Maya came home to find Wren fast asleep, her head resting on her father's lap. She hadn't seen her father that relaxed since her mother's passing. He would always be a father, and Wren always longed for parents. In their own way, they helped each other, became a new family. Maya's eyes watered and she hurried out of the room. Without having seen this, she may not have found the courage to leave and follow Teddy to Amora's Territory.

She raised her eyes again to Amora's Palace. Smoke rose from a soot-covered turret, like some cruel joke of a chimney. The main entrance, a tunnel-like opening Maya remembered being able to walk right into – because *everyone was welcome inside* – was now caved in. No lilting music flowed from the palace, no laughter.

Maya expected devastation – *The capital is gone, along with the fairy,* they'd been told – but seeing it for herself was so much worse. If anything, it reminded her of Bearra when she'd first woken: rotting, dead, a ghost of what it once was.

And yet she didn't shed a tear. Couldn't. She wondered if this was it. If she'd finally seen enough. If she was really broken this time.

Ebony pushed herself to her feet, wiping her eyes. 'Time to go.'

'Wait— We can't just—' Teddy began, tensing at Maya's side.

'You want to find them or not?' Ebony demanded, back to her usual stoic nature. 'You said it yourself. They can't all be dead. Amora is being held somewhere. I know it. Lire wouldn't let all that power go to waste, would she? Her people have fled, and we need to rescue the fairy. Let's go.'

Maya knew the pirates were tough – like Sierra, they could handle a lot – but wasn't this too much to bear? Maya had a pit bigger than her grandmother's mausoleum in her stomach. The exhaustion of their situation weighed on her so heavily she couldn't imagine taking a single step.

'How? Where?' asked Teddy, his voice small. 'Where could we possibly begin?'

'Did you come on this mission expecting it to be easy?' Ebony flipped her enchanted weapon out of her belt. It turned into a knife, which she worked at with her fingers; the only giveaway she was still feeling something. 'We didn't come here to cry. We came here to rescue a fairy and her territory.'

'And we will,' Maya urged. She needed to defend Teddy and give him time to feel his anguish. She couldn't let him bottle up yet another piece of agony. 'But we can also take this one step at a time.'

Ebony opened her mouth to argue, then exhaled, softening. 'It doesn't help us to be bogged down with depression,' she said. 'But if even *Maya Nova* wants to slow down, then I suppose we can take a short break to collect ourselves. Then we get to work.'

Maya nodded. She and Ebony hadn't interacted much when they first met; neither were particularly good at socialising, nor did they particularly enjoy it. Then Sierra told Maya that Ebony had sourced one of her books before knowing who she was. Ebony flushed red and stammered over her words as she explained everything she loved about Maya's work, which led to Maya showing her more books – and Maya was so excited to have a fan that she rushed to make Ebony a storybook all of her own, dedicated to the pirate.

The two were surprisingly alike. They'd spent most of the journey to Amora's Territory talking about books and stories while Teddy sat staring out the window of the carriage. Maya hadn't expected to love the impassive pirate, but she thought she understood her well enough now.

And *thank the fairies*, because having Ebony with them at all times meant Maya and Teddy couldn't talk about the animosity hanging between them. The faith he'd lost in her when she'd suggested they surrender to Lire to save Bearra.

As they often had throughout their relationship, they pushed back their doubts and fears and disagreements in favour of all the good they had together. Maya loved Teddy. Their commitment was never in question.

But what if they did really talk? What if everything came back to the surface? A single word might be strong enough to bring them down.

'Thank you.' Teddy pulled himself apart from Maya but took her hand, leading her towards a bench that was still standing, if a little charred. He slumped down, rubbing his hands over his knees, wiping charcoal on his slacks.

If one good thing had come of this, it was that they didn't have to wear those horrid formal castle clothes anymore. Maya was happy in a loose-fitting top and pants – *pants* – which she could move around in with ease. No one would chastise her if she got them ruined, covered in paint or oil or dirt.

With Teddy in a faded-green shirt and brown pants, Maya thought he looked a little like a half-dead tree. Her summery boy was losing his vibrancy one day at a time. If she were to paint him, he'd be all Autumn, a slow decay, his eyes perpetually rimmed red, his cheeks always hollow.

As if she looked much better. Since she lost her mother, she was barely alive herself. She had to allow Teddy to fall if he needed to, but she had been deep in midwinter from the start. He was the optimist.

He was the sun. If Teddy fell into the cold as well, how would they survive?

It was selfish, but she needed his warmth.

'Where might your mother have taken her?' Ebony asked, and Teddy flinched. It took Maya a moment to realise Ebony meant Lire and Amora.

He shook his head, ash falling from the loose curls of his hair. Maya inched back from him on the bench so she could see his face, scrunched up. 'Lire has her estate outside Bearra,' he mumbled. 'But that seems too obvious.'

Lire's Estate . . . Maya had forgotten about that. The fairy's other home, which she'd stayed in while Bearra spent a century asleep. Teddy had only been there a handful of times, since he and his brother's existence had to remain secret.

'No,' Ebony said, her eyes fixed in the way that meant she was deep in strategy. 'No, if her estate has become her base, then that's where she feels safest. It makes the most sense that she'd have Amora there. She wouldn't be trying to hide her. She wouldn't think she'd need to. If anything, Lire will be showing Amora off. Besides, where else would she keep her?'

At the bottom of a well lined with iron. Maya didn't say it aloud, but if *she* were to imprison a fairy . . .

'It does sound like something she'd do,' Teddy relented.

Maya scratched behind her ear. 'So we're going back to Bearra? What about the Amoran people? We still have to find them.'

Ebony's gaze darkened as she looked out at the buildings that once held so much light. 'We can spend a few days scouting the city, but that's all we have time for. If the Amorans are alive, they can take care of themselves for that long at least.' Maya wasn't sure they could – the people were used to dancing away their time. Could they manage without their fairy's power? 'And if they're already dead . . .'

'Then we can't help them anyway,' Teddy finished. 'But Amora really does need us.'

If she's still alive.

Maya stood, and helped Teddy up. 'We better start, then.'

CHAPTER FOUR

I sputter, gasping. Rhiannon's scaly wing scratches my neck where she pins me to the wall, her strength unflappable even as she's enraptured by the nutcracker.

Zeus's mouth hangs open as he studies it – no longer worried about the fairy that tried to kill him but the strange object that saved his life. 'I thought . . .' he starts. 'It repaired itself before, so I thought it might have some sort of . . .'

Protective qualities. He figured it out even before I could.

I lose focus on the fight we're in, my mind going over what happened again and again. My nutcracker – the one thing I have from my parents – saved Zeus. Candace said it's enchanted, but what is it? It mended itself, but it can also *protect itself from magic?*

I've known for a long time that magic doesn't work on me like it does others. It passes around me, ignores me as if I'm not there at all.

I've always assumed that's because Candace put wards on me, but this toy suggests otherwise. Was it my parents who gave me my immunity to magic, like they did with the nutcracker? Have they been protecting me this whole time without me knowing?

From behind the fairy, Sierra, flanked by Levi and Arden, clears her throat. 'I'm delighted about your special toy, but could we possibly get back to the fight?'

Yes, please. Make her fight so she stops strangling me.

Rhiannon snaps her head to face the pirates. 'Don't tempt me.'

'Well, we've bested you, haven't we?' says Sierra, arms crossed and long legs relaxed. 'Look at our little weapon. Didn't expect that, did you? How are you going to beat us when we have . . .' She glances at me. 'Decorative iron cutlery?'

Not quite. The nutcracker couldn't be iron, or Candace wouldn't have been able to hold it. However, if Rhiannon believes it's made of her only weakness, maybe she'll leave us alone.

'You think that's enough to defeat me?' Rhiannon glows red again. 'I don't need magic to win. I'll strangle you with my bare hands.'

'Go for it,' Sierra mumbles. Arden and Levi elbow her at once. 'I mean, *no, please, don't. Spare us.*'

Rhiannon isn't listening. Intently watching the nutcracker again, she heaves with realisation. 'It's like *you.*' Her eyes bore into mine, and I know it isn't possible, but I swear the pupils narrow into slits.

'Excuse me?' My gut sinks. Can she sense my immunity? Or is there something she knows about me, something she's spied or discovered during our years of being distanced enemies?

She softens into a nasty kind of amusement. 'You don't know who you are. Candace never told you.'

With her wing at my throat, I can't pretend to be strong. The others look at me with a mix of pity and confusion, and I *hate* that there's nothing I can do. 'I-I've never seen the nutcracker before today,' I rasp.

'Poor, lost child,' Rhiannon says, teeth bared in excitement. 'You wondered why I came for you today. Well, I didn't only want you for insurance.' She grins. 'I wanted you because *I know who you are.* Candace's secret weapon. The one who could threaten everything Lire has built.'

I stiffen. Zeus tries to scramble to his feet – as if to protect me, with the nutcracker still held before him – but Rhiannon hisses and he falls back. She presses her scales deeper into my skin, drawing drops of hot blood. I hyperventilate, kicking my feet.

Rhiannon claps like this is the epic finale of a stage play.

I kick and kick, my hands around her wing, my iron dagger on the floor. My boot loosens on my foot. *Fairies,* I didn't tie the laces properly. If I could just work up the strength to boot her, if I still had my dagger in my hand, I could do *something.* I'm defenceless.

'And I'm not going to tell you,' Rhiannon teases. 'Because Candace is right. You don't need to know your own power. No. I'll keep you for myself. But it is so tempting to simply kill you now . . .'

Hot anger bursts through me. Does she know anything at all? She's a strategist, a warrior. She knows how to hit me where it'll hurt. This is manipulation. It could all be lies.

I heave a steaming breath through my closed throat. Raise my foot, readying to punt the fairy. I'll make the strength. Her wings are spread enough I *could* get her in the chest. I don't care if it's a useless attempt. I just want her to hurt – even if it's only a tiny bit.

I swing my leg, but she catches my play and swerves her other wing around to block my ankle. My boot flies off and— *What the fairies?*

She's laughing one second, and then her wings are in front of her, but the shoe, hurtling awkwardly, rises right between them and thwacks her in the forehead.

And *that's* when I remember my boots have metal tips. But not just metal. Iron.

With a gasp, realising in a split second her mistake, her eyes roll into the back of her head and she drops.

I slap my hand over my mouth, stumbling as her wings falter and I crash to the floor. I scramble up, hurrying back as Zeus, Levi, Sierra and Arden stare at me flabbergasted.

As if I have answers! I just knocked out a fairy with my shoe!

'This makes my fairy kill feel a lot less special,' Sierra mumbles.

'Is she . . .' I start. But of course she isn't dead. She's merely unconscious from taking iron to the skull.

'What do we do with her?' Arden asks.

Levi swallows. 'Did Isla *defeat* her with her *boot* . . . ?'

'Mhm. That's General Isla,' Zeus muses.

'But what do we . . .' Arden repeats.

Even with her slacked jaw showing her white teeth, and her limbs and wings sprawled awkwardly, the fairy seems so peaceful in this state. It isn't that she looks beautiful or happy. She looks *human*. Goosebumps rise on my skin; it's horribly unsettling.

It makes me wonder, have the fairies always been immortal and powerful? Were they ever like us? *Are* they like us, when the magic is all gone? Were they born with that power, or did they amass it on their own, like my mother has?

I shake my head, collecting my boot from the floor. 'We get her out of here,' I say, loosening the laces. 'We throw her out of the kingdom before she wakes up. We'll need help.'

'Candace?' Zeus asks.

I nod. I've taken care of the problem. I just need help cleaning it up. 'Candace.'

✦♡✦ 𝚨 ▦ 𝚨 ✦♡✦

'Sugar, you have an unconscious fairy in the hallway?'

I fold my hands calmly. 'We have an unconscious fairy in the hallway.'

Candace is in her nightdress, a pale green that stretches to her toes in soft lace. Her hair is tied into a bun atop her head. 'Alright.' She sighs. 'Let's get rid of her before she wakes up.'

I rub my eyes. It's late, and my lack of sleep – plus the fatigue from Rhiannon choking me – has caught up.

Zeus and Levi, who followed me while we left Sierra and Arden behind to guard the fairy, are too scared to say anything to Candace.

'Come on,' she says, and we scuttle behind.

I don't know what else to tell her, because the only words in my head are: *I know who you are. And I'm not going to tell you.*

How much has Candace kept from me? I haven't told her what the nutcracker did, and I'm not sure I want to. I'm certainly not going to confide in her about Rhiannon's claims. If it's true that Candace lied to me even more than I thought – and I'm sure she has, whether she meant well or not – I can't share that I know. If I do, she'll only shut me down, ruining my chances of getting more information. There's a reason she hasn't told me. I need to have some tact.

In any case, all of that is personal, and right now we have a major security issue to deal with.

We reach the section of hallway with the exploded bricks strewn around and the, well, the . . . dragon wings. The fairy's head sits lopsided between them, her tongue hanging out past her teeth.

Arden breathes a sigh of relief. 'Thank the fairies you're back. What do we do?'

Sierra stands with him, the two of them loyally guarding Rhiannon.

Lark and Wren, the siblings, must be at the Nova house if they still haven't woken. Which is good. I wouldn't have wanted anyone else caught up in this.

'What if we just . . .' Sierra charades tearing Rhiannon's wings off.

Candace raises a brow. 'We aren't savages, Reed.'

Sierra cocks her head. 'Could've fooled me, false fairy.'

Politics. Once again, Dawn's circle proves they can't get anything done without the utmost drama, even if we could all die in the meantime.

'We need to move fast,' says Levi. He rubs his right arm, like he's missing something that should be there. 'She'll be awake soon.'

'What's your plan, General?' Candace asks me.

I pause. We both know she's the real leader, no matter how much responsibility she gives me. My plan was to throw Rhiannon past the borders and hope she's scared enough not to come back in. Candace asking for my orders rather than giving her own is a test to ensure I can take care of Bearra on my own. I need to do this right.

'First we need to take precautions,' I say, mustering all my courage to command the room, 'in case she wakes up before we've dealt with her. That means iron. We have shackles in our encampment. *Then* we dump her outside the kingdom. She'll be so embarrassed going home weakened and unsuccessful that I doubt she'll be back for some time.'

Candace nods at me slightly, in that way she does when she'd be grinning in private. 'Very well.'

Arden clears his throat. 'Shouldn't we ask the *queen* what she thinks?' He gets funny looks from around the room, and Sierra elbows him. He raises his hands, palms out. 'Okay, but she'll be furious when she finds out.'

Zeus waves an unbothered hand. 'Dawn will be fine. Besides—' he eyes me '—Isla is in charge too.' He gives the room a princely stare that I don't think I've ever noticed on him before. 'She knows what she's doing. So *obey*.'

Something heats up in my stomach. *What was that?* 'Uh, thank you. I'll send for people to get those iron shackles. For now, to make sure, I'll just . . .' I wince, giving the fairy's head another good kick with my boot. Her head lolls and her eyes open wide for a second before rolling back into her skull.

'That's one way to do it.' Sierra nods emotionlessly. 'We're sure we don't want to kill her?'

'*No.*' Candace glares at her. 'I hate the fairies as much as anyone else, but that will only cause more chaos. You've done enough of that.'

Sierra shrugs. 'No one appreciates murder like they used to.'

CHAPTER FIVE

'There's something I need to discuss with you.' Candace sits at the desk in her suite, surrounded by papers and inkpots and maps. It's crowded, but everything is in order. She knows if I came in and saw a mess, I'd tidy it myself. 'We've spent long enough establishing our power in Bearra. It's time to decide our next steps. Echo Rhiannon's impatience and keep moving.'

I take a long moment, mulling over the idea. We haven't heard a peep from Rhiannon in the three days since her visit, which means my plan to leave her embarrassed and defeated worked. All because of a *nutcracker* and a *shoe*.

Dawn wasn't happy we didn't tell her our plan, but I made it clear that my decision was the right one, and she would've had no right to oppose it anyway. She's a queen, but I'm a general. She can lead a kingdom. I'm the one who wins wars.

I close Candace's door behind me, giving us some privacy from the castle staff outside. Her room gets more sun than mine, and she basks in it. Her lush dress shimmers. She must have enchanted it to do just that, so she can appear more fairy-like. I shield my eyes and sit at the foot of her bed.

'This is now our base for the war,' I say. 'We should continue securing the kingdom, but we can certainly expand our influence outward from here. Darraport and Naroport would be next.'

'I'm not so sure,' Candace replies, sealing a sheet of parchment with wax, then tilting her head to meet my gaze. 'We're so focused on Bearra and the war that we're forgetting our home. The Ice Empire is falling back into the royals' influence. Our people feel abandoned by us. We can't both be here, fighting the war for Bearra, while leaving our own empire on its own. But we can't leave what we've built here, either.'

I run my eyes over the cracks in the brick floor and massage the palm of my hand. Surely in such a short time, the royals couldn't be usurping us. It took Candace years to overpower them. And our people know we're here for the empire over anything else. Don't they? My soldiers and I are expanding our power, which has always been our goal.

And, yes, saving the world as well. *For* the Ice Empire.

Maybe that doesn't matter. Royals are royals. Their influence runs generations deep. No, they don't have the leadership skills that Candace does – she's not only taking care of the empire, but making it into a worldwide power – but the royals are who the people are familiar with.

'You're planning to spend even less time here?' I ask. 'We need your power at the centre. There's only so much I can do alone.'

'That's not true. You defeated Rhiannon without my help. But . . . I agree with you,' she says, giving me a solemn look. 'I do think that, for now, it's best I stay.'

I frown. She can't really mean— 'You're asking *me* to go home? After all I've done here?' I tilt my chin up and resist the urge to clench her bedsheets in my fists. 'Mother, taking Bearra was my idea. This is my project. My battle. You—'

'I know, sugar.' She stands up from her desk and sits beside me on the bed, holding my hands. 'I won't force you to do anything, but it's a request I must make of you for the sake of our power in the empire. You can show our people once more how formidable we are. How much they need us. You know I trust you entirely, Isla. I know you can retain the empire for us while I work on saving the world out here.'

I take a deep breath and centre myself. Candace isn't being cruel. Besides, I don't even want to be here. I hate this place, its overdramatic people, its wretchedly hot days and blazing nights. I hate always feeling like an outcast.

I'm also desperate to see Elm. Not only to see what they make of the nutcracker, but also to talk over what Rhiannon said about my parents – and what Candace might be hiding from me. I'm backed into a corner in Bearra. I need to talk, and Elm is the only person I can be honest with.

I know it shouldn't be my priority, but is going home the best step I can take towards, well, finding myself?

It's what *I* want the most, and yet going back to the Ice Empire feels like giving up on Bearra, and being shunted out of the war.

'I'll think about it,' I tell Candace.

She smiles, albeit ruefully. 'Thank you, my powerful girl. You know how grateful I am to work alongside you.'

I avert my gaze. There are so many things I want to tell her, but I force myself to keep my mouth shut. Candace has always been someone I can trust without question. I am her daughter, and she raised me to be brave, to be a leader. She has never failed me, never not been there for me, even in all these years of politics and power.

She is my mother. And yet . . . she isn't.

She hid my nutcracker from me for eighteen years. She knows more about who I really am than she's let on. Candace took me in for a reason, and not just because I was a baby she found in the snow. She never planned to have children, and if I were just any baby, why not take me to live with someone else so she could focus on her career? She never *had* to adopt me.

But she did, because she knows I give her some secret edge. Rhiannon knows as much, and I need to find it out for myself.

My hands go cold, still gripped in hers.

She loves me. Whatever her reason for raising me, she *chose* to be a good mother. I don't resent that we're a family, nor do I resent the position I have in the world as her child. I'm privileged to live in castles and lead armies, even if Candace and I had to build everything we have from the ground up.

Still, my heart yearns for the life I never had.

I want to scream it to her. *'Who am I?'*

But I smile softly and squeeze her hands. Despite the climate we hail from, she's always been so warm. She will always be my lifeline, my home, my mother.

'I won't fail you,' I tell her. 'Or our people.'

⋅♡⁺ ⛄ ⋅♡⁺

Dawn, Relia, and I walk along the edge of the cliff on one side of the castle, overlooking the terracotta rooftops of the kingdom. It's cloudy, so the heat is less offensive today, but the canals still have a sparkle to them.

Now that I'm thinking of leaving, I fear I'll miss this place – *slightly.*

I don't tell them I'm leaving. I'm yet to make the final decision. But, I reason with myself, I have to tread the waters. See if Bearra is ready to be without me. Check what final measures I need to put into place before I leave my venture in Candace's hands.

Relia watches me with a polite but genuine smile, speaking every so often to provide a decent insight, but she's otherwise content to be by her lover's side and listen. With that crimson hair and lovely pink face, it's hard to imagine she spent a century dead. But seeing her with Dawn, the way they're like one person in two bodies, it's clear why the young woman fought so hard to come back.

I've done plenty of research on them since my arrival – and been around them more often than I'm comfortable with – but it's still odd speaking with these girls from another time. They're like fables come to life.

I'd always known about Princess – now Queen – Dawn, of the long-respected Triamin royal line. And once I met Lady Relia Rosenway, I did plenty of research into her family too; there was little to find about her birth parents, but the noble family she was adopted into had records.

And though I never knew him well before he left with Maya and Ebony, even Teddy is a legend – a half fairy. The world knows about his existence now; whispers have spread far and wide of Bearra's saviour, Maya Nova, and her partner Teddy Fairyborn.

But none of these people are faceless characters, and all the facts I could dig up have done little to help me understand who they actually are: very real people who are a *pain* to deal with in our very real world.

'I wish to honour our agreement,' says Dawn.

Her posture is strong enough to rival mine, and I force myself to stand even straighter, nearly pulling a muscle in the process. How easy life must be for a perfect, born royal who has never had to fight for her power. But I have to admit she's a good leader.

'Bearra is now – partially – yours,' she says, 'and I don't see the need for your soldiers to have their encampment outside our walls. They're more than welcome to stay there if they like, but I want to see them in the kingdom, mingling with our people. As you expand your empire, I imagine more Imperials will arrive. Encouraging our people to bond now will help everyone acclimatise. In addition, it'll be helpful to teach Bearrans about the outside world and prepare them to become a modern kingdom.'

I keep a blank expression. Dawn and I agreed to be friends. Or, at least, friendly. I want to trust her. I want this to be easy, and with her enchanting, blessed magnetism, it's so tempting to hunger for acceptance into her inner circle. But I have to keep my wits about me and remember I'm in charge. I have to put the Ice Empire first. What if her friendship is all a ploy?

'Very well,' I concede, because I do love her idea. I would be happier leaving Bearra if I knew clear plans like this were in place to support us both. Even if I don't get to oversee it. 'I would prefer to keep my army together, living in the encampment. But whenever they aren't working, there's no reason they shouldn't enjoy all the kingdom has to offer.' I resist adding, *Which is what, exactly?*

'We look forward to seeing more of you around,' Relia offers. She's always been kind to me, much more than any of the others, and I do appreciate it. She gently takes Dawn's hand in hers. *Fairies*, how nice it must be to trust someone, rely on someone, like that . . .

I'm not lonely, am I? That isn't a very good trait for a leader. Dawn seems so happy with Relia and her cats. I should look into that. The cats, I mean. I don't have time for romance.

Besides, if I did find a partner, Zeus might have a heart attack.

I ask Dawn, 'How will you make sure the Bearrans don't resist?'

'However do you mean?' she responds.

As if she doesn't know. 'They may not view the presence of Imperials in the kingdom as an offer of peace and sisterhood, but as a threat. Especially after having Bearra closed off from everyone else for so long. Have you considered what you'll do if this idea only creates more tension?'

The queen raises a brow. 'We aren't a territorial people,' she says. 'Traditional, certainly, and possibly anxious about the new world, but I don't expect a revolt. Of course, there will always be a few troublemakers on either side, but they can be dealt with.'

'I'll have to take your word for it, then?'

'Isla,' Relia says, with a hesitant glance at Dawn. 'We can be honest. You have the most capable army in the world, and we have *citizens* we're doing our best to train with magic and iron. You know that if any tension arises, the Bearrans aren't the ones who'll win the fight.'

Dawn responds to Relia with a betrayed expression, but sighs and nods. '*That* you don't have to take our word for, General. There's a reason I agreed to you being here.'

'Quite right,' I mutter. Of course I'm worried about leaving Bearra without my leadership, but Relia is right.

Dawn wants to help my people as well as hers by assimilating them into Bearra. She's as Wise as her blessing demands, and I feel a bit lighter as I realise I *can* leave the centre of the world under her direction while I save my empire.

I can't rely on Candace to watch over this kingdom and keep its queen and people in line. She's always leaving to fight, to spy, because she trusts no one but me. It's a risk for me to leave Bearra when I'm the only person who can run it effectively *and* make sure the Imperials aren't pushed out.

But I'm starting to truly believe I can trust Dawn. Even if we didn't get off to the best start, we're two powerful young women who can understand each other in ways most people wouldn't. I'd be glad to call her an ally, and one day even a friend.

There's a lot we can do together if we win this war. We could bring peace to the entire world, from its hot centre to its snowy edges.

'So, are you ready to bring our people together,' Dawn asks, 'and begin a new kingdom of both Bearrans and Imperials?'

I give her a sharp, certain nod. 'I'm ready.'

CHAPTER SIX

'I hope some of them fall in love,' Zeus muses, all but skipping alongside me as I walk towards Bearra's gates and the Ice Empire encampment beyond.

Though I still haven't decided whether to go home or stay in Bearra – even several days after speaking with Candace – the idea of leaving Zeus behind and having some time to myself is incredibly tempting.

In fact, it's currently my number-one argument in favour of going.

'Don't you think it's romantic?' he goes on. 'The idea of an Ice Empire soldier, sent to take over an old kingdom, falling in love with one of the people he's been tasked to take the kingdom from. It's very . . . star-crossed.' In my peripheral vision, I catch him making gooey eyes at me. 'Rivals turned lovers, like you and I.'

I make a gagging noise, ambling up an old brick bridge built over one of Bearra's many glistening canals. How lovely a swim might be if

I weren't worried someone would take the chance to drown me. Most Imperials can't swim, but I forced myself to learn long ago. Ice baths are great for the heart.

The kingdom is bustling today. A reminder of the good I've done here. When I arrived and made my offer to Queen Dawn, this place was dissolving between its people's fingers like dry cake.

With my influence and power, as well as my soldiers introducing more trade by buying from the Bearrans, this place is thriving more than it has in over a century.

And people still see me as the enemy.

I weave through market stalls and children laughing as they play, holding myself tall. The crowds don't part to make room for me as they would for Dawn. I squeeze through the orange-bricked streets and terracotta-topped white buildings. Sweat beads on my forehead; I work very hard to resist taking off my army jacket, which to *me* is a very important symbol of my power.

Zeus, meanwhile, dances and dallies along behind me, paying no attention to the world even as people watch him like he's a deity of his own. They move out of his way and shake his hand, waving for their friends to come and lay their eyes upon him. His royal charm, his beauty, and his masculinity evoke such adoration.

Bearrans aren't stupid, but *everyone* is attracted to shiny things. It's easy to see why they were tricked by Lire and her son, thinking they'd been saved by a hero. Easy to see why they abandoned their princess, let her be abused by a monster. If Zeus were a different kind of man, if I suffered at his hand, my people might have turned a blind eye too.

I would have noticed, I think arrogantly – but probably rightfully. *I'd have helped Dawn.* Candace taught me to see through charm and charisma. It's something we had to learn so we didn't get manipulated while rising in the empire's political ranks. It isn't the average person's fault they aren't trained in such ways.

If I'd been raised differently, Zeus may have tricked me into believing he really loved me and wasn't only fixated on the idea of us, the power I could give him. If I were a different kind of woman, we might already be married. It's a match that makes sense.

Of course, in a twisted way, Zeus *is* one of my closest friends, even if we'll always be two powers working against each other. But that's why I see him for what he is, and know that nothing between us would ever work. He's attracted to me like he'd be attracted to a diamond – like he'd be attracted to himself, probably – and only sees my power, my strength, rather than any true part of me that makes me . . . *me.*

Zeus's infatuations, like with Sierra Reed, are a roundabout way of him worshipping himself. He's always claimed to love me, but he'll back off again once he finds someone new.

The prince grins at me, his pale face turned up to the sun as he gleams with perspiration. He doesn't smell, or look oily or tired. He really does gleam.

He doesn't shift in his blazer like I do in my jacket. He wears his clothes with confidence, showing everyone he surely is a born prince. He expects people to love him, so they do. Who wouldn't believe a pretty face like that?

'We should have dinner together this evening,' Zeus says as we pass through the glittering triarue gates.

If he weren't here, stepping outside Bearra would be like taking a breath of fresh air, feeling free from a kingdom that hates me. But he is here, so instead I bristle up and groan. 'We have dinner together all the time.'

'You know what I mean.'

He turns more serious, the way he only always does when the eyes of others are off him. He shows his other nature: a boy who is smart and strategic, who pays attention and remembers, who *might* genuinely care. Sometimes it's enough to make me wonder if this version of him is special for me – until I remind myself that it could all be another political manipulation tactic to crush my defences.

'I've been begging you for months, Isla. Won't you give me a chance?'

We're nearly at the encampment, the empire's thick white tents rising before us like a small village. While we're still alone and out of anyone's earshot, I swirl to face him. 'Would you *stop*?'

He pouts. There: the immaturity is back.

'This isn't a joke to me, Zeus.' Anger heats my stomach to my fingertips. We've had this conversation a thousand times, but with everything happening right now, there's an extra layer of resentment behind my words. I can't deal with this anymore.

'I know you're trying to derail me for your family's sake,' I accuse him. 'Maybe you do love me, in some sense, but you are extremely misguided. You can't keep doing this to me! This isn't just the two of us fighting over the empire anymore. This is *war*. This is the entire *world*. If we can't show a united front, how is anyone supposed to take the Ice Empire seriously? If you're always acting like a fool—'

'Even though it makes you look better?'

I skip a breath.

'You *love* the competition,' he says, not raising his voice. 'Admit it. You love that I'm here as your opposite, to balance you, to challenge you.'

'You have no idea what you're talking about.'

He tilts his chin to gaze down on me through half-lidded eyes. They're icy in colour as always, but there's a fresh coldness in them. I've never seen Zeus so . . . raw. What side of him is *this*?

He says, his voice deep and sincere, 'What would you do without me, General Isla? Yes, sometimes I make your life difficult because you and your mother have done nothing but take everything you can from my family. But as much as I hate Candace, I've always been *your* friend. I've always watched your back, in ways you don't even know. Even if I occasionally like to tease you.'

'You're overstep—'

'Let me finish, because I need you to believe this truth.' He softens. 'Yes, I truly love you. I've never hidden it, and my openness doesn't make it any less true. I wear my heart on my sleeve, and you might think me a fool, but I never lie. I'm exactly who I say I am. So don't pretend you hate me, because I know you care about me too, even if you'll never love me in the way I wish for.'

I stare at him wide-eyed and wordless. The boiling rage in me ebbs even as I try to grasp it. How has he managed to . . . to . . . twist everything around?

Who are you? I want to ask. *Fairies. Who am I?*

'If you want to present a united front,' he says, 'then fine. I'll do that for you. But you *know* I make you look better. You don't need people to like you. I do. I desperately do, Isla. You have to admit that the lazy, charming prince makes the serious, strategic general seem capable and terrifying. They love me but don't respect me. They hate you but they fear you. Hasn't that always worked for us?'

'What are you saying? That all your bumbling is an act for my sake? Because it *isn't* helping me. It's a nuisance.'

'It's no act.' He puts his hands in his pockets, his hair shining, and he looks so sturdy, an unmoving mountain in the face of a blizzard. 'You underestimate me,' he says. 'Just because I'm joyful and loving doesn't mean I can't be intelligent. You think I'm of no use to you, but if you lost me, you would really see how badly you need me.'

I shake my head, trying to think through his words. Of course I care about him. How couldn't I? We grew up together, always by each other's sides. There's a reason I brought him back to the Ice Empire when he went missing and turned into a swan – and why I helped him hide it, *and* helped him heal when the curse broke and he shattered his arm. Why would I do all that if I hated him?

Zeus knows that as much as I want to strangle him sometimes, I can't help but care. It's why he'll never leave me alone, because he thinks he can unlock some secret part of me that sits behind my cold exterior. But even *I* don't know if that person exists. Sometimes I think the cold is all I am.

'Isla?' he whispers, his expression turning concerned. 'Isla, I'm sorry. I went too far. I didn't mean to—'

At the same time, we realise that my hands are trembling and hot tears are spilling down my cheeks. I shift to wipe them away, but Zeus gently entwines our fingers. His are cold – so beautifully cold, reminding me of home. He pulls me into his body, and his steadiness grounds me. The brick road evens out. The hot sun softens its attack.

I can't be seen like this with him. I can't be seen showing this kind of weakness. But somehow I can't let him go. I didn't realise until now how badly I needed comfort.

Even from him.

'I'm such a fool,' he says, his voice reverberating through his chest as I silently cry into it. 'You don't need me. Of course you don't need me. You're brilliant all on your own. You'd be better off without me and I know it. I just wanted to make you feel bad. I'm an idiot. I'm so sorry.'

I shake my head, pulling back from him. 'I don't know who I am,' I admit.

'I do,' he offers. 'You're smart, and so beaut—'

'No. Zeus, what I mean is . . . I snapped at you because I'm upset about something else too, okay? I don't know where I come from. Who my parents are. I was raised to be a leader. Other than that, there's nothing to me. You think you love me, but how can you love an empty shell of a person?'

'Excuse me?'

'Well it's tr—'

'Absolutely not. You are *not* allowed to speak of yourself like that. I won't have it.' He tilts his head. 'How can you not see your own heart? Every day I'm in awe of you. How can you say you're empty when there's so much love and care in all you do? So much intelligence and creativity? You're not a leader just because you've been moulded into one. You're driven and confident. Resilient and level-headed. All of that is part of the *real you*.'

'It's not,' I say, my nose running. I'm beyond embarrassed, but now the tears have started I can't help it. 'The nutcracker. And what Rhiannon said. She knows who I am, and Candace knows who I am, and it's this big secret, and I don't know who I can trust. I'm a mess all the time. Everyone thinks I'm a heartless monster, when in reality all I do is feel, and none of those feelings are good. I control the empire, I try to control *everything*, because I can't control a thing about *myself*.' I whimper, my feet itching to take me away, to run and hide.

'Shh.' He lowers himself onto his knees and looks up at me, gripping my hands. 'You can't keep thinking as if everything is black or white. We've all got problems. We're all distracted, all the time. We're all messy. You think you have to be perfect all the time, but no one other than you expects it. You're *allowed* to have issues, just like the rest of us. Me, for example? Self-obsessed, a little arrogant, only able to fall in love with people who romance will never work out with . . .' He squints. 'But this isn't about me.'

'No, it isn't.' I meet his eyes. Those beautiful, naïve eyes that will never know the kind of pain I go through. 'These are kind words, but you can't simply say I don't have to be perfect. You can do whatever you want and you'll always have your power. You went missing for a year and returned as if nothing happened. But I can't falter for a moment without losing everything. I can't show people how lost I am. I can barely *blink* without being hated. So I have to pretend I don't care, all the while screaming inside and willing myself every second to . . . to not blink.'

'You can blink with me,' he whispers. 'You can do anything you want around me. I might give you a hard time, but that's politics. You're my best friend – as well as Elm, of course – and beyond all the showing off we do for our people, I'll always be here for you. Not just because I love you, but because I care. I want you to know that.'

My boots are still on the dusty ground, though I feel like I'm up in the air. It's the middle of the day. I was on my way to talk to my people, to be their leader. And I've been utterly derailed out of nowhere.

I let out a deep breath. What am I supposed to make of the strange warmth Zeus has evoked in my chest?

Something has shifted between us. All because for the first time in eighteen years, we've been *honest*.

But despite this moment, politics will always stand between us. We can't escape who we are. We could never truly trust each other, as friends or more. And, as he knows, I most definitely am not in love with him. I can't give him what he really wants. The best I can do is try to be civil, even though my mission is to bring his family down.

'I can't promise I'll stop irritating you,' he says, standing and towering over me once more. 'That's part of my job as prince. But I didn't see how badly you were hurting. I'm so sorry I made you feel this way.'

'Thank you for saying that,' I whisper.

'I'll listen more, alright? Relia and Dawn taught me to be a better friend, a kinder person. I need to extend those skills to you. It's hard, because my instinct is to tease you and flirt with you.' He smiles. 'But I'll try.'

I swallow and nod sharply. 'Then I'll try too.'

He uses the hem of his fine shirt to dab away my tears. 'Let's start with allies,' he says. 'For the war, and for our own sakes. At home we might be rivals, but out here we're Imperials, and we're fighting for the empire. Together.'

'Okay.' I manage a smile, a new weight off my shoulders, a puzzle piece falling into place. 'Together.'

CHAPTER SEVEN

SOMEWHERE, SOMETIME . . .

Zeus had spent more time being a bird than most, and he felt this gave him a wisdom and perspective many commoners – *beg your pardon,* people – lacked.

Others saw him as just a pretty face, and he didn't mind that at all, since it *was* a divine fact that he was beautiful, but it did hurt when they lacked faith in him.

Even Isla, who had known him for so very long, didn't want to see his intelligence or his trailblazing leadership skills. Nor did Dawn, who saw how he'd gotten her the enchanted mirror. Nor Sierra, who he'd gotten the iron sword for. These people would be nowhere without him!

Therefore, despite being adored by all, Prince Zeus was often lonely.

Relia was the only person who genuinely appreciated and under-stood him. Maybe because she had no romantic interest in anyone other than Queen Dawn, nor any interest in power. She didn't care for the godly prince but for the man within.

Each day he smiled through his pain. He brushed his hair into a perfect quiff. He waved to people with the perfect angle to show off the muscles in his upper arms. He tried – he really did – to not openly fawn over General Isla. Her beautiful hazel hair and hazel eyes. That commanding, raspy voice, or her arms, toned from weapon-wielding yet blessed with all the grace of a lady.

Zeus fell in love all the time, but she, *her*, oh *fairies*. He'd been drowning in agony over his best friend ever since he understood the concept of love. Before he'd even begun to love himself – because what he loved so much about himself were the traits mirrored in her.

But after their argument yesterday, it was becoming apparent that nothing between them would *ever* happen. Despite what he thought, maybe he didn't know her very well after all.

He firmly knocked on the door to the queen's quarters, and waited for a guard to let him through. It was early morning, but he needed advice. Now.

The royal suite was a little lacking compared to his back at home, though his castle was also much bigger, and had more modern updates. It also wasn't half-collapsed.

Zeus did, however, favour the way the two women had decorated. Soft pink curtains hung over tall windows in the sitting area, with plush seats in the same petal-like shade. The suite was much like an apartment, except if said apartment were incredibly old and didn't have running hot water. The bathroom to the right had beautiful blue triarue fixtures, and the similarly-styled kitchenette was mostly unused but always stocked with fresh fruit.

To his left was Dawn and Relia's bedroom. On this door, he knocked more softly. He needed to wake them, or alert them to his presence if they were doing other private activities, because he did *not* want to walk in on that. The soft knock, though, allowed a guise of politeness.

'Yes?' came Dawn's groggy voice.

Zeus swung open the door. He pursed his lips as he took in the attractive room, comparing the colour and sunlight to his depressingly grey guest room. Relia had made some upgrades in here – the fluffy violet cushions on the wide four-poster bed were new.

The queenly couple were huddled together, Relia wrapped deep within Dawn's arms. Both had their hair out, blending in a cascade of gold and red across the silky pillows. It was all very regal.

They groaned at the influx of light from the open door, squeezing their eyes shut.

Well, if lazing around in bed was their only plan for the morning, they could surely spare some time for their best friend. Zeus cleared his throat. 'I would like to talk.'

'Certainly. Go on,' mumbled Relia. She refused to sit up, too cosy in Dawn's caress.

Zeus pointed his chin towards the door. '*Relia.* Outside, please. I only want a minute of your time. It's just, something happened with Isla, and . . .' He pouted.

She took a deep breath. 'I see.' She rolled over and gave Dawn a quick kiss. 'Excuse me, my love. Our dear friend needs love advice.'

The queen looked ready to kill him, but she often did. It was all jealousy – not his fault.

Relia hopped out of bed, smoothing her satin rose nightgown. She rubbed her eyes and took Zeus's hand, leading him to the balcony. Here – with the stone still smooth, and the uninterrupted, striking view of the kingdom's terracotta roofs and blue canals, its vine-covered walls, and the pale desert beyond – one could pretend half the castle hadn't been ransacked.

They sat in plush seats and Relia tilted her head, giving him a small, gentle smile. Zeus immediately felt at ease. She was entirely genuine and he knew that whatever he told her, she wouldn't judge. She would listen and advise with only his best interests in mind. No manipulation. No trying to gain something from him.

Of course, it also helped that she could read emotions very well – one of her powers as an undead magical being.

It was still remarkable to see Relia in all her glory when he'd first known her as a mousy little maid. The mannerisms of nobility, the sparkling red hair, that beautiful soft face. But just as she saw him for his heart, he saw her for hers. He adored Relia from the start, as he'd always longed for a sister.

'What's wrong, my sweet prince?' she cooed. Her voice was still croaky from sleep. She kicked her feet up to rest in his lap and leaned tiredly on the arm of her chair.

A slight sense of guilt befell him; maybe he shouldn't have deigned to bother her and the queen on one of their extremely rare mornings off.

'Well—' His bottom lip wobbled. How did she do this to him? Relia's kindness brought everything to the surface. 'I think—' He swallowed. 'I think I've lost my chance with Isla. I thought eventually she'd realise . . . But we talked, and she made it very clear, and— And we're going to be—' He blinked back tears. '*Friends.*'

'Oh my,' said Relia. 'I'm so sorry. How awful.'

'I tried to act princely and unbothered, for her sake and mine. I've been trying to hide how wounded I am. But— But—'

She patted his leg. 'Shh. Thank you for coming to me, Zeus. I'm here with you.'

He nodded.

'I know how hard it is to always be around someone you love when you can't act upon it. I spent months watching Dawn from the shadows.'

'And you got your happy ending. What about me? It's *over* for me.'

She shook her head lightly. 'Sometimes, it's only once we relinquish control that what we want falls into place. You have a nasty habit of chasing those who don't return your feelings, Zeus.'

'I—'

'You know it's true. There are hundreds of people who would love to call you theirs, yet you only enjoy love when you feel that it's a competition. You fall in love with the pursuit, with the need to prove yourself, with your need to be adored.' She held up a finger to stop him protesting. 'I'm not saying this to be cruel. But if you give up on chasing her, what if that makes room for something *real* to happen? If you stop begging her to love you, what if that's what makes her fall?'

'So you're telling me this is a . . . good thing? That by not doing anything at all, she might come to *me*?' He frowned, then slapped the arm of his chair. 'Of course! Everything else comes to me without me chasing it. How could I be so stupid!'

'Not stupid.' Relia looked at him through her wide, shimmering eyes. 'You have so much love in your heart, and an incredibly kind soul. It's why you're so confident and giving. I greatly admire that about you. The love you show the world is why so many people love you in return. So if anyone can't see that, it's their loss.'

'But it's my loss too.' He rubbed his hands over his arms – *ah, so wonderfully muscular* – and watched the morning view for a long moment, darkness eating into his gut like a nasty infection. Not that he ever got infections. He was in perfect physical health.

Relia shifted her feet. 'What are your parents like?'

He gave her a befuddled expression. 'My parents? I don't want to talk about them. I want to talk about Isla.'

'Mhm,' Relia murmured. 'Humour me. I'm only trying to understand why you can't seem to simply love someone who already adores you.'

He gulped, his stomach roiling strangely. 'My parents are queen and king of a stunning, powerful empire. My focus has always been to ensure they keep their power, and that we don't lose our land, even though Isla and her mother are trying to steal it.'

'Yes, yes. But what are they *like*?'

His eyes darted from side to side. What an interrogation! He'd come to his friend for *comfort*. 'They're the queen and king, and I am the prince. We work together, I love them very much, and they love me very much. But if you're asking if we're *close*—'

'I am.'

'Then . . . No. Not particularly. They've always been too busy. We have dinners together, spend holidays together, make appearances together, strategise together, but . . . I can't talk to them like I talk to you. I've always had the sense that if they hadn't needed an heir, they wouldn't have been interested in having a child at all.'

She took that in for a moment. 'Do you think that possibly . . .' she started cautiously. 'Do you think that might have something to do with why you seek the attention of people you don't have a chance with? Because if you get their approval, it would fulfil the fantasy you have of being wanted by your parents?'

Zeus made a gagging noise. 'I don't know what on earth you're talking about, future queen.'

'Oh? Then maybe it's just your giant ego.'

'Ugh!' He threw her legs off him – though only gently – and crossed his arms.

Relia crossed her legs and laid her hands atop them. 'Zeus, I love you very, very much, but if we don't get to the root of the problem, how will things change? You'll only go back to chasing Isla, or the next girl, and come to the same conclusion.'

'*Ugh . . .*'

'So, you'll think about it? Why you might be feeling this way?'

She was right, and Zeus, even in all his wisdom, hadn't thought of it himself. He was very upset about the observation. For once, there was something he had to fix about himself, and not something wrong with everyone else.

He wiped his eyes. 'I'll think about it. But for your information, there's no *next girl.* Isla is the one.'

She beamed. 'Then it's time to look within and see if you can be the man she wants and needs.'

'Quite right.' Zeus straightened. He could do this for himself, and for Isla. *There was still a chance.* 'Thank you.'

'Anything for my prince,' she said. 'Would you like to stay together a little longer, or may I return to bed?'

'Go ahead.' She wasn't making him feel guilty for taking her time, but he still felt at fault for disrupting her morning. 'I didn't mean to keep you.'

'You keeping me is my honour.' She giggled, moving onto her feet.

'Wait – don't go,' he stammered, realising he'd been terribly impolite. 'I should've asked, well, how are *you?*'

'Me?' She blushed, lowering back into her seat. 'Oh, well, you know. Fine.'

He looked her up and down. Birds chirped in the distance, as if to signal her deceit. 'You've never been fine in your life, so don't test me, darling.'

'It isn't that I'm being dishonest,' she said. 'It's just that there's nothing anyone can do. As you said, I'm never fine. I'm always worried. And although I'm incredibly happy with Dawn, and fed and sheltered, and alive and myself again— Oh, now that I'm saying it, it feels silly.'

'You could never be silly.'

'We're in a war! There's constant panic and grief, and I take it all in, and I have horrible nightmares, always slipping into people's dreams, and . . . Am I supposed to be alright? The only thing that will make me feel better is stopping the war, so . . .'

Zeus nodded seriously, folding his hands together. 'Then I will stop at nothing to get this war stopped.'

She untensed, laughing. 'Well, thank you.'

'Do you think I'm joking? I already planned to win the war, but knowing that it's weighing on you so terribly, I will work even harder, even faster, and I will protect you, and Dawn, of course, even though she takes so much of the attention off me, and I'll *kill* anyone who gets in—'

Relia took Zeus's hands. 'You don't have to save the world. You and Dawn, you royals, you think so big. Everything is in worldwide proportions, because so much of it is yours. But,' she said, 'you're *human* too. I don't need Dawn as the queen, and I don't need you as the prince. Neither of you has to give me the world. Just give me what you can of yourself, give me your time, and your love, and I will be happy.'

He met her eyes. 'You *deserve* the world.'

'Maybe I do. But let's focus on winning the war first.'

Zeus called on his spies, and they met him in a quiet side of Bearra by a sheep farm. The moon was bright, its glow bouncing off both the clouds of white wool around his feet and the grey clouds above.

'Your Highness,' greeted his primary spy, Delphine. Her two assistant agents flanked her, stoic and silent, blending into the shadows. Delphine had the pale skin of someone from the world's edges, but dark, curly hair that helped her blend into places without being clearly Imperial.

Zeus was pleased to see her. He'd first found her sneaking around his castle stealing jewels, and only caught her because he happened to be in the bath when she entered his quarters, not expecting him. He wanted people of his own to work for him – not just his parents' staff – so he brought Delphine on as his spy. Without her, he'd never have been able to keep track of Sierra and her pirates to get her the iron sword, nor find Dawn and Relia and get them the mirror.

'Do you have any news?' Zeus thought of what he'd said to Relia, about bringing this war to an end. He'd meant it. Relia made him feel better about Isla, and now he was clear-headed and ready to make change. Delphine could help him find the next step towards defeating the fairies.

'It's a good thing you made contact with us,' the spy said, her voice silky. 'We did find something. We can't make much sense of it, though.'

'Something to do with the war? With the fairies?'

'Possibly.' She pulled a scroll from her pack, unrolling it.

Her assistants held it out on the ground as the group of four knelt around it. It was a map of the world, from Bearra to the Ice Empire, and . . . beyond?

Delphine noted Zeus's confusion. 'Exactly. I found this after filing through the remains of Amora's office. We've spent weeks trailing the clue, seeing if it means anything or if it's just . . . fantasy.'

Zeus swallowed. It was hard to make out the map in the moonlight, but there it was – a village past the frozen walls of the world. If it were possible to travel there, it would only be a few days from the Ice Empire.

Of course people imagined what might be beyond the ice, but no one had ever survived an attempt at breaking through it. Zeus always put the thought out of his mind, too afraid of the concept of something more.

'If you're still following it,' he said, 'I suppose you see some truth here.'

Delphine nodded. 'There are hints, clues, legends, Your Highness. I can't give you a certain answer, but why would Amora keep this map if it were fake? There must be at least one settlement beyond the ice, as marked on this map. We would have no way of reaching it, of course, but . . .'

He gazed at the moon. 'But proof of life beyond us could change everything we're fighting for.'

CHAPTER EIGHT

It's far easier to focus on what I need to do now that Zeus has stopped incessantly bothering me. Well, he bothers me occasionally, especially to distract me in front of others – like he said, he's still my rival, even if he's also my friend – but it's quieted enough I've been able to get things done, putting everything in place for me to leave.

If I decide to.

I'm having dinner with the queen's circle, so deep in thought I don't even remember eating my bread roll, when Zeus nudges my shoulder from his seat beside me.

'You ever miss home?' he asks.

'Every day,' I admit, placing down my fork. The cooks always insist on making hot food for us, despite the weather. Why would I want to consume a potato that's only going to bring the kingdom's heat even deeper into my being? 'Every second.'

'We could take a holiday,' he muses.

'A hol—'

He holds up a hand. 'What if we did? Just for a week or so, to check in on the empire, spend some time with Elm, rejuvenate our energy. You know, General Isla, if you never rest, you're actually depleting your ability level.'

I narrow my eyes. 'Did Candace put you up to this?'

'Her?' His expression sours. 'Absolutely not. I thought it was a good idea. Imagine cool air on your skin. Snuggling into furs by a fireplace. Fruits imported from the jungle, baked into a sweet pie. Evenings at Elm's workshop. Oh – and we could do some exploring to see about your nutcracker.'

I shoot him a stare and he lowers his voice. 'Truly. You've always wanted to find your parents, and now you have a clue. Elm's the expert, and Candace found you in the empire, didn't she? Besides, if this war kills us, wouldn't you have wanted to prioritise finding out who you are?'

'No, but I've already been thinking about going back.'

'Oh. You have?' He tries to go on but I elbow him, curious as the pirates' hushed conversation drifts from the other side of the table.

'. . . already said I'd help,' utters Arden. The young man has one hand on his soup spoon and the other resting on Sierra's lap. In their dark clothes, with their raven-like stares, it's clear they belong on a pirate ship or in an army – not in a royal dining room. From the way they fidget and twitch, I sense they don't favour this lifestyle either.

Desperate for freedom. Just like me.

Lark is blushing about something; he often is. Yet in a rare turn of events, his lover isn't with him. 'I appreciate that,' he says, 'but I don't have an idea yet, Captain.'

'You don't think it's too soon . . .' says Sierra.

Levi stirs his soup with melancholy. 'I miss Ebony. She'd say it's too soon.'

'Hush,' Wren tells them. 'What would any of us know about *soon*? What's time after what we've been through?'

'We'll all be dead soon anyway,' Arden adds.

Lark's brows turn up in the middle. 'Don't say that! Besides, this isn't a debate. I'm asking her to marry me because I know it's right. It isn't out of haste because of the state of the world. It's because I love her and see a future with her, and I'm sure she feels the same about me.'

'So that's three votes for the proposal,' Arden says, 'and—'

'We aren't voting on my marriage!'

'Oh,' says Wren. 'But we probably should, though. You know I'm for it, entirely, but it affects us all.'

'I wish Ebony were here,' Levi laments.

The. Constant. Drama.

'You're welcome to use any room in the castle,' offers Dawn, grinning from her place at the head of the table. 'Sorry for eavesdropping. But if you like, any resources I can provide are yours.'

Before Lark can reply with a thank you, Wren cuts in. 'Flowers. Briar loves flowers. And it has to be incredibly romantic.'

'The ballroom,' says Arden, now shifting excitedly. 'At sunset.'

'Ooh,' says Sierra, clutching Arden's arm. 'We should have a string quartet come in!'

'I thought you were voting against?' teases Arden.

'Right, the vote!' Wren counts the five pirates at the table. 'We can assume Ebony would advise against, but then again, she wouldn't say *no*, necessarily . . .'

'Would any of us say no?' asks Sierra. 'I might think it's too soon, but it's none of my business. It isn't as if she'll be joining us on the *Neptune*.'

Arden turns white and faces Lark. 'You'd be leaving the *Neptune?*'

Lark turns whiter. 'I thought a part-time arrangement might work best.'

'I'm going to count Arden as a no, then,' says Wren. 'I'm for it, Lark is for it, obviously. Levi?'

'I wonder what Ebony is doing right now,' he replies.

'Absolutely, so, maybe we should scrap the vote. It doesn't seem to be working.'

'No way,' says Lark, dripping with sarcasm. 'Really?'

'We simply have to be prepared to deal with the consequences if it doesn't work out,' says Sierra.

'Which it will,' says Arden.

'I agree,' says Wren. 'But just in case . . .'

The debate continues until the end of dinner, and by that time I'm ready to cover my ears and scream.

By then, I've had enough time to think. I try not to ever agree with Zeus, but after his suggestion of returning to the Ice Empire, I can't put it off anymore. It seems to be fated that I go. It's what I want, and if that means putting aside my goals here for a few weeks, so be it.

✦♡✦ ⛄ ✦♡✦

We don't waste time. Three mornings later, Zeus and I are readying an enchanted carriage to take us home. We wave to the queen and her circle – except for Relia, who Zeus picks up and spins in the air. He kisses her cheek and she giggles delightedly, even as Dawn looks upon them with admonishment.

The sun is getting high as I say goodbye to Candace with a polite nod – we had our private farewell already, in which she instructed me to take care of myself, and I instructed her not to worry – and I slip into the carriage.

Being stuck in a small space with Zeus is not ideal. But the thought of being home makes me so jittery with excitement and hope that I can move past it.

Within the first few hours, I see Zeus really took my words to heart. He doesn't go out of his way to irritate me. Instead, our time together is *pleasant*. The carriage sails through Adella's Territory, passes south to reach the border – avoiding Rhiannon's Territory – and soon we're approaching the Ice Empire.

We have conversations about our childhoods together, about the empire – and nothing about the past two years. In our stories, our hands and feet are plunged in deep snow, the world forever glittering around us.

And then, as if there's been no oxygen for months and suddenly I can breathe, the stories are true once more.

It feels like I'm shrinking, becoming smaller and smaller as the mountains and pine trees grow gigantic around us, until I feel the same way I do when I look up at the stars: beautifully insignificant.

Two months. I've been holding my breath for two months.

Here, in my world, everything is covered in layers of icing sugar, purest white, from the endless evergreen trees to the frosted rivers. There's a peppermint scent to the air, and although the cold bites into my bones immediately, it wakes me up, as if everything before this moment was a dream.

Zeus's cheeks and nose go pink, the icy prince I know resurfacing. He breathes deeply. 'Nothing compares,' he says over the sounds of birds chirping.

A pack of wolves eyes us in the distance, calm but curious. I watch their large eyes and ivory fur for a while, smiling. They remind me that every creature of the empire is mine, and that I am proud to protect them all.

This wonderful place . . . it's everything, and it's all I have.

A sleigh of silver and diamond awaits us nearby; Candace sent word ahead of our arrival. Like the carriage we took to get here, the sleigh is enchanted. The side opens at Zeus's touch, defrosting before our eyes in veins of ice.

We unpack the carriage and move our things into the sleigh, and the second we're done, the carriage zips away in a storm of azure magic, speeding back to Bearra. It leaves a snowstorm in its wake, powder dusting around us before settling back into the ground, perfectly flat.

Even our footsteps are hardly enough to mar the pristine landscape – they disappear within moments of us leaving them. An enchantment, of course, but still stunning.

We don't enter the sleigh right away. Neither of us can be torn from taking in our homeland. I've seen it a million times, and yet it's still so mesmerising. The snow is so soft it barely feels cold anymore, and the sky is impossibly blue. It's a painting of a fairytale.

'We can't let this place become a memory,' Zeus says.

I can't meet his eyes, because the sheer vision of my empire is enough to make me want to cry, to make me lay down my life to keep it safe. 'Candace will save us.'

'She isn't our only hope.' He turns to me. 'General Isla, we have you.'

My heart warms, but my wonder begins to ebb. We're home, but there's so much danger.

A lone bat sleeps upside-down in a pine tree's spines. It reminds me of Kara, and then of the dark we have to fend off. It blinks an eye open, watching us.

The cold runs down my spine, finally setting in, and I remember this place *isn't* a dream. Zeus is right. It isn't infallible, and it's already being threatened

I take Zeus's hand. 'Let's be on our way. We have an empire to save.'

CHAPTER NINE

The sleigh pulls up in front of my home and Zeus helps me with my luggage before giving me a polite hug goodnight. To my surprise, I don't resist the contact at all, enjoying our familiarity.

He hops back into the sleigh to be taken to the royal castle, and I watch until it becomes a speck in the white landscape. I'm grateful to be alone, but without him nearby it admittedly feels like something is missing.

In the dark evening, I spot my bedroom window glowing a few floors up. I'd expected to step into my home and be met with unwelcoming waves of dust and darkness, but it seems Candace called upon our staff to prepare for my return. Pushing through the heavy front doors, I find each brick wall lined with candles, their flames enchanted to give off extra warmth. The fireplace in the main sitting room roars with heat, and the savoury scent of roasted vegetables wafts from the kitchens below.

I pull myself up the dark-wooden staircase to my quarters. My door swings open and out floods the air of familiar comfort, sweet and earthy. Red brick reaches high ceilings decorated with a burning gold chandelier, meanwhile the furniture and décor elicit warmth in their deep brown, burgundy, and navy. Dark wooden bookshelves along the walls house tomes on history, language, science, culture. War and political strategy. I run my fingers along the leather and cloth bindings, dustless, placing a book in my reading chair to enjoy before bed.

Earlier I told myself I'd greet and thank the staff after a short rest, but it's already impossibly tempting to go straight to sleep. My bed – with its soft sheets, plush blankets, down pillows and thick quilts – is meticulously made, just how I left it, and the freshly fed fireplace makes the room almost too warm. I could curl up and fall asleep right away, even on the carpet. My feet sink into the wool and I breathe, and I breathe, and I *breathe.*

My bath has hot water running within moments, and once I've scrubbed my entire body and felt every muscle relax, I change into my nightclothes. Back in my bedroom, an array of sweets and baked goods awaits me on the vanity.

Their sugary scents tempt me, but before diving in, I tackle open my trunk and dig for the nutcracker. I know exactly where to put it.

On my desk by the window, there's a small, framed painting of me and Candace. Just as I placed the nutcracker by the window in Bearra as a symbol of safety, I replace the portrait with my new protector.

Snuggled in bed, so safe and warm, everything so familiar, it takes me a moment to remember it's my first morning back in my own home.

I stretch for a while and enjoy taking in my sunlit room. Snow glitters outside the large windows, settling on the houses below us. While Candace's castle is nowhere near as large and high-up as the royals', it's still a mansion in its own right, and from my room I have a superb view of the empire. *My* empire.

I dress in thick pants and my army jacket. Instead of stifling me like they did in Bearra, the clothes sit comfortably on my body – like a second layer of skin. My hair goes into one of my favourite braid styles, and by the time I'm pulling on gloves, a maid knocks on my door with a silver tray.

I nearly fall into her arms in appreciation. '*Sadie*,' I almost moan, taking in the scent of toast and marmalade, warm chai, and an Ice Empire delicacy: sweet raisin tarts. After only snacking last night, my stomach has been cramping and screeching.

'General,' says Sadie, the older woman's pale cheeks crinkling with a smile. 'I'm glad to see you home. This house has felt empty with you and your mother travelling so much. You know the empire needs you.'

'And I need sweet raisin tarts.' I take the tray from her with a mumble of gratitude.

I intended to ask for a packed breakfast to eat on the way to the royals' castle – I slept in too long and don't have a moment to spare – but I can't help myself. I *need* to eat this while it's hot.

Peeling off my gloves, I ask Sadie to sit at my desk while I eat over the vanity. As kindly as I can, I interrogate my loyal maid about the Ice Empire's state since I've been gone.

'You're aware Candace's influence has been waning because you've both spent so much time away,' she says. 'That's why you returned, isn't it?'

She tells me the Imperials are confused and looking for guidance. We're military in nature. We like to follow orders and we're used to clean lines, simplicity, and logic. The uncertainty of this war has everyone on edge, searching for a leader.

Candace's power used to be enough to impress them, to give them peace of mind that they were protected. But since Lire destroyed Amora's Territory, proof of the power of a *real* deity has put the fear of all seven – or, six – fairies into the Ice Empire.

I'm licking honey from my fingers when Sadie finishes with, 'I have faith in your mother, as do many people, but the Ice Empire is falling. You're the strength and heart of this place, General Isla. You might be the only person who can piece it back together.'

I wipe my hands on a soft napkin and slide my gloves back on. 'I don't know about that,' I mutter. I stand, and she does too – almost before I do. The poor woman has spent long enough attuning to my needs and movements.

'We've prepared a sleigh to take you to the castle, then to Elm's workshop later today. We thought those would be your first priorities upon your return. Lunch and dinner are packed should you need food.'

Fairies, I missed being around people who are actually useful. 'Thank you,' I tell her. 'Thank you so much. Truly. Extend my gratitude to the chef and the rest of the staff. The empire may need me, but I can't do my job without people like you.'

✦♡✦ ♤ 🎎 ♤ ✦♡✦

My thick boots touch tiled ground – snow-free and slip-proof by enchantment and engineering. The city roars around me like a building storm, people in heavy coats rushing through the streets around the castle. Where my home is, it's quiet, just how Candace and I prefer. *Not here.*

But oh, the castle. I may not like the royals, but I've spent enough time within those marble walls to have fallen in love with the ancient structure. The white building rises over the empire like a deity over its dominion, protective and intimidating. Built into the side of a mountain, each turret jutting out of the frost tells its people, *You are protected if you obey.*

I shake out the snow from my hair, pull down my jacket, and nod to myself. *This is my territory, and today I'm taking it back.* Chin lifted, I take my first prideful step towards the castle's entrance.

Zeus comes bounding down the front steps, much to the chagrin of the guards following him. 'Isla! General! They told me you'd arrived.'

More likely he was watching the streets from his window, waiting for me to show. I've caught him doing it before. 'Good morning, Your Highness,' I say, breathing out a heavy sigh.

He cringes. 'So formal, just because we're at the castle. Come on, *General*, we're supposed to be enjoying our trip home.'

My eye twitches. 'I'm not. I'm here to work.'

A group of young teenagers passing by in colourful fur coats squeal as they catch sight of Zeus, and wave at him frantically while guards usher them back.

Fairies. This already?

Zeus waves back, flashing them a perfect smile, and they jump. He glances at me as if asking my permission to go and talk to them. Since I *do not* care, and I have business to attend to, I strut towards the castle's grand entrance.

He groans and, choosing me over his admirers, trails me all the way up to the strategy chamber. As expected, the queen, king, several council members, and other generals are milling about the room. In the centre of the gloomy chamber is a circular table with a glowing map: the six territories, each shining with its fairy's colour – plus Bearra in lilac, and the other cities and outlying areas shadowed. To the north-west sits the Ice Empire, glowing white.

But today, Amora's Territory is grey, missing the pink glow I always enjoyed watching when councilmembers' speeches went on too long. It hurts to see the map like this, but I must remember Amora's corner of the world isn't my problem. Lire's son is taking care of it.

A royal throat-clearing marks my presence as unwelcome. The queen and king wear stunning white attire, pure and perfect. They look healthier than the last time I saw them, more confident. The other officials in the room are turned toward the royal couple, drawn to them like moths to a flame.

The situation is worse than I thought. It's as if Candace has been entirely forgotten, simply because she's the one out in the world fighting for the empire.

And what are the royals doing? Playing in their war room like children with toys.

'General Isla,' breathes Zeus, moving to stand in front of me and announce me to the room. 'I'd like you all to welcome back our hero, come to visit us after her successful campaign to take Bearra.'

I glance at Zeus. I knew we'd decided to be kinder to each other, but . . . that was *extra* nice.

Heads turn in my direction and, as directed, the councilmembers and generals congratulate me. They shake my hand and ask about Bearra. Most of it they know. The logistics, anyway. How could I possibly explain the absolutely dramatic personal lives of Bearra's leaders, and how that's affected my campaign more than any Imperial could understand?

As I move through the room, I aim to stay polite enough not to give anyone a reason to see me as rude, while being assertive enough to show them I'm serious.

It's an art I've perfected over the past eighteen years, and before long I have nearly everyone but the queen and king eating out of the palm of my hand once again, answering my questions rather than grilling me with their own.

I let myself relish in that small victory; I may not know who I am, but I know what I can do.

'Opinion has been turning in recent weeks,' Councillor Dierdre tells me. Very much on the side of the royals, she's one of the few councilmembers I can never sway. Her hair is enchanted grey, an attempt at reaching the status symbol of light hair and skin that the royals have popularised. It's very trite to me, but many Imperials work hard to have the right look – to display both beauty and power.

Despite Dierdre's efforts, I see the councillor's dark roots peeking through. She has a certain desperation, and while it often leaves her weak, it can make her dangerous. 'General,' she says, 'we know you've been working with the Bearrans on strategies to win this war, but Lire's power is undeniable.'

Something spiky grips at my stomach. 'What are you saying, Councillor?'

The queen stares me down through her clear eyes. Unlike most Imperials, her cheeks are flawlessly pale and white, rather than red and wind-chapped. She wants to appear like an ethereal, powerful being. Fairy-like. As does the king.

Neither have ever gotten as close as my mother.

'General,' the queen says, 'I know Candace will disagree, but we are having to make decisions on our own for the good of the empire – which she and yourself have not been fully part of for *months*. We are at home protecting our land and people while you only thirst for more power elsewhere. We've been listening and making decisions for our subjects' benefit – not just Candace's.'

I grit my teeth. It would do me no good to show anger. So, relaxing my face, I say, 'How lovely it is to see Her Majesty attempting to do something useful. Would you enlighten me on these decisions you're making without our counsel?'

The king, clad in white, circles the table and stands beside his wife above where the Ice Empire glows on the map. He looks so much like Zeus, but with an even more distinct lack of thought behind his eyes. 'Before Lire attacked Bearra, and before she attacked Amora's Territory, she gave both the chance to surrender and survive.'

I can't stop myself from cutting in. 'You don't mean to say—'

'We must consider the option if it means the survival of the empire.'

'*Father*,' Zeus almost seethes, gripping my shoulder. I don't shake him off. 'If you'd seen what I've seen, the devastation Lire has caused in Bearra, you wouldn't even consider this.'

The queen watches her son through half-lidded eyes. 'Watch your tone.'

I'm tempted to jump in and defend him, but that won't help anyone. What I want more than anything is to have Candace beside me, helping me through this sudden *nightmare*.

Hold on. I freeze. Could that be it? A nightmare? Surrender goes against everything the Ice Empire stands for. I was so exhausted last night, maybe I'm still dreaming.

Unfortunately, when I pinch my arm, it only earns me a strange look from Councillor Dierdre. *Fairies.*

I was prepared for trouble, to have to work to regain Candace's influence and get us above the royals again, but *this*?

My mother needs to be here. She's the powerful one that makes us as strong as any territory. It's her ability to protect us that keeps us confident. Yes, we've always had a strong military, but we all know that without Candace, we can't get through the Fairy War.

If I don't take drastic action soon, the world is going to see the Ice Empire as a joke, barely able to figure out who its own leaders are. We're supposed to be terrifying, formidable. But with our army stretched thin in Bearra, with Candace and I being away, and with the leaders arguing amongst themselves with no direction, *considering surrender?*

The fairies are going to see us as vulnerable; our armour of ice thawed to reveal a warm, beating heart for the taking.

CHAPTER TEN

SOMEWHERE, SOMETIME . . .

Sometimes, Sierra Reed couldn't believe how easily her life could go from bad to worse. Again and again, every time she thought she'd seen as foul as it could get, the world never ceased to surprise her.

Her life was a cracked mirror, glass threatening to shatter, shards waiting to fly. No one – friends nor enemies – would be safe if it did. Sierra felt like it was only a matter of time. But if she were to go down, so would *many* of her enemies.

Despite such a lack of hope, there was always her family, and most significantly, *Arden*.

There was rolling in the silken palace sheets, their bodies endlessly warm. There was time laying in the sun on the deck of the *Neptune*. There were cuddles in the evening, or sitting with Lark, Wren and Levi as they played card games. There was the *rolling in the sheets*.

In the hazy early morning light, she laid her lips on his, a soft brush as she matched her quick breaths with his slow, slumbering ones, gently waking him as they faced each other on their sides. His eyes blinked open, his face lightening into a grin.

She glowed with appreciation. Every time he saw Sierra, it was like he suddenly remembered she was all his.

Which was why she *always* made sure he woke up to the sight of her. Besides, Sierra Reed did not suffer from petty human things like bed hair or bad breath.

She was a Gracian deity, and she loved the way Arden worshipped her.

He ran his hands past the sheets and up to her face, running his thumb across her cheek. Unable to resist his charm, she pressed him onto his back and climbed atop him. He wore no shirt, so her fingers ran along his soft, hot skin, electricity running under her nails as if they were tingling with magic. Even after the months they'd spent together, her heart still raced in these moments, her cheeks flushing.

'Morning, beloved,' she whispered, leaning down to kiss him deeply. His lips parted and she ran her tongue across them. They smiled against each other.

How beautiful it was to have him like this. When they first met, their stolen kisses were heavy and tense, boiling hot. They had never been able to keep their hands off each other, fighting or otherwise. Now, though, she could take her time, enjoy him. With the exception of the war that threatened their very lives and their entire world, nothing and no one was keeping them apart. Least of all each other.

Each caress could be lingered in, every kiss could be leisurely. They weren't starving anymore. They savoured each other, every bite a delicacy. Rather than Arden's presence feeling like Sierra's first meal in weeks, he'd become the icing on her dessert. *And* the dessert, and the meal, actually.

She pressed herself up on her strong arms, planning to travel south with her lips, but he held her upper arms and bit his lip, gazing at her chest with his irises almost entirely black, pupils dilated. If Sierra didn't know better, she'd think she changed every night entirely, and became something new for him to study.

Neither of them slept clothed – especially not in Bearran heat – so they were no strangers to each other's bodies. And yet it always seemed a surprise, as exciting as the first time, when they really saw each other.

When they met, she'd spent weeks staring at his toned arms and legs, at his tanned, tight abs, before she'd finally been able to truly gaze upon them. Let alone *touch* them. *Fairies.*

Weren't people supposed to get bored of this eventually? What was it they said about a honeymoon phase?

Sierra didn't think she'd ever tire. She could be a fire as much as she could be a woman – and in either case, he was the oxygen that let her burn.

He reached up, his nails trailing along the sides of her torso and up to her chest. Her skin tingled with delight. She lent down, letting his fingers continue their journey as she tilted her face to kiss him. As his wandering hands met their destinations, she giggled into his mouth – until pleasure dulled her amusement and she bit his bottom lip instead.

His fingers dawdled south again, and she readied for one of her favourite parts of the morning, when he would—

'Good morning, lovers!' shouted Levi, swinging the door open and barging inside.

Sierra fell atop Arden, nearly crashing their teeth together as she scrambled to cover her top half with the sheets. Arden was red as a strawberry, racing to cover his . . . lower half.

Lark and Wren trailed in behind Levi, the three of them seemingly unbothered by what they walked into. *Boundaries.* That was something they weren't used to having. Not on the ship – that was one thing, a small space that made privacy near impossible – but not in the castle either, apparently.

Lark tossed Sierra a button-down shirt hanging from the arm of a chair, and she slipped it on under the covers, glaring daggers at the intruders. These sorts of things wouldn't happen if Ebony were here. She kept the others in line.

Or if Sierra's best friend Maya were here, *she'd* stay away from Sierra's room with a sword held out to avoid unwanted sights.

Even Zeus and Isla were gone, no longer in neighbouring rooms. They were far from her favourite people, but at least they left her alone. Isla because she didn't care, and Zeus because he feared for his life.

Of course, if Opal were here . . .

Sierra shook her head. She couldn't think of her old friend now. The crew had done well with grieving her. They spoke about her often, and they didn't hold back their sadness. But they also couldn't let themselves be constantly distracted by missing her.

They were still learning that delicate balance.

'So,' said Wren, perching at the foot of the bed, 'we've been talking about what we're doing here.'

'We've had this debate a thousand times, I know,' added Lark.

'But we need to finalise our plan,' Levi finished.

Sierra rubbed her eyes. 'What's new? We're here to protect the kingdom, and—'

'Not for that,' Wren sings. 'The *proposal.*'

Great.

Sierra wondered if she should've gone with Maya and Ebony to find Amora. It might've been gloomy, but being stuck in Bearra was worse. She was rooting for Lark and Briar, of course, but why did she personally have to help with the proposal? She'd surely get roped into the wedding. Wasn't that enough?

Though Sierra *did* love the idea of herself and Maya in matching bridesmaids dresses, drinking their body weight in wine and dancing a stunning night away . . .

'I do think roses will be important,' said Arden, sitting up. He'd stopped blushing now. 'So, the ballroom—'

Dawn and Relia appeared in the doorway, flanked by guards and maids. Sierra screamed in frustration, eliciting flinches from more than half the people in her room. She threw a cushion at the window, which it flew out of. She hadn't realised it was open.

'Oh,' remarked Dawn.

'What?' Sierra groaned. 'We are *busy!*'

Her family interrupting her was one thing, but Sierra still disliked the queen, and she certainly didn't trust her resurrected ghost lady lover.

Dawn entered, her hands calmly hanging either side of her blue dress. 'This current predicament is not my fault, so please refrain from yelling at me.' She waited until Sierra stopped heaving and flopped back into her pillows. 'You're finished? Wonderful. Because we need you on the *Neptune* immediately. A messenger was sent ahead from Grace's Territory.'

'And?'

'And, the Reeds are coming to face their traitorous sister.'

Sierra fisted the sheets. '*What?*'

✦♡✦ ♠ 🎩 ♠ ✦♡✦

Arden held Sierra's hand as they stalked to their ship; they'd meet the Reeds in the water to keep them out of Bearra. And then . . . fight them?

Sierra wasn't sure what exactly they'd come for. There'd been no word from her sisters since she broke the curse, and it wasn't as if Sierra had time to go and check on their, well, *humanity*. So, her best guess was they were, in fact, human again, and very angry.

Killing Sierra would be a great way to regain some pride.

She'd be lying if she said she wasn't excited. *Finally, something to do.* And murdering her old family would not only lift a weight off her shoulders but give her a fantastic morale boost.

Besides, even if things got really bad – which they wouldn't – Arden could always transform them again. He was twice as powerful as he'd been the first time, so maybe now a cygnus curse would really stick.

Sierra, Arden, Levi, Lark, and Wren boarded the *Neptune*, their castle-claustrophobia vanishing as they stepped onto the smooth wood they knew so well, into the fresh river breeze.

They were alone. No Bearran guards, no Imperial soldiers. Not even Relia, the ghost-witch with all her magic. Sierra couldn't let herself commit absolutely feral atrocities in front of all of those people, and today she longed for blood on her hands.

She'd grown, of course, as a person, and been *so good* recently, but the chance to take the lives of her insidious sisters? *Not. To. Be. Missed.*

All the crew were itching for a fight; the *Neptune* wasted no time picking up the anchor and setting sail south-east, following the main river system the Reeds were likely taking.

Sierra's skin tingled with the anticipation of her sisters' hot blood running across her skin as she sliced them to pieces . . .

'You seem happy,' Arden said, stepping beside her and pressing his shoulder to hers. Back on their ship, his eyes had come alive, reflecting the blue water below as it rippled in his irises. 'I thought you might be afraid to see your family, after all we've been through.'

Sierra ran her hands up his arms, bare from where his shirt – billowing perfectly – was rolled up at the sleeves. His tanned skin was even darker from the Bearran sun. The sight both invigorated and distracted her.

She'd changed into a fitted black fighting outfit, sleek and shiny, with her hair brushed to perfection. And, alright, yes, she *also* asked Arden to enchant her hair to stay perfectly styled in case of fighting. She wanted her sisters to see her as the flawless warrior she was.

'Why would I be afraid to see them?' she teased. 'Because I went from being a fighter who stopped criminals in Grace's Territory, to one of the pirates who haunts it? Or because according to them, I'm a traitor, a coward . . .' She counted on her fingers.

'You're also in love with the man who cursed them.'

She stopped counting and wrapped her hands around his waist. 'Would you like me to return to killing you, beloved?'

He rolled his eyes. 'I'd like to get this over with and deal with them, so we have one less problem leering over us.'

The five pirates readied themselves to meet the six Reed sisters, watching for the small army of black-haired women. Sierra felt incomplete without Ebony here to round out their team – not to mention Opal – but they were still capable of facing their oncoming adversaries.

Between Sierra's skills and Arden's magic, they could face anyone. They'd defeated a fairy, *for fairies' sakes*.

Lark and Wren continued to drastically improve their skills. Even Levi, who usually relied on strength and defence, was learning to be more precise and graceful.

'One less problem,' Sierra agreed, but that resolve faltered when the Reeds' vessel appeared upon the water and approached the *Neptune*. Rubbing her eyes as if she were imagining things, she stumbled back. 'F . . .'

Snow white hair.

Fully-black eyes.

From the youngest atop the mast, to the eldest at the helm, each of the sisters still bore marks of their curse.

'Wonderful,' said Lark. 'A whole *new* nightmare.'

The *Neptune* sensed their apprehension and halted, nearly sending the pirates careening over the ship's barriers as it tried to change course and back away from the Reeds.

Sierra knew seeing her family again would bring up horrors she didn't wish to face, but nothing could have prepared her for *this*.

Although they were certainly her sisters, it was hard to recognise these monstrosities as the women who had held her face under the shallows, kicked her until she couldn't breathe, torn out her hair. The women who tortured her for years.

And yet, despite how creepy their new swan-like looks were, Sierra wasn't afraid of them. She wasn't the child who fell victim to their relentless torment, or the insecure teenager who strove for their approval. She was stronger, and she was angry. She'd have six fresh kills today, and then all those years and all that pain would finally be over and dealt with.

'How are they even scarier?' whined Wren. 'Not that *I'm* scared, but generally speaking . . .'

'We could always run away,' said Levi, winking at her.

The *Neptune* bubbled back to life. Of course they wouldn't run, so there was no point panicking. Sierra stood tall and met her eldest sister's gaze. Her fingers clenched at her sides as their ships congregated.

'Cygnet!' one of the sisters called. 'Allow us to come aboard!'

'Tea or coffee?' Sierra yelled back. 'Or would you prefer to drink my blood, you—'

Irene sneered. 'Sadly, your death is not what we've come for, little one.'

Sierra's entire body flopped with disappointment. 'I can't have anything, can I?'

'We don't like it either.' Irene's frustrated growl carried across the ships. 'You're Grace's *favourite*. To fight you would be to fight her, *and* fight Bearra and the Ice Empire. As much as I long to wring my hands around your neck—' she motioned with her fingertips, milky white and bony '—it would be an act of war, so it will have to wait. No, cygnet, we're only here to talk.'

Sierra's heart shattered. They weren't even going to fight a little bit?

The hollow-cheeked women leaped onto the *Neptune*, much to Sierra's discomfort. She didn't like them here on their terms. The pirates stood their ground, arms crossed and unwelcoming, but, ever the leader, Irene confidently approached. Her eyes sent a shiver down Sierra's spine; she couldn't tell where her sister was looking, with no irises to follow her deadly gaze. Her white hair was soft and feathery, unlike the thick, silky strands the Reed bloodline had always been blessed with.

Irene said, with her usual utter lack of charm, 'We come on behalf of Grace. She knows we must choose our allies wisely. Our fairy seeks justice for our people and our world. *You* have created a connection with Bearra and therefore the Ice Empire.' She stepped closer to Sierra, talking down to her. 'Neither of these present a threat to us, but Lire does. We want to—'

Sierra punched her in the face, eliciting a screech. The Reed's nose cracked beneath Sierra's strong knuckles. '*Ack*— You—'

'Oh, sorry! I forgot you only wanted to talk.' As the sisters reeled back, Sierra rebalanced and rubbed her hand. *Fairies*, that was satisfying. Irene moved to return the hit, but another white-haired sister held her back. Sierra grinned wickedly, waving her finger back and forth. 'Grace's favourite, remember?'

'You're not untouchable,' snapped Irene, wiping blood from her face. 'Our parents told us what happened, that you were a coward and escaped the curse. We know you betrayed us all in your failure to save us. It may not be today, but I will have your life.'

Sierra's fingers itched to go for another punch – what about a kick in the stomach? – but she felt Arden shaking his head softly. *Fine.*

'Say what you need to say, then.' Sierra stood back with her hands clasped very politely. 'But I wouldn't keep your hopes up regarding killing me. Surely you've heard I took the life of a fairy? *And* I've survived attacks from Lire and Rhiannon. Six squawking swans are hardly competition for me.'

They really were birds, all watching Sierra with their heads cocked. More animal than human. Teddy had warned her that if the curse was broken, the women might not come back as they once were.

And it wasn't just their off-putting new look – they were different inside too. Sierra sensed the imbalance within them, the inner tug of war between animal and human.

The sisters encircled the pirates. The second eldest craned her neck and, ignoring Sierra's taunts, said, 'Grace has been biding her time, waiting to choose a side. With Muse and Amora out of play, and Adella useless, the best path is clear. Rhiannon has been bidding for Grace's alliance, but Bearra now has the Ice Empire, and the Ice Empire has Kara.' She looked Sierra up and down. 'The friendship you've formed with the Bearran queen gives us an in. With Grace and the power of the Reeds allied with Bearra as well, the world stands a chance against Lire.'

'We really could win,' whispered Wren, but she frowned and cleared her throat. 'Let me guess, Grace wants something in return for helping Bearra?'

Levi huffed. 'You'd think saving the world would be enough.'

'Not for the fairy of justice,' said a younger sister. 'Stop fantasising, cygnet.' She must have noted Sierra's growing temptation to maim. 'You would regret not taking this offer seriously. Bearra would have the might of Grace's Territory in the battle against Lire. All you have to do is make Queen Dawn agree to offer Grace some power in return once the war is won. We'll all need to rebuild – not just our cities, but our societies. With fairies losing their influence, the world will have to change. The territories will be reshaped. The queen only must promise to . . . help us how she can.'

Sierra laughed. 'She's not interested. The only reason she allied with the Ice Empire was because she saw absolutely no choice. She had to give up enough for them – she won't give up any more for Grace. The best thing you can all do is protect Grace's Territory and stay out of the way of the rest of us.'

Irene scoffed. 'How easily you betray your territory and fairy.' She waved a hand, so pale it was translucent as it passed through the sunlight. 'You can forsake the Reed family. We never wanted you. But you have a responsibility to your people. Grace blessed you for a reason.'

'*Okay*.' Sierra rolled her eyes. 'I'll ask Dawn about an alliance. But I can't guarantee she'll say yes. She doesn't listen to me as it is.'

'Good little swan,' said a middle sister. 'Run along now and send our message to the queen. If you survive this war, and I sincerely hope you don't, we'll see you on the other side for your long, painful death.'

Sierra was about to strike back when she noticed Arden's hands brimming with magic. The Reeds moved back, watching him.

'Threaten Sierra again,' he said, turning to make eye contact with each Reed, his eyes burning blue, 'and next time you'll find yourselves as something much worse than swans. Hurt her, and you won't live to see her bleed.'

Sierra hadn't seen this deadly version of the pirate captain in weeks, and her stomach fluttered.

Irene snickered. 'Sister, your dog is well trained.'

Oh no, she did not—

Levi stepped between them, staring Irene down. 'Yes, we all are. You will regret it if you try anything. Do you understand?'

Sierra tried to say something, to stop them defending her – she wasn't ungrateful, but she *did* want to fight her sisters eventually.

Wren beat her to it. 'Sierra is *our* sister,' she seethed. 'We were ready to kill you all today. Step out of line and we'll do it gladly.'

The middle Reed tutted. 'Empty threats from criminals don't scare us.'

Arden's magic crept along the floor. 'Do you really want to find out if our threats are empty?'

'Not threats,' said Sierra, her heart warm and her blood pumping, 'promises.'

She whipped a knife from her pocket and tore through the skin of the closest sister's cheek – then kicked her down for good measure.

'Understood?' she teased as the woman writhed, a hand cupped to her cheek.

The Reeds heaved, but had the decorum to not scream or fight back. Sierra quite liked that they were hers to do with whatever she liked. Maybe Grace would give them to her. Six eerie bodyguards . . . that would be something.

She chuckled. Had she ever felt this happy in her life? Her real family by her side, her old one cowering at her new power. *Grace's favourite.*

'Run back home now,' Sierra said. 'Tell Grace we'll think about her alliance. Oh—' she smiled '—and tell mother and father that they're going to *really* regret ever underestimating me.'

CHAPTER ELEVEN

I huff out of the castle in a barely-contained rage, fire beneath my skin. My lungs scream for fresh air and exercise to clear my head, so I walk straight to Elm's workshop, sending away the carriage awaiting me.

All that arguing got me nowhere with the empire's leaders. I *need* to find a stronger way to get my influence back and stop the royals from surrendering. Until I do, I can't see this simmering anger going away.

At least it'll help push me to get things done.

Elm's workshop sits on the edge of the main city, twenty minutes or so from the castle by foot, and halfway to my home. By the time I'm there, I'm only half as rageful.

The dark wooden building is the only single-storey structure on the street; no one would risk putting Elm above or below others. Too many things in the workshop can go *boom*. That's also why, despite living in the castle, their workshop is out here.

The royals, who took in Elm as their ward, found out about the *boom* risk the hard way. But even before they had so much magic to enchant their toys, Elm's genius was worth any trouble it came with. They were set to be a magnificent inventor, someone who could bring our empire new technology, new weapons.

No one expected the toy-loving child to never grow out of that innocent phase, and instead grow up to be the empire's toymaking *wizard.*

I peek through the frosty window, but there are so many toys displayed in it, whirling and gurgling with enchantment, it's near impossible to see past the show area and into the workshop. Still, I can just make out Adellan-brown arms tinkering at a back table, a head of tight curls leaning over a project.

Children nudge me out of the way to watch a miniature enchanted sleigh race along a track made to look like the empire's mountains. I give their parents a small smile and shuffle to the doors as they bow their heads lightly in my direction.

Though I know Elm will be deep in concentration, I knock out of habit. A wave of heat hits me as I enter. The biting cold of the city turns into the steamy, sweet-smelling air of the workshop, as inviting as a fireplace.

'*Elm,*' I call, drawing out the E as I sing their name. 'It's me.'

Their head bounces up from their work, and the goggles atop their head nearly fly off. They fix them sheepishly before recognising me and breaking into a grin. 'Isla!' they sing back, drawing out the A. Wide, deep mahogany eyes magnetise me, a rare warmth in the empire.

I scurry over to my best friend, avoiding the hazards on the floor and ducking under the tools hanging from the wooden beams of the workshop, then reach my arms over their shoulders. They pick me up into a tight hug, spinning me around. I let out a giggle, scrunching my nose as I take them in.

Healthy. Clean. Warm.

They've been just fine without me.

'I didn't expect you home so soon,' Elm says, clenching my forearms like they don't ever want to let me go again. Their overalls are singed to strings across the straps, nearly falling over their shoulders. 'Already finished taking over the world?'

My head droops. 'Not quite. The royals are talking about surrendering to Lire! Candace and I have barely been gone two months, and—'

'I know. I've seen it firsthand, sweet. Everyone is convinced we've already lost.'

'I never should've left.'

They shake their head. 'It isn't your fault you can't be in two places at once.'

If only. 'You can't make some sort of enchantment for that? An Isla puppet for every corner of the world?'

'What a terrifying thought.' They shudder.

I wince. 'Enough about my shortcomings. How are you, my snow angel?'

With a soft smile, they say, 'As well as anyone can be in these times. The war hasn't reached my workshop yet. I've been tinkering as usual, trying to bring joy to the people who need it most.'

My heart melts. I've been away fighting a war – fighting *Rhiannon,* even – while my best friend has been fighting for our people, for hope and fun. Elm wouldn't know it, but they have just as much influence as I do.

'Pssh,' they utter. 'Don't look at me all gooey eyed, please. I'm no deity for trying to be positive in a difficult time.'

'Aren't you?'

They narrow their eyes. 'What's wrong, Isla? You thrive in war. Something else has you all rattled, doesn't it?'

Fairies, I hope I never have a big secret to keep from them. I smuggle the nutcracker out of its place in my coat, wrapped in faux fur. 'Candace gave me this as an Ice Festival gift.'

They take it carefully – the only hands other than mine I trust the nutcracker in, despite its mending ability – turning it over and running their fingers over the red and black paint. 'Not again,' Elm mumbles as they toy with the lever, its mouth opening and closing.

'*Again?*'

'There's something I need to tell you. But you can't get angry, okay?' They pause, and I only offer a very confused expression. 'So, I've been doing some work in secret. And . . . Candace found this at the borders of the world, didn't she?'

'How did you—?' My heartrate rises. 'I mean, yes, this was with me when she found me as a baby, but . . .'

'And I assume you've noticed it reacts strangely to magic, or you wouldn't be so worked up about it.'

'It's from my parents, Elm. I'd be worked up about it if it were a dead rat.'

They stare at me, waiting.

I grit my teeth, realising I'm being defensive, then say, 'It got broken and magically fixed itself. And when Rhiannon attacked us, Zeus used it as a shield, and it deflected her magic.'

'Excuse me.' They blink very slowly. 'Rhiannon attacked you?'

'The point is, I'm fine. Thanks to *that*.' I gesture at the toy. 'It can't be touched by magic.'

'Right. We're coming back to this Rhiannon situation, but, yes. It's like you.'

'Candace enchanted it?'

Their cheeks flush. 'That's what I need to talk to you about. I don't believe she ever warded you against magic. I've been theorising that you were born with a resistance.'

'Why? How?'

'I think . . . I think it's because you're not from here at all, but from a place where magic doesn't exist. Out *there*. Beyond the borders.'

'Elm. I know Candace found me abandoned out in the snow. But my real parents must have been Imperial.'

'I know what it sounds like, but I found that—' They loose a breath and shake their head, curls bouncing over their eyes. Tired eyes. 'I need to start from the beginning.'

From under the workbench, they pull out a toy carriage. Its golden trimmings sit upon fully-functional wheels, just the right size for a little doll. They tap the top with a gentle finger, and orange magic sparks – their Adellan power. The carriage floats on its own, rising above Elm's head, and they hold the nutcracker beneath it. A claw descends from the base of the carriage and clutches the nutcracker. When Elm motions at the carriage, it flies around the room then back to us, dropping the nutcracker back into their hands.

'That's . . .' I start. 'It's a genius invention, but what does it have to do with me?'

'It's a drone.' They scrunch their face. 'And, thank you.' They tap the carriage again; it sparks and, as the enchantment falls, Elm catches it. They place it and the nutcracker neatly on the workbench. 'As you know, I've always had finding your parents in the back of my mind. We just didn't have the tools yet. That's how the experimenting began.'

They gesture to a map of the Ice Empire pinned up on the wall, depicting everything from our eastern borders with Adella and Rhiannon's territories to the surrounding mountains, the city in the centre, and the impenetrable ice beyond. The map looks new in its saturated colours, but it's already scorched in places. *And* damp, like it only recently caught fire and had to be doused.

'Candace says she found you quite far into the borders,' Elm says. 'Though we don't know why she was out there in the first place. What we do know is that you've always been impervious to magic. I never fully bought that Candace warded you, and I wondered if being exposed out in the borders as a baby was what did it instead. Bearra is the heart of magic, of triarue, so doesn't it make sense that there's less and less magic at the borders? Maybe none at all once you get far enough?'

'I don't know,' I say, bristling. 'Does it?'

'That's what I set out to discover. I sent the drones beyond where any human could go, and many of them didn't come back. Whether their enchantments wavered because they were so far from humanity, or the ice took them, or something else, I don't know. But a few *did* return as I learned to make them stronger, and they brought me objects.'

'Objects like the nutcracker?'

'Exactly.' They shuffle over to a wooden trunk by the window, unlocking it with a magical tap, and pull out an array of toys. A mouse with a crown. A babushka filled with tiny echoing figures. Wind-up dolls. A harlequin. 'I've tested them over and over,' they say. 'None of these objects can be touched by magic. They're . . . *anti*-enchanted.'

To prove it, Elm lights their hand with orange power, and picks up a ballerina figurine. The magic flows right around it, not touching the porcelain.

I lean back. '*Oh.*'

Curious, I handle a teddy bear from the trunk, and there's something calming about it. Just like my nutcracker. The anti-enchantment makes it feel quiet, asleep. Not like iron, with its reverse-effects to magic. *This* has a nothingness to it that makes my shoulders drop, like a droning noise you only notice when it stops.

'I don't know what to say.' I meet my best friend's eyes, unable to hide my apprehension. 'What does this mean? What does it mean about *me*?'

'It means that if human-made things exist out there, there must be humans there. In a place so far from magic that anything from there can't be touched by it. Beyond the ice, Isla.'

Goosebumps travel down my arms despite the warmth of the workshop. 'Don't you think if that were true, if more civilisation existed, we'd know about it already?'

I want to argue, to find any excuse to say this isn't true, that there can't be anything beyond what we know, right on our doorstep. That I can't possibly be so foreign, so much more unknown than I already feared.

'There's a reason we could never find your parents,' they say gently. 'They don't exist here. If they're alive, they're from a place deep in the borders, where they can't be traced by magic. A village, a city, an entire world, I don't know.'

'*Fairies.*' I shuffle a pile of haphazardly placed tools off an armchair and fall into it. '*Elm.* What are we going to—'

'Elm!' The door swings open, and behind it stands a giant puppy, panting and grinning wildly, covered in a soft yellow coat. 'And my lady.' Zeus bows to me.

My stomach lurches with motion sickness, even though I'm perfectly still. I'd have preferred an actual dog breaking into the workshop.

'Your Royal Highness,' Elm mutters, expressionless. 'How great of you to visit.'

Zeus waves, nearly knocking down a shelf of hammers. He clears his throat and tumbles over to Elm, picking up the much shorter person in a suffocating hug.

'Ah!' Elm coughs.

Zeus's eyes gleam. *Fairies*, does he have tears in his eyes? 'I missed you so much,' he cries, his gaze not leaving Elm's face. Unfortunately for my best friend, they're possibly the only person in the world Zeus loves as much as me. Well, Relia has to share that responsibility now too. If only she were here to babysit. 'How have you been, cupcake?'

Elm stands back, as if scared of being tackled again. 'How have *I* been? Don't you have yourself to talk about?'

Zeus claps. 'I'm learning to be good at *listening* now. It's all very intriguing. And so charming of me.'

'Is that right,' says Elm. 'Well, everything is normal here, of course. Nothing interesting to report.' They glance at me, asking with their eyes, *What is Zeus allowed to know?*

I sigh. 'Just tell him.' *Or he'll bother us about it until he finds out.*

Elm quickly explains the nutcracker and their findings at the borders while Zeus nods along. 'Hm,' the prince replies. 'Yes. No, I always thought that, actually.'

'You thought people lived beyond the ice?' I ask in disbelief.

'I've seen them,' he says smugly.

'*What?*' Elm and I reply at once.

'Okay, I haven't. But I've always liked to believe.'

Elm and I *sigh* at once.

Zeus holds up his hands. 'We can look up and see the moon, the sun, the stars. None as beautiful and otherworldly as Isla, of course. But doesn't it make you think there's more in the universe than our small world?'

I scowl at him.

'Oh, my apologies. Because you really might be . . .' He shrinks. '. . . *Otherworldly.*'

'I'm done talking about this.' I stand, hands on hips. 'We can reconvene on this . . . whatever . . . once our more serious matters are dealt with. Since we're all here, we need to plan.' I meet Zeus's icy eyes, hoping he lets me change the subject. 'What are we going to do to stop the royals surrendering?'

He crosses his arms. 'Are you sure *we* should be having this conversation? We may not come to a solution we both like.'

'I don't like it either, but if we're going to save the empire, we need to be on the same team. We already agreed on that.'

'In Bearra maybe,' he says quietly, 'but here, we'll never be on the same team.' His shoulders drop. 'How can we be? Your mother is trying to take my parents' empire away from them. Or did you forget that just because we've been so friendly?'

'*Friendly?*' Elm questions. 'You two?'

I hold up a finger. 'We came to a political compromise, that's all. And surely that compromise means saving the world, and putting aside our differences until we do?'

Zeus gives me a sassy expression that makes me want to strangle him. 'You mean *me* putting aside *my* differences and doing what *you* want.'

'Well, yes. My ideas are always better.'

'You think you can just wrap me around your finger—'

'She can,' offers Elm. 'And you know Isla is always right.'

Zeus huffs defeatedly. 'Fine, if Elm agrees too, then I suppose I'm outvoted. But if this starts to backfire on me, I'm out.' He points to the door like he's being *so incredibly serious.* 'So what's your plan to win back our people and make them believe we can save them?'

I shift. 'Well, I don't have one yet.'

'Right. But *my* idea is wrong, no matter what it is.'

'Zeus—'

Elm shushes us. '*I* actually have an idea. One you'll *both* hate. Maybe that'll be a suitable compromise?'

I narrow my eyes. 'Go on.'

'Yes, let's hear it,' says Zeus.

Elm glances between the two of us. 'A united front is what you want, right? You want to show you're on the same team, to reignite faith in your leadership, whether the people are supporters of Candace or the royals. *Think.* What have people always done throughout history to make political alliances?'

All my earlier motion sickness rushes. 'No. No, Elm. That's too much. I've already had a bad day.'

'I'm not saying get *married.* Just . . . pretend to be together until the war is over. Make the people think you've truly joined forces.'

'Wait—' Zeus's feet point to the doorway as if poised to escape. 'Are you saying what I think—?'

Elm nods. 'It's so obvious. Be the allies you need the world to believe you are. Show everyone you can work together and *both* be the leaders they want, rather than being caught up fighting each other.'

'I really don't think . . .' I start, but I can't deny it's a fantastic idea. I just absolutely hate it.

Zeus works his jaw, cringing. At first it seemed like Zeus's dream come true to pretend to be with me, but it hits me why Elm thought he'd hate it too. If Zeus really does love me, and we're not careful, he could be really hurt by a plan like this. It wouldn't just be fooling the empire – it would be toying with Zeus's feelings.

The prince has a lot more to lose. Does he realise that?

'I'll do it.' Zeus stands tall. 'Isla, if you're in, I am. I *want* to work together. But we need to be strategic. Take it slow.' I'm sure he's holding back a wink, because his eye is twitching.

My head drops into my hands. 'I suppose I can't say no. To my very sincere dismay, this could work.'

Elm nods victoriously, if a bit over-excitedly, and I wonder if there's more to this idea than just politics. But they couldn't . . . *no*. They couldn't be trying to get Zeus and me together for *real*?

CHAPTER TWELVE

The absolute last – and possibly worst – thing I thought I could ever be forced to do befalls me. I find myself on a *date* with *Prince Zeus.*

I link my arm through his, reluctantly noticing the slightest spark as we stroll through the Fairy Gardens – a botanic paradise thirty minutes away from the city by sleigh. The sun is high, and the flower fields are crowded with Imperials taking walks in the magically-heated atmosphere.

The gardens are enchanted to stop any and all snow. It's a waste of magic, in my opinion, but it means we have an ever-summer landscape to escape to.

The warm air and the expanses of red roses, purple lavender, pink camellias, and blue buttercups are enough to make the garden a favourite romantic attraction.

Zeus smiles at me. Each colour of every flower reflects in his clear eyes, each shade brightening his features. He's a springtime dream. Anyone else would long to call him theirs.

I *try* to grin back. We need to be the Ice Empire's sparkling new love story. Enemies united by the power of passion. I've got to make it seem real.

Which is why we're pretending to be here on utterly *non*-romantic terms. Two political rivals simply enjoying a day out, but suspiciously unable to keep their hands off each other. Our romance will be more believable if the people think we don't want them to know about it. *An act within an act.* We'll do the true reveal in a few days, once enough rumour has spread.

Selling the love story is the most important part of the plan. We could announce an engagement, but how could our people believe our partnership were founded on anything real? They'd know it was only for appearances.

But if we show we're in love, they'll believe that we *wanted* this. That we're truly on the same page. On the same side.

'A lovely day with my lovely princess,' Zeus muses, and I truly can't tell if he's being genuine. His light hair glints in the sunlight, haloing him as he picks a mottled yellow and pink rose from a colourful bush. Girls giggle behind us, and he passes me the flower with barely-contained excitement. 'I could pick for you every bloom in the universe, yet none would compare to your beauty.'

I wince – but only on the inside. My face aches from resisting its urge to scrunch. We're supposed to be going for *subtly* suspicious behaviour. I need to remain serious, not look like a lovesick fool.

So really, I'm simply trying to not look angry. Which I am.

'Shh.' I push him back lightly as people walk past, gawking. 'Don't be so obvious.'

'That I love you?' he replies, whispering loud enough for people to hear.

I sigh, leading him into the depths of the lavender field, where we'll get at least some privacy hidden amongst the stems. Chatter floats from neighbouring garden displays, but it's quieter here. We can talk and strategise while attempting body language that makes us appear as though we want to be all over each other.

Fairies. This is a terrible idea, isn't it? How have I succumbed to such *lows*?

We spread out a royally soft picnic rug and open a basket of food from the palace: a pile of sweets, jellies, hard candy, liquorice sticks, berries, and strawberry cakes. I hold a lemon jelly between my fingers, letting it wobble in the breeze before popping it into my mouth with a satisfying squelch. *That's better.*

Rain or shine, war or peace, Imperials will never be left without their sugar.

Their? I shake my head. *Our. Our. I'm still one of them. Us.*

I gaze out at the mountains, west of the Fairy Gardens. Snow-topped as always, the ranges touch the skies, shielding our city from the walls of ice that lay not far beyond. The borders. A cold so severe no human has ever passed through.

Except for *me?*

Zeus gently takes my hands, and I realise I've been tearing apart an innocent stick of lavender. Without its petals, it looks as measly as I feel. He pries the stick from my fingers. 'The war, or the nutcracker? Or . . . me?' he asks, a touch of guilt in his tone.

I meet his eyes, hating how he can read me. I've trained my entire life to hide my emotions and appear unshakable. How can he suddenly break past all of that? He never used to be able to. Not before he became all *sensitive* and *selfless*.

'The nutcracker,' I admit, and then a new fear arises: maybe it isn't Zeus being observant at all, and it's actually *me* dropping my guard around him.

A gust of wind sends petals sailing through the air like coloured snowflakes. The scent of the flowers mixes together, the pleasant perfume softening the anxiety in my mind. I shake petals from my hair, and, making sure people are watching us, pick a scarlet piece of rose from Zeus's pale strands. I run my hands through that soft hair much longer than I should. Stare into his eyes as I do.

Fairies, I must be very good at this, because even I have butterflies. Distant giggles meet my ears, and, invigorated with success, I nearly go to touch him again. But he swallows, his eye contact fluttering.

I quickly lift my hand away. 'Sorry,' I stutter. I should've known that was too much. He's too easily enchanted. This false relationship may be annoying to me, but it's dangerous to him.

'Whatever Elm has found,' he says, blinking and moving slightly back from me, 'it doesn't make a difference to who you are.'

It takes me a moment to remember what he's talking about. That I was worried about myself before I got lost in our scheme. I run my fingers over the picnic rug to remind myself where I am.

'Your parents left you with that toy to protect you,' he says, 'and it has. They left you in the Ice Empire, and you've never been anything less than an Imperial. And that's coming from an Imperial royal, so good luck denying it.'

He lifts his chin, all his cool confidence back. 'Darling, we'll figure all of this out, but remember it can't change who you are in your heart.'

'Oh. I— Thank you.' Is my heart *fluttering* now? No. Absolutely not. It's warming, that's all, because we're in enchanted weather, and the butterflies in my stomach aren't butterflies, they're nausea from all the stress.

Like a terrible omen, two real butterflies, blue and shimmery, flitter above us.

Am I superstitious? No. But the way things are going, any kind of sign feels like a threat.

A long shadow appears over us, and I nearly gasp when I turn to see Councillor Dierdre with her brows raised so high they might burst off her lined face. 'How lovely it is,' she says, 'to see the two of you not arguing for once.'

I raise my head; she's in the dominant position, standing over us, but my back is straight as always and I do my best to look down my nose at her. 'Yes, Councillor, even we can place our pride aside for the sake of the empire,' I tell her. 'Especially in the midst of a war.'

'Is that right?' She folds her arms over her cloak. 'If I didn't know better, I would guess this is a romantic rendezvous.'

Zeus gives her a charming smile, feigning the slightest slip of anxiety as his brow twitches. 'Councillor, please. Rumours are the last thing we need at the moment. Don't you agree that too much is at stake in the empire for such immature gossip?'

Her eyes flash. Zeus has struck the right nerve. As much as I detest her presence, Dierdre is the perfect mark. She'll bring our *rumour* right to the palace, while the rest of the garden-goers spread the news through the common people.

Maybe this *is* a good idea.

I lightly brush Zeus's hand, as if on instinct, then pull my fingers back – making sure she sees it. Zeus and I exchange a quick glance that could mean a million things to Dierdre. It's meaningless to me, though, so I'm not sure why it feels magically charged.

'It isn't me you have to worry about,' she says, watching us closely. 'If our precious prince is being wooed, jealousy will spread quickly. Surely the two of you are wise enough to realise that?'

I wave, dismissing the idea. Naturally, she doesn't mention anyone would be jealous of Zeus having *me*. 'If rumours are what we must endure for the sake of peace between the royals and Candace, peace within our leadership . . .'

'How noble you are, General.' She steps back, signalling her intent to leave. *Thank the fairies.* 'Though it won't matter much. Lire will soon be our highest ranking leader. She can protect us in ways Candace cannot. Your mother was never a real fairy, after all.'

I drop my composure for a moment to push myself to my feet, standing at eye level to her. Giving her my most lethal glare, I utter, 'The empire will remember your cowardice when it matters most.'

She grits her teeth, spins, and leaves in a flurry of purple petals.

Zeus offers his hand to help me back down, looking nothing other than impressed. I could burn the world to the ground and he'd still worship me, for some inexplicable reason.

I do take his hand, but I slump to the ground nonetheless, overcome with irritation. 'Less than an hour in, and I'm already tired of this plan,' I groan.

He picks a strawberry from our basket, pinching the leaves at the top. 'That couldn't have gone better, darling lover. What's wrong?'

'She has it out for me!' I nearly slap the strawberry from his hand, but he pops it into his mouth just in time.

Chewing, he brushes my hand to the side, placing it back on the rug. 'Don't lose your composure,' he whispers. 'We're having a good time, remember?'

Fairies. I shudder. I feel like I'm trapped within myself, caged within a mask that I can't survive this world without, can't *save* this world without.

But I can't breathe. I can't show a single emotion without getting criticised, and even then, I get criticised for seeming cold.

It isn't Zeus's fault. He's only trying to help me. He's showing he understands how I need people to see me, that the world is different for me than for him. But it's *him* who gets to live the life I deserve. I can't help but resent him for it.

If only we'd had opposite lives, could we have been happy?

What if I'd been a princess, and he'd been the son of a false-fairy? He could have spent his life searching for his parents and dallying around without consequence, the world not suffering for it, because he wouldn't be bestowed with all his unwanted responsibility.

Meanwhile, I could rise as queen of the world, have no one in my way as I expanded the empire to the ends of the borders – and beyond.

I start to take deep, calming breaths, and it's only when I look at him again that I realise I've subconsciously matched his. Those wide shoulders rise and fall with rhythmic calm, and he runs his hand up and down my back in time.

My instinct is to slap him away, but it does help. Like some kind of meditation, continuing to breathe with him makes my thoughts slow.

He made me feel better?

What is happening to this world?

CHAPTER THIRTEEN

It's rare for me to truly feel the cold, but this afternoon I pull my coat tight around my body, fighting a chill that freezes my skin and sends tingles up and down my spine.

In the Ice Empire, especially in our city deep in the mountains, we're mostly protected from any high wind. But Elm, Zeus and I have taken a sleigh several hours north-west, as far as we could go into the borders – at least, as far as any of us dared to go – and now we huddle in a snow-sugared pine forest that offers only a little reprieve from the blizzarding weather.

Here, the flat expanses of white mist, skies, and ground are un-forgiving. Worse even than the awfully lifeless areas around Kara's

Capital. We may live in the snow too, but we had the sense to at least build our city where it's habitable.

Fairies, that reminds me. I hope Candace has been handling Kara well enough. I haven't had much to do with that front, since I've been too busy with Bearra. But the death fairy was displeased when we allied with Queen Dawn without consulting her first. Then again, it isn't my fault Kara tried to kidnap Dawn – and that was after cursing her to die a century ago. *She* burnt that bridge first.

Zeus's cheeks and nose are red and wind chapped. He shivers in the icy wind, arms crossed over his wide chest as he leans against the sleigh. 'Elm – you've been – doing this – alone – for – months?'

The Adellan grins; they've always loved the cold as much as me, despite coming from the most temperate territory. In a fluffy scarf that wraps around their head, sparkling with magic that keeps their ears warm, they say, 'The drones get the worst of it, travelling as deep as possible before coming back. I've never been further than this – though I'd like to. I just didn't dare do it alone.'

'If there is life out here,' Zeus says, rubbing his throat as if to warm his vocal cords, 'I c-can't imagine why they bother.'

I glare at him. That's my family he's talking about. Possibly.

'Oh – Isla – I meant—'

'Forget it.'

We venture a little deeper into the pine forest, careful not to slip on the layers of ice that occasionally appear beneath the thick snow. We trudge on through in our heavy boots. Little avalanches slide from pine needles as we bump the trees. It's slow moving, but we're used to walking this kind of terrain.

Elm holds two drones: one is shaped like a butterfly with automated fluttering iridescent wings, and the other is a goldfish, its agile body and twirling fins ready to cut through damp air.

'It'll be different today,' Elm says. 'Isla, with you here, there's so much more I can surmise from what we find. Who knows – maybe this place will respond to you as one of its own.'

A gust of wet wind nearly has me running back to the comfort of the sleigh. 'I don't think it's showing me any favouritism,' I say, shoving my hands deeper into my coat pockets.

With a flash of orange enchantment, Elm sends the butterfly and goldfish soaring out into the mist, flapping and swimming. Their resemblance to real creatures is so uncanny I have to blink to remind myself they're only toys.

With magic glittering in their wake, they speed into the borders until the golden sparkles dim entirely. Lost in a place we'll never reach.

'How long do they need?' Zeus asks, teeth chattering.

'No more than half an hour.' Elm tugs their gloves on, magic complete. 'So far my drones have spent twenty minutes on average before returning. That's six drones over three visits. Ten minutes there – to as far as they can manage – and then ten back. Give or take a few minutes as they look around for objects to collect. These newer drones are hardier, so I'm hoping they'll get further and find more.'

I watch their analysing eyes with a confusing blend of pride and caution. Elm has always been brilliant, a creative marvel. Their toys have consistency and massively improved over their many years in the empire. They can be a brilliant engineer *and* magic user when they want to be. But this level of scientific discovery is new. Elm is a tinkerer, not an explorer.

As usual, I wish I could convince Elm to help the empire create weapons for the war. Does this new, more exploratory side mean their help could be an option somewhere down the line?

When they were brought to the empire as a child for their engineering skills, they were given absurd amounts of magic in the hopes they'd expand the empire with their abilities. Instead, Elm has lived to bring the empire happiness and whimsy, which is why the toymaker is so beloved. Their creations are stunning, wholly unique.

Even so, those creations were never brilliant enough to travel beyond where a person could, deep into the borders. Elm has gone beyond humanity's previous limits.

To win this war, having them crafting weapons instead of toys could change the tide entirely. And yet, how can I keep asking that of my best friend, who I adore so much because of their *kindness*? How can I ask someone who is all heart to indirectly kill hundreds, thousands, even?

But if they don't, and Lire wins because of it, how many more people could be hurt?

'You're brilliant, Elm,' Zeus says, echoing my unspoken admiration. He clamps his hands over his heart. 'I'm so lucky you're my best friend.'

'Wow,' Elm deadpans. 'Thanks.'

Zeus nods emphatically. 'You are so very welcome.'

The logical part of my mind is yelling at me: *This is the man you're pretending to be in love with?* But at least he's being nice, and if I'm being honest, I admire Zeus's authenticity.

Once, that authenticity showed very little promise, like a glass window into an empty room, but there's more to him now.

Even when he's being silly, he's always coming from a place of love. Love for others, for himself, for the world around him. Zeus *is* love and joy. And though I've spent my life keeping him at arm's length because of our parents' feud . . . I can't help but lean into the soft feeling that's warming my heart now. Especially seeing him be so nice to Elm, the person *I* love most.

Why in the seven fairies am I feeling like this?

For such a long time, the prince was a burden, a parasite attached to me and Elm. Suddenly I feel . . . *lucky* . . . to be one of the chosen few he pours all his love towards.

People with hearts that big are rare, and he's finally learned to make that heart look outwards instead of only within. Truly, what did Relia and Dawn hit him over the head with?

'I'll be back at the sleigh working on some papers,' Elm says, buttoning up their satchel and throwing it over their shoulder. 'Why don't you two have a stroll? There's a beautiful lake just a couple minutes' walk east. Take a compass and some skates. I already packed them in the sleigh – we'll grab them on the way.'

I narrow my eyes. Elm is acting nonchalant, but this feels too planned to be an idea they've just come up with. Sending Zeus and I off on our own? With skates they happened to have packed?

Once again I wonder if Elm is trying to create romance where there is definitely none.

Fine, I'll admit I'm *confused* about whether or not there's *none*, but there certainly shouldn't be any. Especially not from me.

Because Zeus isn't what I want – he's what stands in the way of what I want. He's just been very friendly lately, that's all, making things complicated. I'm not used to having friends – so it's quite possible these sudden nice feelings I have towards him are only platonic.

'That sounds lovely,' I say, giving Elm a glare but trudging back to the sleigh to collect what we'll need. I don't have the heart to shut their schemes down. Besides, I do need something to get on with while we wait. If I stand around, I'll go out of my mind. 'We'll be back soon.'

Elm gives me a gratified smile. 'I'll scream if I need you, sweet.'

'Right back at you, snow angel.'

Zeus claps. 'Skating with my lovely general! Just when I thought this day couldn't get better.'

I could've sworn he was complaining a few minutes ago, but . . .

We head back to the sleigh and Zeus grabs the bag Elm packed with water, snacks and skates, carrying everything over his broad shoulders while I check the compass. Something jingles suspiciously in the bag as we travel, but I figure it's metal brushing against metal, our thermal water packs.

It isn't that I walk *close*-close, but we keep managing to brush hands, our bare fingers warm against each other. Each feathery touch is a small spark, a taste of something bigger.

Something I do not want.

The urge to hold his hand is merely an instinct to stay warm using his body heat.

My breath hitches as we reach the lake, the mist dispersing around a silver and white sheet of ice that stretches as far as I can see, meeting faraway hills.

I rarely feel truly alone – even when I'm lonely. Constantly under scrutiny, I'm always looking out for someone to catch me making a mistake. I watch every word, every movement. Even when I'm by myself, it's as if I'm performing for invisible people.

Here, deep in the borders, there is absolutely no one near – except Zeus, that is, but even his presence can't bother me. There's no life, no noise except the wind. Even though each breath scratches my lungs with frost, I breathe deeply, feeling my shoulders drop.

Have I been that tense all day?

Out in this beautifully pure world, I'm as close to home as I could possibly get. The lack of stimulation from noise, from colour, from any scent other than the ice threatening the inside of my nose and mouth . . . I could drop into the soft snow and fall right to sleep.

Here, everything is in its place. Here, though the world is deadly, though it constantly moves and changes, the landscape knows exactly what it is. It is strong and unbreakable, and yet it flows with each change of the wind.

Is this my parents' legacy? There may not be any enchantment out here, but surely, *surely* this place must be considered magical.

A breeze blows through my hair and drops snowflakes on my coat. Zeus laughs, reaching out a finger to wipe a snowflake from the tip of my nose. In this greyscale world, he's the only colour, his pink cheeks warm as the sun.

He places our ice skates on the snowy ground – there's that jingling sound again – and we sit to put them on before going near the ice. We're Imperials; we can walk on it if we must, but we've had enough bumps and bruises to know we don't want to.

At the edge of the lake – was it ever truly a lake, or was it always frozen over? – we shiver together as we unlace our boots and squeeze our thickly-furred socks into the skates.

Zeus and I moan simultaneously as our feet slip inside. With a spark of orange, the skates heat up from within, sending waves of warmth up to the tip of my head, relaxing my body all over.

'Elm,' I utter. 'They're too good.'

'You don't have to tell me,' Zeus says, blinking slowly with relief. Once he's spent a long moment yawning, he asks, 'Might I have this dance, my lady?' He stands, steady on his skates, and holds out his hand for me as I finish tying my laces.

The skates fit snugly, even with my layers of socks, and the blades are easy to adjust to. I'm a brilliant skater, but it helps to have royal-quality, enchanted equipment.

'Certainly, Your Highness.' I take his hand with a small smile.

I hate to admit it, but I'm finding I quite like being friends with Zeus. Friends have boundaries, and maybe all along I only needed to tell him how I really felt about his annoying habits for us to be able to stand each other.

That day by the Imperial encampment in Bearra might have changed everything, even though I didn't realise it at the time. He hasn't changed overnight, and I'd never expect him to. But I didn't think he could change at *all* when I'd only seen an immature boy who expected everything to be handed to him.

Now, Zeus is a man who could become a king. A man with a generous heart, persuasive charm, the smarts to find the right allies, and the bravery to speak his mind.

Maybe I never saw this in him before because I was afraid of what it meant if I came to respect him. I can't forget that he's an enemy to what Candace and I are trying to build.

Or is that all part of it? Is my new affection for Zeus just my mind's way of rebelling against my mother?

Everything has been different since the nutcracker entered my life. I can't trust my mother anymore, so is that why I'm putting my emotions in the wrong places? Can I even trust myself?

Or, maybe none of it is that meaningful at all, and I'm simply torturing myself with all this overthinking.

Zeus's eyes light up, our gloved fingers entwined as he helps me to my feet, and my worries dissolve into the fog. *Let me enjoy this.*

I'm tall on my skates, but the Imperial prince still towers over me. He steps onto the frozen lake and, sliding backwards, pulls me forward.

I exhale as the steadiness of the ground turns into blissful gliding. I take off, flying, floating. Otherworldly.

Skating has always made me feel as if I'm in a dream.

Zeus lets go of my hand and spins, mist billowing around him. Ice sprays as he comes to a stop. 'If only there was music. I'm hardly as good at dancing without a rhythm.'

'Zeus, you're hardly good at dancing.'

He smirks. 'I suppose you'll find out, won't you? At least I can skate better than you.'

'Now don't even— Wait.' Resisting the appeal of challenging him to a race, or a competition of skill, I remember the jingling in our bag. I glide back to the edge of the ice, opening the pack. Sitting inside is a music box, a beautiful dark wood etched with triarue.

I knew it. Elm had this all planned out.

Zeus skates up to me, dropping to his knees so he can see. 'Did I just wish that to life?' He squeezes his eyes shut. 'I wish for Candace's demise.' He glances at me with one eye open. 'Oops. Sorry. No I don't. Well, not in front of Isla, Magical Wishing Lake.'

'*Zeus,*' I hiss. Well, that's some of his spell over me broken, at least. 'Shut up.'

I open the lid of the music box, revealing a beautiful ballerina within. Her posy skirt falls from her frame in waves, delicate ribbons tied to her arms and the skirt's hem. On one side of the box is a key to wind it up, and beneath the ballerina is the music contraption – the keys locked into a sequence to recite a song. Like a tiny piano that needs no player.

'Elm is—' Zeus begins.

'We need to start inventing new words for how amazing Elm Is,' I say.

'Wind it up,' he insists. 'And I shall twirl you around this ice in enchanting ways you could never even imagine.' He lifts a finger before I can reply. 'With your consent, darling.'

I spin the key and the box *dings*, a sweet, high-pitched bell. I spin and spin, hoping to wind it up fully so the song lasts for a full dance. When I release the key, a classic Imperial melody plays in the soft chimes of the music box's keys. The ballerina turns slowly, the ribbons tied to her twirling around her like magical tendrils. Mesmerising and magical.

'Well, then?' I say to Zeus, setting down the music box and motioning for him to take my hand once more.

CHAPTER FOURTEEN

We softly sway to the music, letting our skates slide as they take us together across the ice. As we gain confidence, Zeus spins me around, ice spraying as I circle perfectly. He places my hands over his shoulders while his own wrap around my waist, holding the sensitive area above my hips and next to my stomach.

The music trills and sways in rhythms we match with each glide, and I throw my head back, a childlike laugh bubbling out of me. 'It has been far too long,' I say, catching my breath.

His gaze is soft, his hair covered in snowflakes. 'I haven't seen you smile like this in years.'

'I can't remember the last time I had . . .' I pull him back so we can continue swaying to the music. '*Fun.*'

'We'd best make the most of this, then.' He doesn't miss a beat, placing his arms around me and moving us along the ice with soft treads that have us soaring. I keep my eyes locked on his, still fighting a giggle as the wind blows through my hair.

Soon we're sailing, gliding far from the music box, though I can still hear it well. The melody changes to beautiful harmonies, long, drawling notes.

Then: strings.

I nearly topple. 'Do you hear that?'

Zeus listens intently. 'Someone invited a very talented flautist.'

That's right – there's woodwind now as well, and a light percussion building on top of the strings. The same melody plays, but as we dance, the orchestra grows.

Is this . . . *possible*? To contain the sound of a dozen musicians in a box that's only supposed to ding like bells?

The ballerina glows with orange magic as she turns – I can see her even from here – and more beautiful notes fly out of the box and over to our dancing bodies.

What has Elm created? I didn't know manipulating sound was an option for magic, except for using it to create shields that block or warp noise. Is this an evolution from that? How did they come up with—

'Stop it,' Zeus utters, moving his hand from my waist to tap my forehead. 'You don't need to understand it. Just dance with me and *enjoy* it.'

My first instinct is to disagree with him, because it's *him*, but he's right. I take a breath, clear my mind – as well as I can, at least – and focus on listening to the melody and moving my feet.

Heat rushes through me as Zeus lets go and stretches out the space between us, letting me do another spin. I glide first around him, then open my arms wide, soaring like a swan as I race across the ice with my eyes closed.

It's like my heart is filled with the colour yellow, like my soul is blossoming with daisies. Another laugh escapes me, my skin tingling. *Joy.* Pure, senseless, wonderful joy.

Zeus catches up to me, and he's smiling so widely his eyes are half closed, his head still craned to take in the orchestra. 'I'd stay here forever,' he says, panting. 'With you. I'd stay in this moment forever. I don't care how cold it is.'

I could say the same, but the words don't pass my lips. It would be so easy right now, with the snow falling around us, with the harmonies lilting, all alone, and so happy, to make this moment even more exciting by giving him what he wants most – me.

He takes my hand and I shiver as he pulls me to him. We're so close, and we're sliding – sliding down a slippery slope, and I don't mean the ice. I shiver, electrified, my eyes locked on his.

My heart is racing, my stomach fluttering, and my lips feel so sensitive, awaiting a kiss I secretly long for. *Fairies,* I must be weak if after only a few good days with Zeus – after eighteen *years* of wishing he'd disappear – I'm having fantasies about kissing him.

I try to pull away but he inches closer. *Is this really happening? Could I let this happen and . . . enjoy it?*

But what if this is all part of his scheme? What if he doesn't care for me at all, and this new act is just a way to distract me? To hurt me?

We may not be enemies, but we've never been on the same side. If I'm too busy being in love with him, I could lose focus on my leadership.

He crouches, looking up at me as he floats along the ice, running a hand along the soft sheet of the lake. He's laughing, and I know, I have to be sure . . . this is real, isn't it?

This can't be pretend. Not all this joy. There's no one here to see our false partnership.

So could it be that something real is growing in the shadows of our politics?

Zeus rises back up, and we glide together, dancing in the wind. I let my doubts go as we put our hands out, laughing like we did when we were kids. How many times have we skated together?

But never like this.

The rhythm quickens, snappier, the chords still deep and romantic but with a new urgency. We skate quickly, more playful in the way we spin each other, attempting small jumps.

A silver flicker behind Zeus draws my eye. In the falling snow and the heavy mist, at first I think I imagined it. But then, again – a light like a tiny diamond floating in the air. It disappears as quickly as it came.

I shake my head. Am I dizzy?

But when Zeus and I turn, a masterpiece builds before us: a spattering of stars, flying through the mist, through the snowflakes.

Zeus gasps. 'Fireflies?'

'*White* fireflies?'

One of them flutters right up to me, and I place out my palm. I gasp as it lands in the centre, unfolding its wings and blinking its little light. Like a miniature fairy.

With no natural predators out here, they must be trusting creatures.

'Diamonds of the borders,' Zeus says. 'Mystical and beautiful. Like you.'

I can't help it – I smile as the firefly flutters back into the mist, returning to its star-like sisters. Zeus and I clasp our hands again, this time gliding right into the cluster, and they move around us like glitter, alighting the snow, the mist, turning my world into a realm of shimmering gems.

Yet my eyes are drawn only to *him*. His clear eyes, gazing at me with such tenderness. His perfect lips, that sharp jaw. The royal suit he wears with the thick down coat. His near-white hair, brushed perfectly out of his eyes.

I never cared about his looks, and though I don't *dislike* gazing at him, what I see now is beyond even that. What I see is the boy I've cared for since we were children. The boy I could never admit to myself was my friend. The boy it hurt too much to not hate, when we were always working against each other.

'Truly, it's easy to believe you're from out here,' he says, lowering himself and leading my glide. 'It's as perfect as you are.'

I blink slowly, and I'm not sure which of us does it, or if it's the skates, the dance, the fireflies, the waltzing snowflakes, but we're pulled closer to each other, and he rises again, our bodies nearly touching as our hands reach out at our sides, fingers entwined.

'Zeus,' I whisper. 'Thank you.'

He leans his head down. The music sways, still urgent, still building. 'Whatever for, General?'

'For always showing me who I am,' I say. Before I can stop myself, my hands leave his and reach up of their own accord, cradling his jaw. We stop moving, and instead glide with the momentum left from our dance. I'm in a dream, I think. I've fallen into another world.

He swallows, teeth clenching under my palm. 'Isla.'

Heat rushes through me from where our skin touches. I can't get my face to reach his – I can't stand on my toes in skates – so I gently tug him down towards me.

I might *burst*. Truly, there's a fire in me that might explode out of every crevice. His lips part, as do mine, and as he comes closer, our chests press together and his hot breath touches my cheeks.

I tilt my head up that last touch, and—

'Isla.' He gasps. Pulls back. I move forward again, but he stops me. 'You know there's nothing more I want. So, please. *Don't.*'

I drop my hands. The fireflies flitter away, blinking out. Even the music stops. The spell broken. 'I— I'm so sorry.' *Fairies*, how selfish could I be? 'I was caught up in the moment, Zeus. I didn't mean to toy with you like that.'

He shakes his head. 'I know – don't be sorry. It's my fault too. You capture me so easily. I just . . . I can't let this go too far. Not if it's never going to be real.'

I don't know what to say. It could be, one day, couldn't it? But in the midst of a war, now is hardly the time to find out. Not in the midst of all that lies between us.

'*Isla.*' His eyes are so filled with hurt that I can't breathe for a second.

I didn't want to bring him pain. I've never seen him truly let his guard down like this. Even when I've had to save him, he has always saved face. Even when I brought him back to the empire after being kidnapped by Sierra Reed, and after he broke his arm, he always stayed cocky.

Now my gut pulls with guilt and disappointment.

'We should get back,' I tell him, looking away. 'The drones have probably returned, and Elm will be waiting in the cold.'

This time, as we skate, he doesn't hold my hand. Our glides aren't synchronised as we return to our bag, our shoes, and the music box. In heavy silence, we change back into our boots and trudge back to the sleigh.

Elm waves as they see us through the mist, a mischievous expression on their face. 'Have fun?' they shout into the wind. They must catch our depressed air, though, because they quickly suck in a breath and say, 'Skating can be exhausting, can't it?'

I quicken my pace and meet them at the sleigh. 'Find anything yet?'

'Not yet. They're taking their time, which is good news. Hopefully not too long, though. I need a hot bath.'

Me too.

Zeus shifts between his feet, avoiding our eyes. *Fairies,* what have I done to him? 'I do need to get back,' he says. 'For . . . meetings. Yes. Many meetings this afternoon.'

Elm raises their brows. 'You have meetings every afternoon. You never go to them.'

A flash of orange catches my eye and, thanking the seven fairies, or however many there are these days, I point into the mist. 'They're coming back!'

The wide wings of a butterfly flap, and beside it is the fish, a streak of gold. Clasped in claws that extend from their bellies are an assortment of objects from the deep borders.

Zeus sighs with relief, then quickly covers by clearing his throat.

Elm reaches towards their creations, jumping with excitement. 'Things!' The drones land in their hands. Elm hops into the sleigh to lay them out on the seat along with their gatherings.

I lean over for a better look, Zeus close behind me. The butterfly holds a tattered old dress, a soft ball for a sport I can't place, and a metal knife and fork. The goldfish has returned with two teddies and a . . . *book*.

While Zeus plays with the knife and fork, clanging them together, and Elm studies the material of the dress, I reach over the side of the sleigh and take the old book. It reminds me of the old ones I've seen in Bearra, those Nova tomes they're all so proud of. The cloth cover is worn but soft under my fingertips, tied with a loose string.

I open it gently, my breath halting, though I don't know why. Maybe Elm was right, that I'd have a connection to these things, because I just know – I can sense something about this. My eyes go blurry, my fingertips sparking with anticipation.

As the pages fall open, I expect them to be thick and printed, but they're thin and lined, each word scrawled in handwriting. This is no book – it's someone's journal.

Someone's journal from the *borders*. Someone outside our world.

My next exhale is a shudder, and I force myself to calm my breathing. Zeus and Elm are talking about something, but their words are muted, dissolving into the mist and the cold as the journal enraptures me.

I skim each page. The words, the names I read, the glimpses of the stories and the dates – none of it makes any sense. I know the things it talks about are from a place far from here, and at first I wonder, hope, even, that it's all a fantasy. A joke. Because what I'm reading right now can't be real. What this says about *me* can't be true.

We'd thought people might live out here, that there might even be worlds beyond ours, that that's who I am. But what this journal details nearly makes me lose my footing.

I grip the sleigh, blinking hard. Snow must have gotten into my eyes. Zeus's distant voice asks if I'm okay, but I'm not here at all.

He taps my shoulder. 'What's that?'

I snap the journal shut and stick it in my coat. 'Nothing. Some child's musings.'

The first page: *This journal belongs to Kara Kennedy, age twenty-six.*

CHAPTER FIFTEEN

The foyer of our small castle bustles with a whirl of dancing feet and dramatic music. Tucked into the corner of a downstairs room and gazing into my mint tea, I squeeze my eyes and try to will some energy back into my body. I've spent the last hour speaking with Candace's carefully selected party attendees, trying to win people back to our side.

She's visiting, and it isn't the relief I'd hoped it would be.

She threw this party in my honour, for being such a *great leader of the empire* and *taking Bearra* and whatnot, but this is the last thing I want.

It isn't that I'm ungrateful, but if she really wanted to congratulate me, we would've had a quiet night in. This is about showing my victories to the Imperials.

The dark wood, crackling fireplace, and books along the walls of this sitting room tempt a quiet evening. But the only way I'd get that is if I abandoned the party and made myself look like a brat. So I stare, from my dark corner, at the grandfather clock on the other side of the room, watching it tick, tick, tick, the owl carving atop it winking at me as flashes of light pass over its jewelled eyes.

A glint of twinkling emerald warns me to move from the wall and paste on a smile in time for Candace to shimmy over. Her strawberry-blonde hair is braided in a crown on top of her head. A glittery enchantment makes the air shimmer around her as she walks.

It won't be long until my mother has a pair of wings.

'Sugar,' she hums, and all I can think is, *You know the truth and you lied to me.* 'You've done so well here already. I wish I could stay longer.' Her voice slurs ever so slightly. She's had a bit too much mulled wine. I'm not sure where her train of thought is going when she continues, 'It's so strange. I've brought it up before, and you've always said no, so I know it *can't* be true, but I keep hearing whispers of rumours about you and—'

Zeus rounds a corner and his jaw goes slack when he sees me. After a very long moment with our eyes locked – at least, the moment *feels* long – his attention travels to Candace. He straightens his back, his expression morphing into his signature cocky grin. 'Greetings, ladies,' he says, approaching. His fists are clenched.

So he also doesn't want to be here, only bearing it for appearances. We haven't seen each other in four days. Not since the kiss he rejected at the borders.

It isn't a great look for two people who are supposed to be in love, and yet I went to Elm's workshop yesterday and caught Zeus sneaking out the back. To be quite honest, I would've done the same. Just not gotten caught.

'Your Highness,' offers Candace. 'Thank you for attending tonight.'

'Wouldn't miss it.' He takes a sip of his drink, the glass dangerously small and breakable in his big hand. 'Thank you for the invitation.'

Even from here, the lights of the royal's castle can be seen lighting up the city like a beacon of warmth; but it's in *my* castle where the most powerful Imperials are gathered tonight. Including the prince.

Candace glances between us. 'Look at you two. Interacting for a good fifteen seconds and neither of you has been snippy or irritating. Did Bearra's traditional ways teach you some civility?'

My blood goes cold. 'Uh . . .'

She stiffens, lowering her voice. 'The rumours are true? The two of you are . . . *seeing each other*?'

'Shh,' Zeus urges, loud enough the entire room turns their heads. I can't tell if he's done it on purpose or not, but he acts surprised. 'Candace, the last thing we want is a scandal.'

Right on time, Councillor Dierdre – our biggest fan – pops her head around the corner, like a wolf who can smell fear. She doesn't approach, but she cranes her neck.

My mother has gone pale, but she tries to cover. 'We'll discuss it later. If this is to happen, there are rules and limits we need to put in place to ensure everyone's safety, and . . .'

'I wouldn't let anything bad happen,' I tell her. I should give her a hint that it isn't real, but after all the lies she's told me, I enjoy the idea of keeping her in the dark about something. Well, something else. *Fairies know* I'm going to keep her as far from Kara's journal as possible.

She untenses. 'I know that, sugar. Whatever happens, I support you.'

I try to smile. If only Elm were here, they'd distract her and the guests with their lovable demeanour and displays of their latest toys. But Elm hates political events, and can never be convinced to attend unless the queen and king themselves demand it.

'Anyway, back to the festivities,' says Candace, clasping her hands. That wine-tinged cheeky glint has re-entered her eyes. 'I have a surprise for you, Isla.'

My expression falls. 'What?' The only thing worse than a party is a party with a surprise. That's what happened when she gave me the nutcracker, and my life has only been nightmarish since.

'Ooh,' Zeus teases, before remembering we aren't talking and pressing his lips together.

Candace waves off my hesitation. 'Just a little fun for the night. A treat for us all.' She takes my hand, leading me out into the courtyard, which has been cleared of snow. Amongst the finely-cut hedges and under the sprawling starlight is a *stage*. She explains, 'I saw this troupe perform when I was last visiting Muse's Territory. They come from all over the world, and they're fantastic. I had to bring them here.'

She isn't usually so . . . enthusiastic. It makes me wonder if she's up to something. Candace, the fairy, the politician, is charming but powerful, always the perfect balance of likable and commanding. It may be the drinks and the guests, but she's unusually friendly, and I wish I could talk to her without her mask on. Figure out what her game is.

Though it isn't as if there's much to say, or much I want to hear from her. I can't wrap my head around my conflicting emotions. How can I loathe Candace the leader, but long for the Candace who has always been my mother?

Servants seat us in the largest chairs – throne like, plush couches – in the front row before the stage, ensuring we block many others' view. Zeus is not invited to sit beside us. They try to usher him away, but in an attempt to solidify our plan and our political alliance, I request for him to be seated beside me.

I'm *trying* to make this work.

An orchestra reveals themselves as music sounds from behind a sheer screen at the back of the stage. Their circles of instruments and musicians glow with yellow magic, and it's as if they've appeared out of nowhere.

Yellow-clad dancers scurry onto the stage en pointe, and I clap as eagerly as I can manage. With a build of harmonising strings, the Musan entertainers spring to life like little birds. The orchestra's magic wraps around them like sunlight.

Their precise, beautiful steps force me to soften. This *is* beautiful, and though it's more for our guests than for me . . . Candace must have had me in mind at least a little. I can never turn down the ballet.

A few minutes later, the music slows to a stop and the crowd applauds. I expect them to start a second dance, but they scurry back off the stage and disappear behind the screen, the star-like magic dimming until all is hidden again.

That's it?

I bristle as new light brightens – this time an enchanted blue. More dancers appear, but they're Gracian, with their straight black hair pulled into ribbons over azure dresses. Long strips of silk attached to their arms ripple like water as the light turns the stage into an underwater fairytale.

The music is stronger, with deep echoes that reflect the vastness of rivers and lakes. I almost hold my breath, so convinced by their display. The dancers move in slow, flowing movements, exquisite in every step.

Mesmerised, my head nearly spins. I could remain in the magic of this scene forever, but just like the Musan dancers, the Gracians bow and leave the stage all too soon, returning us to reality.

Candace grips my forearm in excitement. *Thank you,* I try to tell her with my eyes.

Beautiful art is exactly what I've needed to bring my hope back. To be reminded that I'm trying to save the world not just for my own sake, but for every incredible human and what they can create.

They say the fairies have all the power, but when I look at marvels like this, I know we have so much of our own magic to offer.

As the stage brightens with rosy hues, the newest set of dancers – two Amorans in baby pink costumes resembling flowers – pick themselves off the floor, rising as if blooming. The orchestra builds, starting with pretty flute trills and increasing into a romantic harmony that tugs at my heart with the push and pull of the instruments.

The dancers perform a love story between two flowers, from their first meeting, cautious and sweet, to nearly breaking apart as the music strikes with drama – and a final kiss that makes the crowd *aww*.

The *pas de deux* ends with the dancers wilting, returning to the stage floor.

I grin widely, closing my fists over the material of my coat. They're taking us clockwise through the territories, which means next is—

Bang. The orchestra explodes from romantic lulling into heavy percussion. Red magic builds until even the audience is bathed in it like a consuming fire. Ten long-limbed athletes of Rhiannon's Territory march onstage.

The melody takes on a subtler note – building tension with strong beats – as the dancers climb atop each other's shoulders, performing leaps and flips while others twirl bars of fire.

I duck as a flame passes across the front row, and Candace laughs at my reaction.

In the name of the seven fairies.

So much is happening, I have to strain to catch it all: the woman backflipping through a firelit hoop barely bigger than her waist, the man holding up four others as they stand on one leg – *is that one upside down?*

There *must* be magic involved, because I have no idea how any of it is possible.

The scarlet light surges, focusing into a strong beam that silhouettes the athletes. My breath hitches as they line up on either edge of the stage, and with a clash of cymbals they flip onto the ground and march backstage to the orchestra.

Thankfully, a more calming orange light forms and I release my breath. A single dancer in gold twirls shimmering ribbons as gentle, dawdling music plays. The melody sends ripples of relaxation through my veins, and I breathe deeply while the dancer turns to liquid gold.

The Adellan's brown curls turn to copper amongst the magic, reminding me of Elm in their workshop. I'm so entranced that for a moment I forget everything else, losing where I am entirely. My vision blurs and the music quietens. It's only the dancer and me in a psychedelic dream.

But the orchestra rises again, the Adellan's routine becoming complex and fast. I blink back to reality – only to realise Zeus has moved his hand atop mine.

I stifle a gasp. Isn't he angry with me? Aren't we avoiding each other, both of us unsure how to continue as if there's nothing between us? Aren't we . . .

The dancer's routine ends and the crowd claps with delight, and I remember – this is part of *our* show. I glance at Zeus's hand, breathe in his signature coolness, and remember this isn't for me. It's a tactic, not a romantic gesture.

Unless . . .

I shake my head and return to the performance. The finale arrives in a wash of darkness. Grey mist spreads across the stage, no magic this time. Six dancers appear with white light held in their hands and topping their feet, like tiny moons.

I'm not sure how the white glow is possible, some sort of combination of different fairies' magic? Zeus's voice in the back of my mind tells me to stop thinking about it, to enjoy the beautiful and blinding aura.

The dancers of Kara's Territory have sickly-pale skin and dark hair, their movements as eerie as they are graceful. Their dresses are decorated with snowflakes of lace, and I'm reminded of mine and Zeus's dance in the borders – drifting snow, mist, white fireflies.

It's like a magical joke, like they're trying to embarrass me.

He squeezes my hand, and I wonder if he's reliving the same memory. But if he is, does he think of this part fondly like I do, or does he only resent my horrific blunder at the end?

I shiver as the dancers skip across the stage with their lit-up hands and feet, asteroids in a night sky. The music swells in dark minor chords, sending goosebumps over my arms.

Finally the dance ends with an eruption of applause, and Zeus moves his hands back into his lap.

All the dancers appear back on the stage in their six distinct colours, bowing with wide smiles. The curtain hiding the orchestra lifts. The dancers gesture to the musicians, and the crowd applauds for them just as loudly.

I turn to Candace, her eyes bright with enjoyment. 'That was so beautiful,' I tell her genuinely. 'Thank you.'

She turns as if to hug me, but we can't – not in these seats nor in this company – so she says, 'I wanted you to have a taste of all that you deserve, sugar.'

The world.

I nod, my heart warm, but just as soon it freezes over. I grit my jaw, trying to hide my discontent. *Liar.*

She can put on a show like this, but she's the person who has manipulated me the most. I think of the crowd, the prince beside me, the world Candace and I are trying to take – and remember none of this is really for me.

⋅♡⋅ ☖ ♔ ☖ ⋅♡⋅

Alone in my room, I open the diary. Some of the pages stick together, crispy and tainted by the snow it laid in for possibly hundreds of years.

With my party makeup removed, my hair down, and my dress off, I enjoy the sensation of being clean against my sheets in my warm bed. The dark walls of my castle room press in on me comfortingly as the fireplace simmers, and my nutcracker sits on my desk by the window, watching and waiting, protecting me from the snowstorm that's built up outside.

No one can bother me here, not even myself. Candace can't lie to me. Elm can't make me see things positively. Zeus can't distract me. This is something I need to learn on my own. I won't give this information to another soul until I know what to make of it myself.

So I pry open each page of Kara's diary, ready to find out every detail of who I am, who the fairies really are, and what the world beyond truly is.

'March nineteenth, waxing moon,' I whisper, reading the first page. I curl up into my pillows and pull the diary close, moving my candle to better light the writing and tempt away my shivers. 'Every day, the world becomes more dangerous for witches . . .'

CHAPTER SIXTEEN

SOMEWHERE, SOMETIME...

Kara shifted her satchel; the books were weighing on her bad shoulder, weak from three years of carting volumes around the university.

She used to use little spells to ease the weight, but in these times? Witches had to be cautious. Displays of magic were fine in the confines of a classroom or laboratory, but where regular people could see? One was only asking for trouble.

Lire waved from across the green. With a wide smile, Kara jumped into a sprint. The old brick buildings that Kara so deeply admired faded to the background as she found her best friend.

Kara and Lire crashed into each other, nearly toppling as they hugged and hopped with excitement. They hadn't seen each other all summer.

The pair didn't live together, nor were they in any of the same classes, but the two had stuck together since their first day. It was hard enough being a woman in academia – that was why they started their coven in the first place. They pulled each other through the best and worst of it.

'Why, would you look at that *tan*,' said Lire, looking her friend up and down. 'You summered by the coast?'

Kara nodded. Were Lire's eyes brighter for seeing her, or was she only imagining it? 'The seaside was the only bearable part of it all,' Kara said. 'My family are deathly boring.'

'Oh, don't get me started.' Lire gestured to get moving and the two began walking between the buildings of the university, following a route it seemed only they knew; the grass under their feet was vivid green rather than padded down to brown from footsteps.

'My family forbade me from practising all summer,' Lire said. 'I still did, of course, but you know what they're like. *God forbid* I look into a crystal ball. People outside the city are the worst dissenters of magic. My parents don't want our family name *tainted* by *witchcraft*. Backwards, degenerate—'

They'd entered a hallway, and male students scooted past them, whistling. Lire ignored them, her blonde waves swishing behind her. Kara sneered – but still pulled at her skirt. Men couldn't bother her unless she let them, at least she told herself so. Yet there was always an underpinning fear when they hassled the girls.

With a quick spell – a click of her fingers and a white spark – Lire unlocked the heavy old door that sat unnoticed at the end of the corridor. They followed a long tunnel through the back of the building and, finally, entered their hidden courtyard.

Kara took in a deep breath. Her skin tingled with both comfort and anticipation. After two months, she was home. Ready for another year of learning, of expanding. Of changing the world.

Under the protection of a weeping willow, and cut through by a stream that seemed to run to and from nowhere, their secret garden was only a few metres in diameter. It was a perfect circle hemmed in by brick walls, as if they were at the bottom of a well. Blossoms smiled under the bright sunlight that dappled through the willow's branches, and while the university was loud, the only sounds in the courtyard were chirping birds.

The other five were already awaiting them, sitting in the grass with their packed lunches: analytical law student Grace and her athletic best friend Rhiannon; sweet social science Adella and romantic psychologist Amora; and Muse, a violin prodigy two years younger than the rest at just nineteen, adopted into their circle for her exceptional talent.

Each young woman was hand-picked by Kara and Lire for their coven – the best of the best.

Muse's eyes widened when she saw Lire step into the garden. She shuffled to make room for her, but Kara sat beside Amora and Lire followed, leaving Muse seated just outside the circle.

Poor thing, Kara thought. Muse worshipped Lire, and with the six of them doubled up, it must have been difficult for the shy girl to fit in. Muse *was* beloved; their baby. But it couldn't have been easy to always be on the outside.

Still, it thrilled Kara to have Lire sit beside her, to always choose her above the rest. With Lire, Kara could be sure there would always be someone by her side – someone to share magic with, to feel safe with, unconditionally. Always someone to love, and to be loved by.

Adella and Amora whispered between themselves, sharing the treats they'd brought for lunch. The sweet girls were more often than not in their own little world.

Meanwhile, Grace put her hands in her lap, smoothing her pleated skirt. 'Shall we start? I've been writing essays on the politics of magic.' Her eyes bored into each of her friends', sharp and serious. 'The population grows more afraid of witchcraft by the day. Men will keep spreading fear about who we are. They want us to hide. Our coven needs plans in place to handle the hatred brewing against us.'

'Your suggestion?' asked Kara, fishing through her satchel for a rare snack between her stacks of books.

'I've tried sending my essays to politicians, to convince them to move against these fear campaigns. But magical women are the last people they want to help. All we are is a threat to their power, as far as they see it.'

'A threat,' Lire repeated with a sly grin. 'I like that.'

Rhiannon licked her lips, flipping her braids over her shoulder. 'It is delightful. But I do agree we should prepare for the worst.'

'What's the worst?' Muse asked. 'What could they do? Stop us practising?' Nervous magic sprung under her fingertips in the form of pure white flickers as her hands clenched.

'Imprison us, have us killed,' offered Grace. 'It's happened before. Patriarchy calls for the demonisation of powerful women – just look at history. This is no game.' She drummed her fingers against her skirt. 'We have a lot to lose. The university didn't only recruit us for our smarts. They see potential in our magical practise across our industries. The respect and safety they offer is the positive side of a dangerous coin. Many witches will go into hiding or stop practising. But because we're known, we can't simply pretend we don't use magic if it becomes criminalised.'

'If only there were a place like this where we could live forever,' Lire mused, running her fingers through the courtyard's soft grass. 'I dream of it. A secret place just for us, for magic to run wild, for women to be free. A place where we're in charge.'

'Oh, give the people credit,' Kara said. She liked the sound of that fantasy world, but she wasn't ready to give up on the real one. 'Most still appreciate us. It's only a small handful of dissenters who happen to yell the loudest. As long as we can show people the strength and hope in our magic, they won't be manipulated by fear. Like Grace said, we were chosen to study, to better ourselves, because each of us shows exceptional promise. What we should do is use the opportunities we've been given to *expand* magic and *help* the world.'

Lire shrugged, biting into an apple. Her eyes went to the sky, her thoughts elsewhere. Kara noticed the fairy books spilling from Lire's bag, splayed in the grass. Illustrations of winged creatures, generous beings, magical and mysterious.

Kara had always known Lire to love fairies; her parents told her she'd been consumed by them as a child. She often got distracted inking wings onto her hands, her wrists, drawing little butterflies.

If fairies were real, would they help us now?

Kara wished there were magical creatures out there who might stand by their side.

Maybe that hope, even in just a legend, was what Lire needed to survive. But Kara wanted their reality to be enough for Lire. *She* wanted to be enough. Couldn't their coven be all she needed? If they focused on the here and now, they could still have their fantasy.

•♡⁺ ♣ 🍺 ♣ ⁺♡•

Grace's fears came to light within four years – years that were slow in their terror, yet fast as academia consumed the coven. Propaganda spread, a blazing fire no one could put out. Magic was no longer a beautiful gift.

It was danger.

A threat to all who lacked it, and a mark of corruption upon every woman who used it.

The secret courtyard was the only place the coven could meet, else they'd be at risk of the many men who hated them. They stayed at the university so they could remain together, stayed in academia to build their credibility and hope that one day, they might be able to use their magic more openly again.

But even on their campus, even in the city, they weren't safe. The persecution of magic strained all their relationships. The once inseparable group of friends now felt more like colleagues forced to work together. Arguments broke out easily. Balance between the seven never lasted.

They loved each other dearly, but their days of fun were long behind them.

Kara and Lire no longer returned to their families in the summer. It was too dangerous. In outer villages, people caught using magic were shunned – if not burned alive. Besides, Kara and Lire hated being apart. Why leave each other, dangerous or otherwise?

They moved into an apartment together by the university, with large windows they could stargaze through, and water that ran hot *most* of the time. Academia didn't pay the women well, and they let their candles burn low every night as they stayed up reading and writing.

Their work was never done. As self-made women given an opportunity to research and experiment, to never stop learning, they had to put their power to good use. Their original studies were of little use now. Kara once thought she might be a healer who used magic to benefit her patients. Now, the exploration and expansion of magic was her entire life.

Kara and Lire had each other, and no matter what else befell them, they hung onto their bond as if it were their lifeblood.

That is, until it all came crashing down, one eerily moonlit night in their apartment.

Kara was cuddled on the sofa when she reluctantly decided to clean some of Lire's mess before she came back. The entire apartment was a flurry of books and papers and ink. Lire had left that morning in a hurry, and her things were even more scattered than their usual organised chaos.

Kara cleared away the remains of Lire's hasty breakfast, and returned to the table to push the open journals to the side so they would have somewhere to eat dinner.

There she found the illustrations of a new world.

She held a hand to her mouth and sunk into a dining chair, flipping through the pages. Each was filled past the margins with drawings, inspirations, meticulously detailed schemes.

This place Lire detailed was walled by ice, separated from the real world. A circular landscape with many terrains and cultures. Magic held deep in its centre. A gemstone that would be housed at the heart, filled with power seeped from this world and poured into the new one.

Not just enough for them; Lire intended to take *all* the magic from this world and create an entirely new enchanted realm.

The witches had spent many years refining their practise. Lire knew *exactly* what she was doing, and with the seven of them using their power together . . .

This plan was insane, foolish – and entirely possible. Kara shivered. She wouldn't let this happen, but she also didn't know what to do about Lire's dangerous delusion.

What had become of her best friend? The person she loved and trusted most?

How did I not see this coming?

Afraid Lire could come home and catch her at any moment, Kara tore through the pages, absorbing as much as possible. They'd been going through hard times, of course, but how had Kara not noticed Lire going mad right under her nose?

A wad of watercolours dropped out of a journal and Kara's stomach squeezed. Lire *had* gone over the edges of sanity.

Dozens of illustrations showed the seven coven members as fairies, each with stunning wings and an aspect of magic to be the guardian of in this new world. Rhiannon, a fairy in red with scaled dragon's wings and the attributes of war and strength . . . Amora with rainbow wings that represented love and passion . . .

Magic was always white, but in Lire's world, it was fractured into seven colours, one for each fairy. They would be immortalised, and watch over their world together as deities.

Deities.

Kara's throat tightened as she found a full-page painting of herself, her dark hair flowing over wings of starlight, her magic green like an aurora. A fairy of the night sky. Everything about it was absolutely breathtaking, and she knew Lire had chosen this beautiful persona with great care. No one knew her like Lire did.

But apparently Kara didn't know Lire at all, if she was planning this – to take them into a new place, to turn them into something else. Did she expect the witches to go willingly?

Frozen, her eyes glued to the pages, Kara forced herself to put the paintings back. Her hands felt like lead. The deckled pages crunched together. '*Hell below.*'

'Everything alright, my love?' Lire slipped into the apartment.

Kara flung her hands off the papers and stepped away. She tried to smile warmly, but her lip wobbled. 'Of— Of course.'

Lire's eyes dropped to the journals, then slowly rose back to Kara's stiffened gaze. 'What did you see?'

'I don't know what you mean.' Kara turned, facing the window. Arms crossed.

Lire stumbled over, climbing the stacks of books. 'Don't be childish.' She grabbed Kara's arm and spun her back to face her. 'You saw my plans? It's okay. I was going to tell you soon.'

'It's not *okay*!' Kara's breath came out hot. 'This isn't the answer to our problems. You— I understand fantasising, but you truly want this?'

'I've thought it all through. We'll be happy. Free. Together for eternity.'

'An entire world to the seven of us?' *Together for eternity.* Kara wanted that, of course she did, but not like this. 'How would we survive? What would we do? What about our families?'

'*I'm* your family.' Lire's eyes shadowed. 'Besides, you can invite whomever you like. We'll have to bring a few hundred or thousand humans to begin our new society.'

Kara leaned away. 'What, against their will? To be like slaves?'

'When have they ever cared about our will? Witches are being killed for the *crime* of using the beautiful tool we're blessed to wield. If we don't escape soon, we won't make it out alive. It's them or us if we stay. This way no one has to die.'

'I . . .' Kara paced the room, half to get away from the ever-approaching Lire, half to think. 'The others. Have you told them about this?'

Lire looked out the window at the half-moon. 'Muse is already with me. She's helped with the plans. I wanted to tell you first, but I had to make it all real, because I knew you'd be hard to convince. Rhiannon will be easy; she'd love to rule. Grace will come around soon enough, and Amora and Adella will follow the pack.'

Lire was right. Each member of their coven would agree in time – unless Kara could convince them otherwise. But Lire would need all seven for this to work. She needed the power of the full coven.

Lire picked up her journals with trembling hands – she wasn't as calm and sure as she wanted Kara to think – and flipped to the page with Kara's illustration. 'You saw this? You see what I want for you?'

The fairy of the night sky softly smiled back at them.

'But Lire, *I* don't want that.'

'My love, you will!'

'No!' Kara exploded, clutching her skirt and cowering back. 'I will not be part of this! We cannot simply run and make a new world. There are millions here who we can use our magic to help. We keep studying, we keep fighting, we protect others like us, and—'

'Coward,' Lire seethed, mirroring Kara's anger. 'I'm trying to give you *everything*. I have loved you more than I love myself. We are doing this whether or not you agree. This is the only future we have.'

'You can't force me! And you can't do this without me.' Kara blinked out the tears in her eyes. 'Consider this finished. Say goodbye to your foolish plans before anyone else sees this madness.'

Lire's eyes glowed lilac – had she already been experimenting with her new forms of magic? 'You are *mine*. You're supposed to be happy!' She became a fiery craze. 'Be happy! Be— Be—'

Kara scrambled backwards. Hot, white magic pooled in her fists.

Lire caught the defensive move, and all her fire snuffed out. She turned entirely cold, her grimace dropping into nonchalance. 'So you would choose having *nothing* over having me, over having an entire world.'

'I choose *this* world. I'll always choose this world. Not over you. But for both of our sakes.' She grabbed her bag where it hung from the corner of a dining chair and began throwing things into it. 'I can't stay here,' she mumbled.

'Don't run away from me. Don't you dare.'

'Because I'm *yours*? Because I belong to you, and have to sacrifice all my dreams because you say so?'

Lire's shoulders dropped. '*Yes*. Kara, please, if you—'

'Do not come after me.' Kara made it to the door. 'I'll be back to collect my things another day.' She exhaled, taking in Lire's crazed expression with a confusing blend of pity and fear. 'I would have helped you, Lire. I would have tried. But you don't care about me at all – you want to own me. You cannot force me to do this.'

'You think I want you now?' Lire spat. 'Someone as weak as you?'

Kara stood in the doorway, fingers trembling over the knob. 'Anything that was between us – you and I, this coven – it's over.'

Lire's head tilted slowly to one side. 'Well, if that's how it must be,' she said.

Kara opened the door slowly, swallowing her terror.

'But know I'll have what I want. Whether you like it or not. And in my new world, everyone will see you for the weakling – no, the *monster* that you are.'

It was a year before Kara saw Lire again. She spoke to the other coven members on occasion, passing them in the hallways of the university, but never her old best friend. Never the person she thought she could never live without. But she couldn't go back there. As much as it broke her heart, she had to be strong enough to live her own life instead of sacrificing her values to be with Lire.

The five others kept their mouths shut on the details of Lire's plan, afraid of what Lire might do if she thought they were siding with Kara. Besides, Kara couldn't go to their secret garden anymore, so there was nowhere safe to talk.

Their lives using magic, their lives in a coven, were over.

Outside the city, witches were hunted. Even within the university, they were now banned from practising. They were only allowed to study, and even then they were under harsh restrictions.

If Lire was caught, her plans would never make it to fruition.

Would that be so terrible?

✦♡✦ ♠ ⛉ ♠ ✦♡✦

Kara was half asleep, the hot summer night making her toss and turn, when she was shocked awake by bright lights in her room.

She cursed the place – a cheap house shared with younger students. It never felt like home the way her apartment with Lire had.

Were those cursed teenagers throwing *another* party?

She rubbed her eyes and sat up, trying to decide whether it was worth confronting the partiers or easier to cover her ears with her pillow.

But in the flashes between the light's glare, she was met with a loud silence. Not a party. This glow – it was *magic.*

Her heart skipped a beat as her eyes adjusted.

The coven was in her room.

Kara sprang up, heart racing. 'What are you doing?' she demanded, hands out in front of her now with glimmering magic of her own.

'I'm sorry,' said Grace, jumping onto her, kicking the wind from her chest. Grace placed a hand on Kara's forehead.

And her eyes rolled back until . . .

Until . . .

·♡' ♙ 📦 ♙ '♡·

Her head pounded and voices filled her ears. Chanting, shouting, harsh whispers, humming. Kara was afraid to look. This had to be some plan of Lire's. *Revenge?* After an entire year?

She'd been furious, but even this seemed too far.

What were they going to do, sacrifice Kara? *Holy,* were they?

Kara forced one eye open. It was still night, so she couldn't have been passed out long, and the landscape didn't look much different from the university's. They couldn't have gone far. *I can escape.*

All seven coven members were gathered in a forest clearing, a wide circle surrounded by wilting trees. The witches' hands were raised to the sky, magic pouring in, around, through them. But the magic wasn't white – it was split into different colours. Like Lire had schemed.

No.

Lire was bathed in purple, Muse in yellow . . . Each of them had their own striking aura.

Kara, however, was still in the darkness, crumpled outside their circle. No candles, no moonlight.

Was she here to watch? To be gloated at by Lire? She couldn't be part of this. *Wouldn't* be. They couldn't force her.

A shimmering at her feet made her realise there *was* magic around her – a black, shadowy power crawling between her body and the sky just like the others'. As she fully regained consciousness, it tingled and tickled over and under her skin. She pulled her knees to her chest.

This wasn't like magic's usual heat – this was *cold*.

Was it possible they could force her to do this? Lire was mad enough to try.

Kara didn't know what to do, but she wouldn't sit there and let this go on. She crawled towards the circle, weak as she was, her palms and bare feet crunching over the forest floor. Maybe, just maybe, she could put a stop to this before too many people got hurt.

Even if it meant hurting herself and her friends.

Lire sensed her coming. She shook out of her trance, still humming in the shower of magic. With a gleeful laugh, she turned to Kara, grinning victoriously. 'So, the traitor has decided to join us.'

'Decided?' Kara rasped. 'Lire – let me *go*.'

The others began to lose focus, turning to watch Kara and Lire. The enchantment around them dimmed, if only slightly, the colours threatening to reconnect and turn back to white.

Lire ignored them and faced down Kara. 'That magic at your feet? It will be all yours, my love. But your fate is yours to choose. I'll give you one last chance. Will you join my world willingly and stand by my side, or take the place of my enemy?'

Kara struggled to breathe – was she injured, or only in deep panic? 'Do this to me, and I will only ever be your enemy. That's *your* choice.'

Lire lifted her hands and shrugged, lilac pooling between her fingers. 'Well, I tried my best. All I ever did was love you. And you threw it back in my face. You'll spend eternity regretting it, my fairy of death.'

Kara turned cold. What did that mean? The black magic pulled at her now, forcing her closer to the circle. The dirty ground tore her nightdress as she was dragged across it. Amora gave her a sorry, frightened look, but the witches were all too enraptured by the magic to stop it. If they ever had doubts, it was too late to change their minds now.

Kara tried to fight it, but she was too late and too weak. She had been stripped of her will. Whatever was next, her life would never truly be hers again.

Above them, a rainbow formed in a full circle, peaking white in the centre. The halo grew and grew as the witches absorbed the magic.

Lire had found her way to leech all the magic from this world and redirect it to the coven. How could she possibly think this was okay? How could she know they'd survive this? That this wouldn't destroy the Earth, levelling life in its overflowing greed?

Lire's voice circled in Kara's head: *We deserve this. This world doesn't deserve to keep its magic. It'll be put to good use now.*

But what about all the people who still needed it? The hundreds of witches outside their coven, without their privilege, who would now suffer, utterly powerless? The millions of people in poverty who could have been helped with the enchantments they were studying? Clean water, more nutritious food, *infinite* possibilities to heal the world.

The enchantment forced Kara into the circle and to her feet, her arms raising of their own accord as blackness flooded over her body, into the earth, and up to the sky. Her heart squeezed as she tried to pull away. Her body was no longer her own.

The rainbow was so enormous it must have consumed the entire forest by now. Maybe the university campus, the city, further. Was that Lire's idea, to consume an entire part of the existing world and turn it into her own? How could she possibly make that work? *How? How?*

An even stronger wave of magic sent shudders through Kara's body. It was happening to the others as well. Adella nearly fell as golden magic consumed her; she looked as terrified as she was awed.

All the magic of the world in seven bodies. It was surely too much for them to take. But they wouldn't be human anymore. Not if Lire's fantasy came to light.

Tears spilled over Kara's cheeks. She struggled to watch without her stomach turning, but she couldn't close her eyes.

Lire was changing, *laughing* as purple wings formed behind her back, stretching upwards into stunning points. She gasped, fluttering the wings as more and more magic absorbed into her body. The rainbow above them stretched as far as the eye could see.

Kara watched as her old friends became the immortal illustrations that had terrified her a year ago. Muse a stunning yellow songbird; Grace an artwork of water droplets, her wings like tears. The six fairies glanced at each other in delight.

When they turned to Kara, some of their doubt returned. Their *guilt.*

Kara tried once more to move, to run, but her feet were still stuck to the ground, bare and cold. Her hands, though, she could control. Her breath hitched as she reached behind her back. She knew what would be there, and yet it wasn't real. She could still pretend, even if she couldn't run.

There was a powdery softness between her fingers. The *wings* – they were weightless, but so wrong, like something she needed to throw or scratch off. A parasite glued to her, growing from her. She could move them with barely a thought. A limb. She brought them forward to look.

Kara shuddered. She was not the illustration Lire had so beautifully made of a starlit fairy bathed in green light. *Fairy of death. You will be the monster.* Kara's wings were those of a moth, with huge patterned eyes that bored down on her. Her magic was black as a starless night.

Her veins turned to ice, her skin paling, a picture of the undead.

Kara dropped to her knees, the wings scraping the forest floor. Panic roared in feverish waves within her.

She couldn't make sense of it. It was a nightmare. Not real. But so terrifyingly vivid that she knew it was happening. That there was no escape.

'Please!' she screamed to Lire. *I can't– I can't do this– I–* 'Please, let me go!'

The rainbow above them exploded into millions of fractures of light, echoing with a *boom* that crashed like thunder.

Suddenly it was a dark night again, the only light caged within the seven fairies, glowing in seven colours.

It was done.

Kara was a deity, to be forever trapped in a world she hated. Her wings flopped around her. How she wished she could pry them off. Now free of the spell's power, she was buzzing with so much magic she thought maybe she could. She could do *anything*.

This was their world to shape as they saw fit. Seven sisters, each with a fragment of infinite power.

Did Lire have more magic than the rest? If Kara was to be the villain, could she reverse what had been done? Could she fight?

Maybe not now. But she could do something, some day.

The fairies heaved and laughed and gazed upon their wings.

Amora and Adella's doubts were long gone – arm in arm, they jumped with glee. Muse was already at Lire's side again, yellow dancing upon her as she showered Lire with admiration, with gratitude.

But Lire was not celebrating.

She stared daggers at Kara and pointed away from the coven. '*That way.* You will travel as far as possible until you hit impenetrable walls of ice. That is where our world ends, and that is where you'll rule. Over nothing but darkness.'

'Lire—' Kara choked out.

'Do not attempt to see the warmth again, monster. It's not yours anymore. All you own is death.' She crept closer, and whispered in Kara's ear, 'No one will ever love you again. No one will make my mistake.'

CHAPTER SEVENTEEN

I dream and dream of Kara and Lire, of the stories about them and their friends that I read, years of their lives ingrained behind my eyes. Years in another world.

The world my parents must live in, a thousand years after the fairies left it. Searching for me, a little girl who slipped through the walls of ice and ended up in an enchanted land with nothing but a nutcracker.

As I sleep, a mother and father cradle me, brothers and sisters watch over me, all with my hazel eyes until Candace, in a flurry of ice, tears me from their arms. Lire and Kara await me, giants looming above, wrapping me in their wings until I'm consumed by lilac and grey.

I wake in a cold sweat, the morning light dappling through the windows of my bedroom. Panting, I throw my sheets off me and wipe at my eyes. The nutcracker sits in its place by the window, its red paint silhouetted by the sunrise. For once it doesn't comfort me – it sends waves of chills across my skin.

I can't stay here. I need to talk to Elm and Zeus. *Now.*

I haul myself into my bathroom while trying to shake my anxiety. I wash quickly and dress myself. Servants in the halls try to ask me if I'm alright, but I hurry past them and out the door. I can't talk to anyone right now. Can't even ask for a carriage ride.

It crosses my mind that I'm experiencing an anxiety attack, or some type of mental breakdown. But I run and run. Like I can leave everything I've learned in my wake if only I move fast enough.

Soon, Candace will get up and wonder where I've gone. I can only hope she assumes I've left to see Zeus for romantic matters instead of political, world-shattering ones.

Because now I know. Why she adopted me. What this was all for.

It isn't until I'm halfway into the city that I realise I've forgotten my coat, dressed only in a thick wool dress that touches the floor, snow soaking the hem. I tug the sleeves over my fingers and shiver.

Too late. I'll grab Zeus from the castle and borrow a coat there to get me to Elm's workshop. We'll probably take a royal carriage. I'll be fine. What I need more than anything is my friends. *Now.*

Imperials look my way as I pass; their famed general in a wild state, hair unbrushed, eyes black around the edges.

It's no matter, because, well, none of this is even *real*, is it? All the power I've spent my life attaining is for a world that shouldn't exist.

One good thing about everyone thinking I'm the prince's lover is that no one questions me as I storm into the castle and up to his suite, still covered in snow. A servant tries to knock and announce my arrival, but I usher them out of the way and throw open the doors to Zeus's ridiculously large bedroom.

There's a lump under layers of fur on the bed – twice the size of mine, *fairies* – which I assume is him. '*Zeus!*' I shout, shaking said lump. 'Get up!'

Servants gasp from the door, slamming it behind them as they scurry away.

'Zeus!' I grab a pillow and whack him. If this is some sort of joke and he's somewhere else, I'm going to—

The lump shifts. 'Mmm?'

'Get. Up.' I whack him again, though I'm so grateful he's here I let out a long breath. I didn't realise I was hyperventilating.

He stretches out and gives birth to himself as he peels the layers of fur off him. His head emerges. His eyes widen. 'Isla? Uh. What's this?'

'We're going to Elm's. Now. Call a carriage.' I turn to go.

'But—'

'Zeus!' I argue, turning back to pull his bare arm, my fingers sticky over his skin.

He looks me up and down, and I catch fear in his gaze. Not of me, but for me. 'Are you quite alright?'

'I . . .' I'm speechless. What on earth could I say to even *begin* explaining all of this? I shake my head, tears filling my eyes. 'I . . . '

'Isla, give yourself a minute.' He pulls me onto the bed and wraps his arms around me, despite the wet snow getting all over his furs.

My shoulders fall as I press my forehead into his warm bicep. Tears fall softly, my back shuddering.

I'm crying in front of the prince.

And I don't even *care*.

'Elm stayed in their quarters here last night,' Zeus explains, his voice reverberating calmly through his chest as he holds me tightly against him. 'They won't have gone to the workshop yet, so I can have someone bring them here.'

'Please,' I murmur.

We sit in silence for a long time and I match Zeus's slow, deep breaths. He runs his hand up and down my back, patting off snow and detangling my hair. Finally I'm back in my right mind enough to remember we've been avoiding each other all week, and I flush with embarrassment.

'Oh, Zeus,' I stutter, pulling myself away from him. It feels like tearing off a part of myself, like my skin is left behind touching his. 'I'm so sorry. I shouldn't have come here. I didn't want to put you through that. I . . .'

After everything in the borders, I come to him and have him hold me for comfort? What kind of monster—

'You're my best friend,' he says, eyes locked on mine. 'Whatever's happened between us, I'll always be here for you. Please don't be sorry.'

'But you were so clear. You told me I can't do things like this. That we can't be—' I take a breath. 'I don't want to hurt you.'

He plants his hand on my arm steadily, his gaze soft. So soft I could melt into it, that there's nothing more I want to do than crawl back into his arms. 'My darling, the last thing I want to do is push you away. A kiss would be too far, but being here for you isn't.'

Fresh tears spring to my eyes, and for a harrowing moment, I wonder if I could really be his princess, if he'd only have me after everything we've been through. Because I don't understand it. When did entitled, irritating Zeus – the boy I've spent my life resenting – become the person I run to after a nightmare?

He calls for Elm and within a few minutes a rapping on the window makes us both jolt. Elm's head pops into view, covering the white mountains. 'Let me in,' they mouth.

Zeus stops me as I try to get up, patting my arm and placing a blanket over me on his way to the window. 'Morning, gorgeous,' he says to Elm, opening the panes to a gust of freezing air. I pull the blanket tighter around me and wipe my eyes.

Elm rolls through the window with a sack full of toys. 'Morning, my sweets!' They see my face and their smile drops. 'What's wrong?'

'I—' I start. 'Why'd you come through the window?'

'Didn't want to talk to anyone on the way. Why are you crying? What's wrong?'

I flop back on the bed. '*Everything.*' I reach to simply hand them the journal, but in my haste to get here I must've left it hidden under my sheets. *Fairies.*

Zeus and Elm sit either side of me, cradling me in the centre. 'Did something happen with your—' Elm clears their throat. 'With Candace?'

'Sort of. Not really.' My voice cracks. 'But yes.'

'I never liked her,' Zeus mumbles, and I hit him with a pillow. At least it elicits a soft laugh from my chest.

'From the beginning,' Elm encourages. Usually they'd tell me to wait until I'm ready to talk. Even they know we're in a war with no time to lose.

I cover my mouth. 'I lied about the book we found at the borders,' I say, and it all tumbles out from there – the truth about the fairies, about our world, about me and where Candace must have found me. All my doubts and fears flood from the pit of my stomach and the tornado in my mind until my throat is sore.

Zeus and Elm sit staring at me slack-jawed, and I wouldn't be surprised if they think I've lost my mind. I have no proof – just years of manically searching for answers, and a lot of stress that would certainly be enough to make me start seeing things that aren't real.

Oh, no. *Have* I lost my mind?

Zeus places his hands in his lap calmly, collecting himself. 'Delphine was right . . .' he mutters under his breath.

'Excuse me?' I ask.

'My spies,' he explains. 'They found a map showing a village in the borders. It was in the ruins of Amora's castle, so we knew it must be important, but we didn't understand why.'

'Zeus!' Elm whisper-screams. 'That would've been great for us to know! Last week when we were *at the borders*!'

Zeus raises his hands innocently. 'I didn't know it meant anything yet! You wouldn't have taken me seriously!'

I gesture for them both to quiet down. 'We know the truth now. That's what matters. But Zeus, next time you have information pertaining to the end of the world, consider *sharing it.*'

'My mistake. Sure. So what's our next move? Do we confront Candace while she's still here?'

'Confront her?' Elm says, voice small. 'As far as we know, after all these lies, she's the enemy.'

'She isn't the enemy,' I whisper. 'I mean, I don't know. But I really do think she cares about me, whether or not her adopting me started as a political move. I . . . I don't think she's a bad person. She's just done things that aren't exactly morally perfect because it was her only way to get power.'

I hate myself for defending her, but it's my first instinct, even though I feel completely betrayed.

'Well that's our only option, then.' Zeus has a flush on his cheeks, and I remember yet again, with another pang of guilt, that I've been avoiding him. *Why, oh* why, *do I ruin everything?* 'We have to talk to Candace and find out what she knows. This information is useless to us if we don't understand how she's fitting it into the bigger picture.'

My stomach knots itself, and I have to swallow the lump in my throat – but he's right. My *mother* is the only person who can help us make sense of this, and it's time to tell her I know she's been lying.

✦♡✦ ▲ 🎩 ▲ ✦♡✦

A royal carriage gets us back to my home quickly, but before we left, Zeus insisted I change – into a very fine dress that fit me perfectly, which he *happened* to have sitting around – so I'd be warm and dry. I wear one of his coats over the top, stark-white with blue snowflakes embroidered across the thick material. The royal clothing could be worth a lifetime of food to some people, and because it's so large on me, it drags along the floor, collecting snow and mud. Zeus doesn't blink an eye, though.

He'd give me the world and not blink an eye.

The pale leather of the carriage seats becomes the dark crimson décor of Candace's castle. Though I feel more settled after talking things through with my friends, it's all still a blur.

Elm goes first, opening the doors and leading us past the servants – who they ask for hot tea and cakes – and to the sitting room where Candace is meeting with – *no* – Councillor Dierdre.

This woman has the most impeccable timing I've ever seen.

Before we can enter, my maid, Sadie, rushes to announce us, and it's all very formal and I am still very much in the midst of a breakdown. I tap my foot on the dark hardwood and fantasise about kicking Dierdre off the plush sofa she's sitting on, cross-legged and grinning venomously.

For both show and comfort, I take Zeus's hand, allowing my breathing to calm with his presence at my back. *'Mother,'* I say as we step inside. Candace and Dierdre don't stand, despite the prince entering. A clear sign of how highly they think of themselves.

Still, Candace's eyes flash. She can tell I'm angry. 'Good morning, sugar. Elm – lovely to see you. And Zeus.' She grimaces. 'You're also here.'

'Of course he is,' I say, cutting off Dierdre as she half attempts a greeting. I do not have time. 'My *partner* goes where I go, and we have urgent business to discuss with you.'

Dierdre's mouth twitches. 'Surely not an announcement of—'

'Have a lovely day, Councillor.' I motion for Sadie to collect her teacup and show her out. Dierdre shuffles up quickly. But not without a look of horror at my brashness.

Once she's gone, Zeus shuts the door, leaving the three of us trapped in the small room with Candace, the air charged with tension that has the hairs on my arms raised.

'Your eyes are so red,' says Candace, a look of such motherly concern on her face that it's hard not to forget everything. 'Are you okay? Come and sit down. All of you.'

I shake my head. 'Don't— I know, Candace. I know every-thing.' The lump in my throat returns, and I struggle to talk around it. 'I know what's beyond the borders. I know that's where I'm from. You only adopted me because you thought I'd be useful to you. I'm immune to magic because I'm from a world without it. And you've spent my entire life hiding it even though you know how desperate I've been for answers. I *know*.'

Tears build and drop, but I'm not ashamed to show them. Not to the people in this room, who are possibly the only people in the world who know I have the capacity to feel anything at all.

Candace grips the arm of her chair, startled magic building beneath her fingertips in several colours. 'Sugar . . .' Her brows pinch upwards. 'I-I don't know what to say. I'm so sorry.'

'Don't tell me that. I have no reason to believe you.' My jaw tenses. '*Explain.*'

'I should have told you. I know. But you've always been an Imper-ial, through and through. Imagine telling that little girl who loved her land and worked so hard for her power that none of it was ever meant to exist.'

Her fingers press into her temples. 'I *couldn't*. I couldn't shatter your world. It isn't as if I ever found a way out. I couldn't get you home. The best I could do for you was love you and give you a good life here. Please— Please try to understand.'

My hands shake, and I stuff them into the folds of my dress. 'A good life *you* would benefit from. Because you thought I could serve as a weapon, didn't you? You thought because I'm from outside the borders, because I'm immune to magic, I might be the key to your power.'

'*Isla*.' Her eyes are filled with guilt. With love. 'You're my baby. I always wanted power, yes, but it was adopting you that made me realise the truth about our world. I've always known you could be a formidable tool against the fairies, but you are my daughter before anything else.' She holds out her hands. Pleading. 'It wasn't power I fell in love with when I saw your big hazel eyes in the borders. I saw a child who needed help – your little hands, they were blue, and so tiny – and I knew you were destined to be mine. I never anticipated for you to become so powerful, not only because of your birthplace but because of your own brilliant nature. I swear.'

I swallow, my eyes darting around the room because I can no longer meet hers. 'You're telling me what I want to hear.'

'I'm telling you the truth. I won't say I've never been selfish, but I need you to know that I love you. You are my child above any benefit you might bring me. I only ever wanted to protect your heart. That's why I lied. I'll tell you everything I know if that's what you want.'

'Everything?' asks Elm. 'What else is there we don't already know?'

Candace's expression flattens, turning diplomatic. I follow suit instinctively, but it makes my blood boil – why can't we just *fight*? Why does everything have to be about appearances?

Why does she have to love me when I want to hurt her so terribly? When I want her to feel all the uncertainty and heartbreak I've felt?

'This war is larger than you think,' she says. 'You may know how our world came to be, but you don't realise yet the importance of it now.' She grips the arms of her chair once more. 'Lire never intended to stay here forever. She and the other fairies built all of this for themselves. But not all of them see our world as enough. Lire means to extend her empire into the outside world.'

'She'd open the borders?' I ask, too enthusiastically. If my parents are still beyond them, I could find them. Those impenetrable walls of ice would be gone, and we could be together again.

'We already know it's possible to get through, in extremely rare cases,' Candace says, gesturing at me. 'The fairies built the borders, so they have the power to take them down. Whatever has become of *out there* in the past thousand or so years, Lire wants it for herself. She's bored of this war. Why stay here, with much of the population rebelling, when she can simply create a new empire? I . . . I don't know how much damage the process of rejoining the worlds would cause, but I don't like our odds.'

Any delusional hope I had falls. *Of course.* If Lire opens the borders, even if it means I could get my family back, it would put both worlds at risk.

'So we don't only have to win this war for ourselves,' I say. 'We have to win it to protect a world we don't even know.'

Candace nods. 'We have our fight here, but we can't fail all those outside as well. We may not know that world, but I know you, Isla. If the people there are anything like my daughter, I want to protect them too.'

I bite my lip. My people in here, and my people out there. They all need me to fight for them. And *fairies know* I will.

If it doesn't break me first.

'How do we stop her?' asks Zeus, playing with the hem of Elm's jacket. Elm lets him, enraptured by Candace's revelations.

'Lire has a plan.' The sun falls behind a tall building outside, casting a shadow over us. Candace's sombre expression flitters in the dim firelight. 'I don't know everything, but I've gathered plenty between what she's gloated about and what I've managed to spy from her people. One thing we have on our side is that she needs the power of all seven fairies, and she has no access to Muse anymore.'

'Great,' says Zeus. 'What are we worrying about, then?'

'Muse may not be able to help Lire, but her magic still exists. Many people have that power within them. I've got plenty, and when Muse died, I have a gut feeling it didn't just disappear. It's gone somewhere, and Lire is either trying to find it or already has. Beyond that, all she has to do is convince the other fairies. It may seem like a difficult task, but she managed it last time – as you know, even Kara was roped in against her will.'

'Why's Lire still fighting us, then?' I ask. 'If all it would take for her to expand her power is gathering the seven fairies' magic and undoing their original enchantment, why hasn't she already?'

Candace raises a brow. 'Her pride, first of all. Lire would hate to leave this war unfinished. And secondly, this world-level enchantment can't be undone easily. The borders were sealed with a lot of magic to make sure no one would ever get in or out. They need a key to unlock their way back into the outer world.'

My fingers itch. 'What key? If we can just get it first and destroy it—'

'It's . . . You, Isla.' Candace's eyes turn glassy, and the sight of her emotion nearly makes me reel back before I've even registered her words. 'A soul from the outside, immune to magic. A soul with great determination and strength. That would be the key to unlocking the enchantment and reconnecting the worlds.'

Zeus takes my arm and stands in front of me. 'Well they aren't getting her.' He points at Candace. 'And you aren't touching her, either. This innocent act doesn't fool me.'

My cheeks burn, and I fight the weakness creeping into my legs. 'Candace, the fairies already *know* I'm the key. Rhiannon saw it when she attacked us in Bearra. The others will figure it out if they haven't already, and they'll come for me. If you'd told me this years ago, I could've made a plan, gotten ahead, but now . . .'

'We can't just put you into hiding,' says Elm. 'We need you to lead the fight.'

'I . . .' I pry Zeus off me, gripping an armchair and lowering myself into it. 'They won't get me without a fight. I'll kill Lire long before she can use me for any harm.' The shaking in my voice doesn't quite convey the strong message I'm trying to convince myself of.

'I'm going to keep you safe,' Candace assures. 'I always have, although you don't often need it. Your immunity to magic will make you a formidable enemy to Lire. But she's smarter than she is strong. If she can't use brute force to make you her key, she'll manipulate you until you agree.' She glances at Elm and Zeus. 'It's the people you love that are most in danger. She'll hurt them to get to you, sugar. That's why I'm trying to keep you all safe in the empire.'

So there *was* another reason for her sending me away from Bearra. I lower my head into my hands and close my eyes. *Fairies.*

I've found out everything. I've gotten exactly what I always wanted. I know who I am, where I'm from, and . . . What's the cost? I don't feel relieved. I don't feel full or warm or joyful.

I'm more confused and scared than I've ever been. At least when I knew nothing, I could live in fantasies.

'We can't stay here,' I mumble. 'We have to return to Bearra. We have to fight.'

'Isla, you can't leave—' Elm starts.

'The Imperials already want to surrender to Lire,' I say, new plans already forming in the back of my mind. 'I can make bigger moves with Queen Dawn at my side. I have to tell her and the other Bearrans what's really happening. We can win this war together, stop Lire expanding her world, *then* get back to dealing with our own empire. One step at a time.'

'Sugar,' Candace says softly. 'Take your time to absorb all of this. Please. I don't want you to fall apart because you keep moving without rest.'

I push myself to my feet. 'I'll rest when I know every world is safe.'

CHAPTER EIGHTEEN

Zeus, Candace, and I prepare to abandon our home once again, knowing that leaving could cause the empire's downfall.

For seven nights I bury my face into my pillows and squeeze my blankets in my fists, trying to imprint the feeling of home into my heart forever. I'm well aware I might never come back – whether it's because I'm dead, or because the empire doesn't make it through the war, destroyed like Amora's Capital.

Zeus prepares his final goodbye to his parents. Elm – who can't be convinced to stay back – packs up their workshop, toy by toy. Candace and I spend each night scheming until late, and each day debating with the council and royals in the castle.

I check on my army, the soldiers I've spent the last few years leading, and organise who will join the division in Bearra and who will stay behind to protect the empire. Ideally we'd pick one battle, as we can't spread ourselves too thin, but with the royals still wanting to surrender, our troops don't have a clear goal. Some will follow me, and some will stay with the royals.

All I can do is leave the choice to them and hope for loyalty and strength from the ones that come.

Zeus and I hold hands at the end of the throne room, a crowd of people – mostly aristocrats and gossips – gathered for our announcement. A blizzard hammers the small windows, but the blazing fire at our backs makes the room stifling. The traditional dress wrapped around me in its thick layers of red and green wool chokes my body, while red roses from the Fairy Gardens tug at my braided hair.

Candace stands behind us, next to the royals. None of them particularly love the idea of this, especially considering they believe it to be real, but they know the benefits to the empire outweigh the disdain between our families.

So I lift my chin and focus on my fingers intertwined with Zeus's.

The prince clears his throat, and the echoing mumbles and footsteps disappear at once, like magic. He stands tall in his white suit, adorned with silver along each hemline that matches the silver crown in his hair. 'Thank you all for being here for this announcement,' he says, glancing at me with puppy dog eyes and squeezing my hand.

I attempt a smitten expression, biting my bottom lip, and nod for him to continue.

'Much as we've tried, for our own privacy, to keep it a secret,' he says, 'it seems many of you have noticed that General Isla and I have been touched by romance.'

People *aww*, and Zeus manages to go bright red – *how can he do that on command?*

'I would like to confirm for you all, today, that we are indeed in love. But in these terrible times, with so many unknowns facing us, we want to show the world our devotion and immortalise it, despite whatever may happen next.'

He turns to face me, taking my other hand. Our gazes lock, and I can't tell if it's part of the show or real, but I can't look away from those ice-blue eyes.

My heart flutters.

'And that is why my beloved won't be General Isla Khirina for much longer. She will be *Princess* Isla of the Ice Empire. As my—' he pauses, unable to speak over his grin '—wife.'

Gasps fill the room until Candace starts clapping behind us, and our guests quickly right themselves and applaud. Except for the two googly-eyed women in the back who faint.

It's no secret amongst our people that Zeus and I have always hated each other. They surely never expected this romance to go so far. But an engagement is the last card we have left to play save pregnancy, and I am *not* doing that.

We leave tomorrow, and we need to show our unity now more than ever – before we're gone and the politics and protection of our home are left to the council and royals.

If they can believe in this love, can they believe we'll save them? Can this alliance be enough to keep them from surrendering?

I drop Zeus's hands and turn to my people. 'Thank you for your support,' I say, projecting my voice. 'You all know the Ice Empire means the world to me, and I will be incredibly proud to be its princess. I will always protect you, whether that's at the head of an army or atop a throne. And—' I attempt a flush like Zeus's, but fear I only scrunch my face off-puttingly '—you may all consider yourselves invited to our wedding, which will occur once the two of us win this war.'

People in the crowd tear up, their hands clasped together.

'We leave today.' Zeus places his hands over his heart. 'And we will not return until we're victorious. I will keep each one of your faces etched into my mind and heart as I fight for you. I will surrender my life for you if I must, even if it means saying goodbye to my beloved princess. But you, my dear subjects, must remember the strength of your prince, and honour my sacrifice by always fighting. By never surrendering to Lire.'

The quiet cries of his fans turn into cheers as he raises a fisted hand. I put mine up along with his, lifting both our arms, and the cheers turn even louder, bouncing through the throne room and searing my eardrums.

But it's . . . *nice*. A real smile fights its way onto my face. With all these people cheering for us – for me – I imagine myself truly as the princess of this empire. Not a general, who has to work every day to keep her position, but a royal whose leadership can't be questioned.

Someone who truly belongs here. Not an orphan, but a princess.

His princess.

They chant our names, and I wonder if being his partner, *really* this time, would be such an awful idea.

✦♡✦ ⛄ 🎩 ⛄ ✦♡✦

We pile into the royal carriage that will take Zeus, Elm, and me to the sleigh at the edge of the city – which will take us to a second carriage to bring us to Bearra. To that awful, stinking hot place.

Word has spread across the world of the legendary place's rise back into our world, calling it the *woken kingdom*. In my opinion, it's very much still asleep. A *nightmare*.

Oh, how I can't *wait* to be back amongst all the drama of the Bearrans and their friends. The constant arguing, the immaturity. *Fairies.*

Zeus will be spending time with Relia again, which means I won't see him as much. Not that I'm jealous. It's best we spend as much time apart as possible, except to keep up appearances and for strategy sessions. Our emotions are becoming dangerously entwined.

But what if Relia sees how this plan hurts Zeus, and convinces him to break off the fake engagement? She won't be fooled by our story. What if she takes him away from me?

Zeus gives me a sweet smile from across the carriage as it rocks to life.

Truly, what am I going to do about him? What if we win the war and actually have to get married, fated to live in unease forever, always at arm's length so we don't hurt each other with the real feelings we can't help?

I tear my eyes from him and brush aside the curtain to take one final glance at my city. The streets are lined with the warmth of homes, shops of dark brick and logs, while the castle reaches up from the mountainside. My home is to the east, the tips of the castle peeking into view. The snowy mountains behind stretch as far as I can see, and they go much further, those endless hills I've always looked to for protection. The icy roads fly below us, a blur of a home I may never return to.

But I'll try. I swear, wiping my eyes, that I'll try to keep this place safe.

This cold city that took an orphan from another world and made her its own.

I'll come back. I have to.

When I can't stop crying, Zeus hands me his handkerchief, and Elm lets me lay my head in their lap.

I'll try.

CHAPTER NINETEEN

SOMEWHERE, SOMETIME...

Despite the circumstances, Maya Nova was delighted to see a familiar face. The blue-draped boy on the other side of the apartment doorway grinned so widely his dimples showed, and even Teddy – as lethargic as he'd been these past weeks – bounced on his toes at the sight of his old friend.

'*Fairies,*' Gus breathed. 'Where have you been? You look like you just stepped out of an apocalypse.'

'Not quite,' Maya replied. 'We're just on our way to one.'

He stepped to the side and gestured them in. 'It has been that sort of year, hasn't it?'

The apartment emerged around them, Maya sighing in relief to be somewhere she could relax after so long on the road. *Familiarity.*

The city shimmering around and below them, past the windows. The modern furniture that was stiff but covered in the softest blankets. The kitchen and bathroom with all their magical appliances. Maya couldn't wait to let hot water run over her sore back.

Ebony crept in last, a cautious cat, and Gus ran his azure eyes over her. 'And who is this Amoran beauty?'

She grimaced at him. Maya already told her Gus helped them when they were searching for the crown, offering them new clothes and a place to stay. Maya would always be indebted to him. When she'd been faced with infinite unknowns, Gus offered her friendship.

He was also one of few people who knew about Teddy's parentage. Like Amora and Dawn, Gus was part of Teddy's chosen family. And, by extension, Maya's.

That didn't mean Ebony had to like him, though. She picked and chose who she was nice to. Maya learned this well over the weeks they'd spent together. She was grateful books had brought them together, or their travels would've been very awkward.

'Of course,' realised Gus, his smile dropping. 'Your city. I never had the chance to visit, but I was sorry to hear of its fall.'

She gave him a short nod and went to explore the apartment, peeking into drawers and behind curtains.

'You haven't found Amora yet?' Gus asked Teddy, who sat beside him on the long couch while Ebony continued prying and Maya found a cushion on the floor.

Maya's skin prickled. 'How did you know we're looking for her?'

Gus was a friend, of course, but so much had happened lately, she was always waiting for the next betrayal.

He cocked his head. 'Teddy told me.'

Maya raised her brows at her red-haired boy.

'What? I write Gus letters,' he said, wringing his fingers. 'Last time we were here, he was mad I didn't keep in touch, so this time . . .'

'Yes,' Gus said, 'this time I got *all* the gory details.'

A little bit of the knot in Maya's stomach unravelled. At least she wouldn't have to explain the entirety of the past few months. Even if she felt a little strange about Teddy communicating with his friend without telling her. She'd have loved to say hello.

Then again, she enjoyed talking to her sisters privately, so it was only fair Teddy had someone of his own. *Fairies knew* Dawn was busy most of the time between her resurrected lover and her new role as queen. Teddy needed a confidant.

But Maya told her sisters *intimate* details of her life with Teddy – and some of the things she'd heard from Sierra about Arden were unspeakable in most company – so what was he telling Gus about her?

'Up until we left Bearra,' said Teddy. 'I'm sorry I haven't written since.'

'You should be. I've been worried,' Gus said. 'Well?'

They covered the last few weeks, since finding out what happened to Amora and her territory: discovering the place abandoned and demolished; searching for clues; making their way back north – slower than they should've, and without learning much new, but they'd all needed space to breathe – and finally their arrival in Darraport.

Lire's estate wasn't far from here, so they would spend a night or two, maybe go and scout it, before their rescue mission to get Amora out of there.

If she even *was* there.

Regardless, sneaking into Lire's estate – risky as it was – meant an opportunity to learn information about her, so it wouldn't be an entire waste unless they didn't survive.

Gus nodded. 'You're going to spend today here, resting. That's non-negotiable. I'll cook up a big dinner while you three try to take your minds off things. Then first thing tomorrow, we'll head out to the estate to assess it and make a plan.'

Maya felt like she was being given a warm hug. If anything, Gus's kindness reminded her of her mother.

She bit her lip. *I won't cry.*

But the bittersweet feeling pooled in her gut. No matter how terrible things got, at least she knew there would always be someone to hold her. No matter where she turned, friends or family always appeared to lead her out of darkness.

She could take another step. And another. And another. Until the war was won.

Teddy tossed and turned, huddled in blankets and within arm's reach of Maya, but never able to rest. Nightmares haunted him: Amora screaming in pain as Lire tore at her rainbow wings; himself stuck in a jail cell in Amora's Capital with Maya on the other side of metal bars as the city burned around them; Dawn and Relia in the destructive wake of a killing blow of magic, a faceless fairy cackling over them as their castle collapsed.

He periodically woke soaked in sweat, trying to breathe deeply and watch Maya's peacefully closed eyes until he fell back into fitful sleep.

Now he stood over the graves of Gus and his mother, in a cemetery that stretched on as far as the eye could see. It reminded him of the endless grey in Glassine, where Maya's grandmother was buried. But here, the sky was dark grey, thunder rumbled, and fog snaked amongst the concrete headstones.

A red glimmer in the distance drew his attention. A young woman was walking towards him, almost floating, with a lilac aura surrounding her. Her bright hair floated as if she were in water, and her pink dress moved like the ripple of raindrops hitting a puddle.

She appeared before him, the dream bringing her to his side in the blink of an eye.

'What happened?' Teddy asked. In some sense, he was relieved this was only a dream; Gus was still alive, in his room just a few metres away. But he also knew Relia didn't visit people like this anymore unless it was an emergency. 'Is Dawn okay?'

Relia nodded quickly. 'We're all as okay as we can be.' She ran a hand over his arm reassuringly and a wave of peace washed over him. 'I'll explain everything. Would you like to take a seat?' She motioned behind him, where a soft couch appeared.

He turned to sit, and when he looked back at Relia, they were in Amora's Palace, in a comfortable room he'd stayed in a few times as a child. The sofa morphed to match his memory.

'You feel safe here,' Relia said. 'It's beautiful.'

'It was.' His voice was raspy even in the dream, a reflection of his grief and exhaustion. 'What did you come here to tell me?'

'There's been a development in the Ice Empire.'

Relia appeared fine, but she could manipulate her appearance in dreams. Despite her calm demeanour, Teddy could sense a tension below the surface that she was hiding. Maybe it was because their magic was the same; they were like siblings in some ways, both magical children of Lire. He could look past her magic and he *knew* she wasn't okay.

'Information was discovered by Zeus and Isla,' she said. 'They're already on their way back to Bearra.'

Teddy sat upright. What could the Imperials have found out that affected them all? When had they even left? Or was that the problem – was it Zeus and Isla who were planning to take even more of Bearra for their own empire?

'Shh.' Relia shook her head. 'I told you, we're all fine. They left a few weeks ago to visit the Ice Empire, and I've been checking in with Zeus by visiting his dreams. Usually I only pop in to make sure he's okay, but earlier tonight, he sought me out and wanted to talk . . .'

'If everything's fine, what are you so hesitant to tell me?'

'I'm trying to find the words to put it delicately. In short, we've discovered Lire's true plan.'

He leaned away, fists clenching. 'True plan?'

It all tumbled out of her in nervous, confused stops and starts as Teddy asked question after question she didn't have the answer to.

He was left with one realisation that gave him hope: Lire had not always been a fairy, an immortal.

Maybe Teddy was more human than he'd thought.

•♡• ⛄ •♡•

It was difficult for the four of them to concentrate the next morning, but they stuck to their mission and hopped in the carriage, headed for Lire's Estate. Maya's veins were cold with a constant undercurrent of sparks that had her jumping at every shadow. Since Teddy told her everything Relia had revealed to him, she'd been shaken up far more than usual.

Gus seemed to still be wrapping his head around it. Teddy seemed angry, if anything. Ebony wasn't shocked; instead she went into analytical mode, dissecting the information against everything she already knew.

Maya found her mind running in circles. One moment she felt deep fear of what might lie beyond all she knew, and the next, hope that a better world might be out there, and then: endless questions about, well, everything.

She thought she'd been facing a villain that threatened all life, and yet there was indefinitely *more* life beyond with no idea of Lire's existence. Maya struggled with two conflicting truths: their world was smaller than they thought, and yet if Lire succeeded, the power hungry fairy could be a threat to a much larger universe.

She felt tiny. Like all her problems were meaningless. What was the loss of one city, the loss of a fairy, the loss of her aunt, her *mother* – when there could be *millions* of people, *thousands* of cities, at stake?

And if none of her problems mattered, why did she still feel so gut-wrenchingly terrible?

Why couldn't she just . . . fix things?

Fix her grief. Fix her and Teddy's relationship. Fix all the mistakes she'd made.

Go back to who she was before all of this – a girl fuelled by spite, instead of a girl under crushing tonnes of sadness and fear.

When she destroyed the crown, she thought she'd won. Lire would be back, she knew, but it felt like she'd really done something. That object, which could have changed her life, seemed so meaningless now. She'd given up riches and Lire was still going to destroy their world, destroy *more* than their world. All Maya had done was delay it.

Hadn't she lost enough, sacrificed enough?

If she'd just made the selfish choice and kept the crown to herself, she could have everything now. Saving this world would be up to someone else. She'd be sitting in a castle with her family, eating delicacies from silver spoons, watching the world end around her.

Teddy guided them to Lire's Estate, Maya seated with a hand on her plunging stomach, her eyelids heavy. As their carriage approached, they could already see Lire's soldiers milling about the surrounding villages. There was a distinct distrust written on their faces, and a glow of magic around their fingers.

Teddy stopped the carriage in a small clearing in a nearby forest, the estate appearing in a large, flat expanse of greenery-lined buildings.

They crouched at the brow of a hill for cover. Maya's chin itched as she stayed pressed to the grass, eyes fixed on the estate below. It was maybe ten minutes' walk from their hiding place.

Lire's Estate wasn't a castle, nor was it quite a village. It consisted of about twenty brick buildings of various sizes, connected by concrete pathways. Gardens lay between the structures, some squares of grass left for people to sit and walk on, others inlaid with shaped hedges.

Maya wasn't sure what the buildings were used for. They didn't look like shops or houses, but they had to be one or the other.

The largest structure in the centre, according to Teddy, was Lire's residence. The bricks of this one had a faint purple hue, almost a glow, and it reached the tallest, though it was still no more than four or five storeys high. In a different stone, lighter than the aged brick elsewhere, turrets had been added to the rooftops of Lire's residence, making it castle-like.

Surely Amora was hidden away in this place.

✦♡✦ ♠ 🎒 ♠ ✦♡✦

Between Ebony's fighting skills and Teddy's magic, Maya knew it was more likely than not that they'd be fine. She was reminded of the adrenaline and success of their break-in to Grace's Fortress. She'd faced something like this before. As long as they didn't run into Lire herself, they could survive anything.

Goosebumps ran up her bare arms as they snuck through the cold tunnel at the edge of the estate that Teddy and his brother Jacob used when Lire would bring them here. The brick-lined passageway glistened with dampness. The buildings were very old – from before this world was made, Maya guessed – and filled with many hideaways and secret tunnels Teddy explored as a child.

Ebony led the pack, slashing cobwebs with her weapon, its enchantment forming it into a curved knife. Teddy used a glow of lilac magic to light their way. Gus, to Maya's surprise, didn't complain despite the fear he was clearly trying to keep from his expression. At first they told him not to come, but he had the advantage of not being recognisable as one of them. Lire probably had a bounty on the rest of their heads. If they needed him to, he could sneak around more areas without notice.

The tunnel ended at a wooden door, and Teddy peeked through the cracks, then motioned Maya forward. 'There's a latch,' he explained, his cheeks reddening. 'I had smaller fingers when I was last here. Can you . . .'

She thought of that little boy, so lost and afraid, searching for ways out of this place. Away from his mother. It made her bite her lip as she nodded. 'I've got it.'

He smiled his gratitude. It was such a small thing, but Maya felt pride that he wanted her help with something. She couldn't deny that his power was so great that there was an imbalance between them. She hated feeling like he didn't need her. He *did* – he'd be lost without her – but she needed these moments to remember.

She squeezed her fingers through a hole in the wood, wincing as she caught a splinter, and unhooked the latch. Teddy pressed his face to the cracks again, then they swung open the door.

Maya stuck her pricked finger in her mouth as she took in the room. An old classroom with desks facing one wall and bookshelves lining the perimeter. The door swung shut behind them, also lined with books – *a secret door*. And these books, they were *old*. Older than she'd ever seen, but in wonderful condition considering.

She couldn't help but run her fingers along the cracking leather spines and yellowing pages. *From the other world.*

'No one uses this room,' said Teddy. 'At least, no one did when I was here. This estate is so big half of it is abandoned.'

It didn't look abandoned, with everything in perfect condition, not a spot of dust in sight. But Maya supposed that was an enchantment. 'And this is where you think Amora will be?' she asked. 'Hidden in the abandoned parts?'

'Or would she be kept close to Lire, nearer her quarters?' Ebony added, but her attention was on the old books.

Teddy shrugged like it wasn't overly serious, but a darkness to his eyes showed his determination. 'We'll search everywhere until we find her.'

They coursed through countless rooms like this one, down endless corridors with endless doors, and every time someone approached, Teddy shielded them with masking magic. Despite not running into trouble, it felt like they weren't running into anything at all.

There were no signs of Amora, or even anything about the war.

They split up, Maya and Teddy exploring on their own so they could save time. They'd already been in Lire's Estate too long.

Climbing to the top floor, they peered out the windows for any clues. The estate was beautiful – Maya had to give it that – but the energy around them was unruly and irate, like the place was rippling with Lire's catastrophic magic, her fury.

Teddy was observing the main building, Lire's *castle*, and Maya caught the glassiness in his eyes.

She chided herself. What was she doing? She should have been softer, should have supported him more. Instead she was solely focused on their search.

This must be such a difficult place for him to return to. They'd both been so deep in their own sadness and anxiety for so long she'd almost forgotten. Forgotten he still needed help.

Maya placed her hand atop Teddy's on the windowsill. His eyes. Those lovely brown eyes that held so much warmth. She hated seeing them so sad. Teddy was a happy person. He was sunshine. And she would always love him deeply, even in the dark times, but this wasn't *him*. This wasn't *them*.

'I'm sorry,' she whispered.

He turned to her, lowering his head to look her in the eyes. 'What's wrong?'

She exhaled. Of course his first instinct was to check on her. 'All of it. But that's not the point.' She paused. 'Teddy, I'm trying to tell you that . . .' She rolled her head back. 'I don't know! I don't know. That I love you. And I hate it because, because— Why can't we just love each other? Why not? Why do we have to face all of this? Why does there have to be so much conflict between us?'

His mouth fell open. 'Maya, I love you too. Nothing could ever come between us – not in any way we can't face. You know that, don't you?'

'We never talk about anything,' she said, fingertips buzzing – she felt suddenly distraught. Words splattered out of her mind and through her lips in ways she wasn't sure made sense, but she couldn't hold them back. 'All we went through with the crown. Do you know how badly you hurt me? Don't you know how hard I find it to trust anyone? And what about my stint as the princess? I don't know if you've forgiven me for suggesting we surrender to Lire to protect Bearra. Because we don't *talk*. We pretend everything is okay. And I thought I was okay with that – to just come back to things once we're safe. But what if we're never safe? What if we never talk, and there's betrayal and resentment between us forever? What if—'

'*Maya.*' He took her hands, his face a flush of pink. Tears sparkled in his eyes. 'I'm so sorry. I don't know what to say.'

'I'm sorry too. I think I'm losing my mind. But I know we can't go on like this.'

'I know . . . I just . . . I haven't been myself, and . . .'

'Because you don't even know who you *are*.'

'I—'

'I see your heart, Teddy,' she said, and he closed his mouth. 'You're one of the best people I know. But you were a runaway, and then a liar, and now we're both so consumed by guilt and anger and grief that we can't tell up from down. I love you so much. But I also can't keep doing this. I can't keep living with a brick wall between us that I have to either ignore or climb just to talk to you.'

'I don't know who I am,' he echoed softly. 'Do you think . . . Do *you* know who I am?'

'I want to help you find out.' She rubbed her thumb over his hand. 'And me as well.'

His shoulders went limp with acceptance. 'Which means we can't keep brushing everything under the rug.'

She nodded, a sense of calm washing over her. *We can fix this.* 'I love you.'

He smiled. 'I love you, too.'

⁘

Exiting the building at least an hour since they entered – still with no clues as to Amora's location – Teddy masked them again and they moved on. The next brick structure was identical to the first, but more populated. Here, the classrooms had been turned into dorms for Lire's soldiers, and even though they couldn't be seen, the four of them had to press themselves to the edges of the corridors so they wouldn't bump into people – the *cowards* who had joined Lire.

Maya wanted to hit every one of them right in the face.

There were whispers, and she keenly listened in on what she could, but the soldiers knew little of Lire's actual plans. Nothing at all about how she intended to reopen their world. Even her own people didn't know the truth.

If she was being completely honest, though, Maya wasn't paying as much attention as she should be. After her breakthrough – or break*down* – with Teddy, a huge weight was off her shoulders, and it was hard to concentrate.

They were going to talk, really talk, and she knew now that it wouldn't break them apart. Honesty would bring them closer together.

Even if they didn't make it through this war, they would at least be in the best place they could with each other before it all ended.

Fairies, she loved him. With all that she had. He filled every gap in her heart. He taught her so much, every day. He'd taught her *how* to love.

The world was ending, but she knew this: she was lucky, because she had found a one in a million soulmate. And no matter how bad things got, she would always be grateful.

Another building, and then another, but none held good news. Hours later, they were in Lire's residence at last. If there was one word for this part of the estate, that word was *purple.* Maya's stomach turned at the glow of the building, emanating from the lavender walls within, the royal purple sofas and amethyst spires that reached from the deep mauve tiles to the orchid ceilings.

When she returned home to her art, she wouldn't be able to use any shade of purple for a long while.

Here, Lire's people weren't dressed in regular clothes. The soldiers closest to the fairy wore uniforms of deep elderberry, with lilac sashes over their chests. They bowled through the residence with such force Maya had to keep shifting out of their way to avoid being knocked down.

Teddy took Maya's hand and led her through yet more corridors, until they found a grand staircase of magenta oak. The group of four rose through the centre as soldiers and staff moved down the sides, using the amethyst handrails.

Maya shivered. Purple would be *banned* from her art. She didn't think she could ever look at it again after this.

At the top of the staircase lay a grand hallway, off of which other corridors led to doors on doors. *Wonderful.* She sighed, then, realising someone was right in front of her, held her breath and scurried on.

Teddy continued upwards, leading them onto another staircase, and then another, until they reached a turret. Here it was quieter, with fewer people moving about. Still, the energy was tense. Something was amiss up there.

Maya locked eyes with Teddy; it was clear they both felt sure Amora was nearby. Teddy strode across the hallway to one of the doors, like a wolf with a caught scent. Maya, still gripping his hand, hurried along to follow.

Her heart raced. She hated seeing Teddy like this, like his mother's son, angry and unforgiving. A renewed vigour overtook him. He *would* find Amora. And *fairies knew* what he'd do when he did.

Ebony eyed Maya, and they shared a quick, uncertain glance. After all their training together with Bearra's army, Ebony trusted Teddy. But she was still cautious of his power. Maya understood that, because how couldn't she be? The pirate trusted Arden like a brother and still did, but power had caused him to make big mistakes.

How did she know Teddy wouldn't be swayed by the temptation to use all he had?

They reached closed double-doors and Teddy went to fling them open, but Gus held him back. 'Listen first,' he whispered. 'If she's in there, we need to know what we're going into.'

Teddy exhaled and nodded, some of that forceful energy leaving him as his oldest friend brought him back.

Maya pursed her lips. She was glad to not have to be the one to intervene. She observed the door, looking for any cracks to peek through, but found no imperfections in the light wood. Yet at the edges, light peeked through.

A soft, pink glow.

So the relief she'd felt, and Teddy's willingness to wait, weren't all natural. Amora was in there, enchanting the room with her dizzying haze.

Ebony's eyes turned wide and hopeful. Her fairy was alive – and her family might be, too. Maya put her ear to the crack in the door on the left, and pulled Teddy to place his ear under hers.

His breaths came quickly and he gripped Maya's hand with harsh hope. The anticipation was deadly. Could they really save the fairy who had done so much for them? Could they right this terrible wrong?

Maya's heart burned with guilt and desperation. Amora had begged them to go and hide in the safety of her territory. They'd refused, and within weeks the city was gone.

Could they have stopped it? Could they have saved her?

We will now, Maya promised.

'. . . and what about my people?' said Amora, in her unmistakably charming, beautiful voice.

'What about them?' came another voice, and Maya seized. Lire. 'I'm taking care of them here. And besides, if they don't make it into the new world, I'll get you *new* people. We'll be starting afresh.'

Teddy's breath hitched, and Maya pulled him into her shoulder.

Amora sighed. 'Not ideal, sister, but if that's what you want.'

'It isn't about what I want,' Lire snapped. 'This is for you. For the six of us. Well, for those of us who choose the right side.' She tutted. 'This experiment has failed. It's time to move on.'

'Failed,' echoed Amora. 'I quite liked it. Until you destroyed everything I built.'

'Don't be so dramatic. We'll rebuild. We're together now, and that's what matters most. Once we bring the others—'

'I know you aren't naïve enough to think Kara would ever join us.'

Join *us?* Maya grasped Teddy with more force, helping to balance him as his legs turned wobbly. Why did it sound like Amora wasn't as much of a victim as they'd thought?

'We managed last time,' said Lire.

'Well, you could kidnap Kara and destroy her city as well,' said Amora, darkly.

'If it were up to me, she'd not be part of this at all. But we've already lost Muse, which will hurt our ability to open the world. Besides, I won't give Kara the satisfaction of my wrath. She wants to pick a fight? She can come here herself.'

'Certainly,' Amora replied, boredly. 'And once the worlds are re-connected, we won't need her power anymore, will we? We'll kill her together. Take that magic for ourselves, et cetera . . .'

Lire's voice turned jovial. 'See, kidnapping you and destroying your city wasn't so bad of me, was it? You did come around, and you now see I'm right. I only ever do what's best for us.'

'I am endlessly grateful, of course.'

'You won't be here much longer, so don't lose your wings. By my spies' estimations, my son should be here for your *rescue* within the next few days. You'll return to Bearra with him and ensure the death of him and everyone he loves. Having you on the inside is the turn we need to make this war ours.'

'I'll do what I must for the coven,' Amora said.

Ebony shook her head. 'What is she talking about?'

Teddy was tremoring, and Maya pulled him from the door. 'She's protecting herself,' he said, then added more quietly, 'She's only pretending to be on Lire's side.'

Maya wasn't so sure. She hated suspecting Amora, but the fairy *had* kept the secret of how their world was formed from them. If she'd told the truth, they would've had the advantage of that knowledge long ago.

As far as Maya knew now, Amora was a stranger. How had she been so blinded by their plan to save her that she'd never thought to doubt her?

'Or she let herself get kidnapped,' said Ebony, dejected and quiet, 'and this was always her plan. To join Lire again.'

Because why would a fairy get so close to Teddy, knowing he was Lire's son, if not to use that to her advantage? Lire always had a plan, was always ten steps ahead – a hundred, a thousand *years* ahead.

Teddy might only be a pawn to the immortals in that room. To them, he was nothing but a blink. Maybe Amora never loved him at all.

'It's all lies.' Teddy was adamant, but he was on his knees. 'She wouldn't betray us. I know her.'

'Whatever the reason is for her words,' Gus said, 'she's safe here. If she's betrayed you, we mustn't bring her back to Bearra. If she's still on our side, she has a plan, and we shouldn't intervene.'

'But—' Teddy began, eyes red-rimmed. 'But I *have* to save her.'

Maya pulled him to his feet. 'We need to go. Gus is right – she's clearly taking care of herself. We've wasted enough time.'

In a daze, Teddy let his friends lead him out of Lire's residence, back past the other buildings they'd searched, and into the old school building. They followed corridors until they found the room with the tunnel, and Maya clutched Teddy's arms. 'Whatever this is, my love, we're going to be okay.'

But when he met her gaze, she didn't know anymore. This boy had been hurt so many times, had trusted so few, despite his big heart. He was in enough strife when he thought he'd lost Amora. But for her to have betrayed him . . .

Maya didn't know if he could make it past that.

As she worked to unlock the latch behind the bookshelf to the tunnel, her worry dissipated into anger, into fury. Her hands heated, and her teeth ground together.

How dare the fairies put them through this? How dare anyone hurt Teddy like this? Especially his own mother, and this other woman who had, what, only pretended to love him?

No. She was *done* letting anyone hurt Teddy. No more.

They were going to have their future together. She'd make sure of it. No more numbness, no more pushing everything away. She'd remember who she was – the stubborn girl who would traverse an unknown world to save her family. Maya might be different now, she might have grown up, but she could still tap into that undeterrable, spiteful flame within.

She got the door open and let the others enter the tunnel before her. As they slipped through, she ran her fingers along the spines of those beautiful books that existed long before she did, and a spark entered her mind. The heat in her cooled as she focused on the forming idea.

With a breath that sent a shiver up her spine and an excitement through her core, she had her plan.

I know how to defeat Lire.

CHAPTER TWENTY

The Bearran heat hits me like a punch in the face. Like I'm sitting right in front of a fireplace. But it isn't a cosy, homely warmth. I'm wrapped and smothered.

My soldiers are exactly how I left them as we visit their encampment – if antsier to fight. Bearra itself is much the same as I left it, the rivers sparkling but the people weary. My room in the castle is cold and impersonal with a fine layer of dust. I place my nutcracker back in the window, and we set up Elm in the next room. Zeus and I tell the Bearrans we're engaged, to everyone's disbelief.

We make one thing very clear: we can't keep waiting for the fight to come to us, wasting time holding down the fort. We need to take control and finish this. I didn't come back to sit around.

I came here to lead, to win the war.

'And you expect to do that by . . .?' questions Queen Dawn from her place at the head of the table. At her left is Relia, followed by Zeus. The two friends are practically on top of each other, thrilled to be reunited.

And I'm sitting like a fool by my 'fiancé', who is showing no notice to me, the Imperial general – and *future princess* – everyone still doesn't quite trust.

We're in a newly-made strategy room in a wing of the castle I haven't visited before, since it's only just been rebuilt. And by rebuilt, I don't mean rebuilt *well*. We'd be better off in a tent, but a room is a room.

I straighten my back, casting my eyes around the table – which contains all of Dawn's inner circle except for Maya, Teddy, and Ebony, who are yet to return.

'By now, each of us knows the truth about our world,' I say, channelling all my years of inspirational political speeches. 'We have the advantage of knowing what Lire wants most. She has a need to be in control and to win. She hates that her big plan to have her own world has backfired. We can use that psychology against her.'

Sierra huffs. 'Psychology? Is your plan to speak to her nicely and request she back down?'

I blink very slowly, willing myself not to react. 'My plan is to come up with a plan, Reed. Or do you not want to take the next step and fight Lire?'

She rolls back in her seat. 'I want her dead, General, but if all you're telling us is we need to do *something*, you aren't making the big move you think you are.'

'Dawn.' I turn my attention to the queen. 'Once we invite Lire to Bearra to face us, we'll be in control, rather than waiting in fear for her inevitable arrival. She won't be able to refuse us without looking like a coward. She'll meet us on *our* terms, and we'll have strategies in place to ensure we win. Backup plans on backup plans so we can't fail.' I give Dawn a long stare. 'Are you with me, or not?'

I shouldn't have to ask. This kingdom is mine – we made a deal, and I should by all rights be in charge. Or at least half in charge, along with her. But for this to work, we must be on the same side. I need the Bearrans to stand with me willingly – enthusiastically, even, if it's possible.

Dawn takes a moment to consider, glancing at Relia before nodding gently. 'I'm with you, Isla. You're right. We gain nothing by doing nothing. If we bring the fight to us, we have an advantage.'

A smile threatens to pinch my cheeks, and I fight it without much luck. 'Then it's time to prepare for battle.'

That gets Sierra more excited. She gives me a conspiratorial grin.

Zeus touches my hand, which makes my skin tingle with an irritating level of distraction that I secretly relish. He says to me, making sure the others can hear, 'You're going to lead us into victory, my princess.'

For a moment, as I intertwine my fingers with his, the rest of the room disappears. I'm ice skating with him again to an enchanted melody, the world glittering around us as my heart beats louder and stronger – for him.

My princess.

Relia clears her throat, shattering my delusion. 'You know, at first I thought you two might be faking it.' There's a delighted ring to her voice. 'But seeing you together, and feeling the emotions coming off you, I can tell you're really in love. I'm so happy for you both.'

I drop Zeus's hand, blood rushing to my cheeks. He responds without missing a beat, wrapping his dropped hand over my shoulders as if that's what we meant to do all along. 'Thank you, Relia,' he says. 'Love does find you in the most unexpected places.'

✦♡✦ ♠ 🥁 ♠ ✦♡✦

I can't look Zeus in the eye for several hours, even once we're finally left alone together.

You're really in love.

But the empath could be wrong, couldn't she? Zeus loves me, I know that, but it's always been . . . shallow. Hasn't it? Before, I knew he loved me, but he wasn't *in love* with me, not truly. Not the real me.

And maybe I've thought about how much I care for him, and he keeps becoming a different person in my mind, a person I might actually consider being with, but our boundaries have been so clear.

We can't be together, because we're both fighting for the same thing, and we both stand to get hurt too badly. We both could betray each other at any turn to take everything the other has.

I do not love Prince Zeus.

I pace around my room, glancing every few steps at my nutcracker, as if it'll give me answers. But unfortunately, the answers it's given me so far have only proven to confuse me further.

'What on earth is on your mind?' says Elm, tinkering on my bed.

I jump, having forgotten they were there. 'Huh?'

The teddy bear in their hands lights up, its eyes glowing orange, but they quickly put it down and the light dims. 'Oh, no.' They feign horror, but the corners of their lips twitch. 'It's Zeus, isn't it? Relia was right. I can see it in your face. You're having fe—'

I spin to argue, but Zeus himself beats me to it, stealing in through the door.

I startle, again. 'Zeus!'

'Good evening, my darling,' he says, shutting the door behind him. 'And my other darling,' he directs at Elm.

'Honey,' Elm replies with a small wave. They look between us and sit up. 'I just remembered I need to do something in the—'

'No, don't—' Zeus and I say at the same time. With the same high pitch.

We all go silent, the tension hanging torturously in the air.

Elm flashes me 'sorry' eyes and shuffles out the door.

Traitor.

Zeus gazes across the room, tapping his palms, then spits out, 'I'm so sorry about what Relia said. I didn't want to make you feel awkward. I mean, you know I have real feelings for you, but you didn't need to be put in that position. Well, it does help the lie about us being engaged, but I know it all makes you uncomfortable and I told you I wouldn't do that anymore, and— And I know you don't feel the same way, and that Relia was wrong. So you don't need to worry about me getting hurt. I'm just— I'm sorry, Isla.'

'*Zeus,*' I say, sitting at the end of the bed. The mattress sinks too much, and I feel like I'll lose myself in it. Apparently this kingdom has nothing for me to sleep on that's between a concrete slab and a sponge cake. I straighten and try to look him in the eyes. 'Please don't be sorry. It isn't your fault.'

He takes a step back, not from me, but *for* me, as if his proximity might hurt me. 'Isn't it?' he says. 'All I've wanted for years is you. And yet all I manage to do is sabotage any potential of us being together. I'm not saying this to make you feel guilty. You have no obligation to love me in return. I don't resent you for it. I spent so long making it a joke so I wouldn't be truly hurt by your rejections, but I've learned my lesson, Isla. I listened to your wishes and stopped. But now it isn't a joke. It's so real, it's so painful, and I don't want you to feel any of that pain.'

I raise my hands as if to calm him, the blood rushing from my face. '*Me* feel that pain? Zeus, all I've been doing these past weeks is trying to save *you* from more pain. Who cares what I feel? I—'

'*Who cares?*' His eyes flash with desperation. 'I'd do anything for you. I'd go to the ends of the earth – I did! We did! That's why I would never want someone's comments like Relia's to affect you.'

In all my confusion, my defences begin to shatter. Against my will, I blurt, 'You're wrong about why her comments affected me.'

'I'm so sorry,' he repeats, staring at the wall, then his eyes snap to me. 'What?'

'Do you really love me?' I ask him, earnestly. 'Is it real, or just . . .'

'An act?' He laughs darkly. 'I'll always love you. Even when I've claimed not to, no one else has ever compared, nor will they ever. Sometimes I feel as if all I know for certain is that I love you. Even before I knew *why* I loved you. And these past weeks I've learned why again and again. I've fallen deeper and deeper and it's *miserable*. But why else would Relia's comments affect you, if not because of how uncomfortable I've made you feel?'

'Because what I feel isn't discomfort!' I slap my hands on the silken sheets, more frustrated with myself than anything else. 'Not anymore. You've gotten what you wanted! You've wormed your way into my heart. You're different to what I thought, Zeus, and I'm so sorry I realised it too late.'

I rub my eyes. 'This is such awful timing. I've known I love you since we nearly kissed on the ice that day in the borders, but you pushed me away, and I got scared, because I realised if these feelings are anything less than genuine, we both stand to find ourselves heart-broken, and even then, we could never be together, because—'

He falls to his knees before me, the most vulnerable look in his icy features. 'This could be *real* for you? If it could, tell me, and I am yours. I only pushed you away because I feared we'd regret it.'

My eyes go wide; I'm not sure what expression is on my face, exactly, but I know I can't shift it. I think my lashes are twitching. 'It's already real for me. But you know I can't really be with you.'

'Why? Isla, *why*?'

'I wish it was simpler. That there wasn't all this *trouble*. If I could go back to hating you, I would, because it was far easier.' I swallow at the lump in my throat. 'You don't seem to understand it. You never have, because everything comes so easily to you. You don't have to care about these things like I do. But we can't be together when you're my ... my ...'

'Enemy?' He shatters. 'Just because Candace says so?'

'*Rival*. Because I know so. Because that's how the world has pitted us against each other. We're competing for the same power. We can't both have it. And I can't have you distracting me from it. You'll always be a royal, and I'll always be the daughter of the woman trying to overthrow your family. How could we ever love each other, ever be vulnerable with each other, when at any turn we might destroy each other?'

'So,' he utters, quietly and desperately, 'you wouldn't be my princess? You wouldn't make this union real and have all the power you want? Being with me, being a royal, wouldn't be enough for you?'

'No, it wouldn't.' My eyes blur. He's making me seem like a monster, but he doesn't get it. He never has, and he never will. 'Because I don't want your power. I want my own.'

I squeeze my eyelids shut and think back to the past – the years of competing, of avoiding him, the years he taunted and teased me. I thought we weren't true friends, but was that only the political side of me keeping him at arm's length? He always said we were closer than we were. I thought he was the delusional one, but was it me lying to myself, thinking I didn't care?

I must have known somehow that I needed him, because *I'm* the one that went and found him after Sierra kidnapped him. I was the one who helped him with his transformations, making sure he was hidden every night, out of the public eye so no one could see their famous prince turn into a swan. I didn't do all that for no reason.

And when he fell from the sky and broke his arm, the day the curse was broken, I got him to safety. I lied to the nurses about the injury.

Despite how much I complained about it, *of course* I cared. I checked every day to make sure he was alright.

When I finally broke down a few weeks ago and was honest about how much his teasing distressed me, he changed. Right away. For me. He showed me this other side of himself, the side that cares, and I was finally able to see the boy I was drawn to rather than the prince I loathed.

Would it truly not be enough for me to be his princess, and one day his queen? To join the family I've been trying to overthrow?

I've spent so many years following Candace's footsteps, carving out victories with our power. Wouldn't I be throwing away all of that hard work if I simply married into royalty?

If we were normal people, with normal lives, without politics, I wouldn't give it a second thought. We love each other, we care about each other, so why shouldn't we be together?

But that isn't our lives.

I open my mouth to explain this all to him, but freeze as he places his cool hand on my cheek, pulling me back to the moment. '*Zeus*,' I warn.

He's bringing his face closer, that porcelain skin glittering in the evening light, his expression a blend of serious pain, genuine desperation, and true love.

'If that's so,' he whispers, his breath hot on my lips, 'if we can't be together, but you do love me, and you wanted that kiss, then just give me *one*. Then we'll leave it all in the past. We'll both try to forget.'

I try to inhale, but my breath hitches and my heart skips a beat – truly, I might have died for a split second. A warmth spreads through my body that I can't shake, deeper than the Bearran heat, something that emanates from my soul, that resonates in my heart. 'Zeus,' I urge again, but my body betrays me and I nod slowly.

He licks his lips, still on his knees but remaining nearly as tall as me seated on the bed. His hand manoeuvres to the back of my neck and guides my face down. Every muscle within me, usually tensed like stone, relaxes at once. I go utterly limp, utterly in his control. And I should be scared, but I *love* it.

His mouth lightly brushes mine, our noses touching as his hands cup the nape of my neck. Mine hang limply by my sides. His breath is minty, reminding me of the forests at home, the freshness of the constant snow.

I shudder as he presses his lips to mine fully, kissing me hard before melting back. We push our foreheads together for a moment. Everything is stifling hot. Everything is as electrified as a swim in ice water.

He comes back, kissing me lightly, and then harder again, alternating between the soft longing of sweet kisses and the heavy desperation of deeper ones. *Just give me one.* The strength finally returns to my body as his attention pulses more blood through my veins, and with quick breaths I'm finally able to kiss him back, parting his lips and bringing my hands around his shoulders.

I push at him to sit back and slide off the bed, into his lap, Zeus simply taking my weight and adjusting his hands and mouth accordingly. His fingers run below the hem of my shirt, brushing my skin, and I nearly lose my mind entirely.

This is what I've spent years avoiding? *This?*

I could be his princess, if it meant kissing him every day, and *fairies forbid*, even more – oh, *fairies*, how I long for even *more* from him. I'll shatter without it.

But the powers of the world must have different plans for me.

A knock on the door sends me soaring from Zeus's grip and to the far wall.

'One second!' I squeak as Zeus and I stare at each other. He looks as flustered and bewildered and bewitched as I feel.

I straighten my shirt and my hair and I fan my cheeks and *try not to panic* before opening the door. I sigh to find it's only Elm, but unfortunately that means I'll have to explain this to them.

Their doe eyes glance between Zeus and I, but they blink and cough. 'Sorry for interrupting, uh – nothing, of course, because I can clearly see that absolutely nothing has been going on in here.' They puff out their cheeks and brush back a stray curl. 'Dawn wants you both. Teddy and Maya? Her friends? They're back. They don't have Amora, but apparently there's news about the fairies.'

I press my lips together and nod quickly. *Fairies.*

What on earth am I meant to do now?

CHAPTER TWENTY-ONE

SOMEWHERE, SOMETIME...

Sierra Reed was so thrilled to have Maya back that she almost forgot about everything else going on. War? Panic? Death?

Maya!

Her best friend returned sallow-faced, with matted hair and purple under-eyes. Not the partying mood Sierra hoped for, although she'd known this Amora mission might not end well.

And it hadn't.

Mostly she felt bad for Ebony. The pirate was in much better shape than Maya, and Levi nearly bowled her over upon their arrival. But Sierra was fluent in Ebony's language, and she was as devastated as the others.

A few hours after their return, Sierra paced outside Maya and Teddy's room, waiting for them to finish bathing so she could talk to Maya. *Finally* Teddy opened the door, fresh and flushed, eyes all red. Sierra groaned. This man was always in her way. 'Maya?' she asked.

'She's in bed,' he replied, nonplussed. 'Resting.'

Sierra bristled. Why was he trying to keep her away? This stupid, jealous fairy baby. 'And you're going . . .?'

He tapped his foot, annoyed. 'Out, I suppose. I'll go and visit Dawn.'

'Take your time.' Sierra nodded – politely. She pushed past him into the room and he shut the door.

'Sierra? That you?' came a muffled voice from below layers of blankets. *In this heat?* Maya definitely wasn't in a party mood.

'Uh huh,' Sierra affirmed. She found the spot she hoped Maya's head was buried, and unearthed her eyes, then nose, then mouth. The girl looked up at Sierra with pursed lips. 'Wallowing?'

'Uh huh,' Maya replied, ducking her mouth back below the blankets. 'It's bad. Teddy's devastated. Not only did we not save Amora – she's switched sides.'

Sierra cringed and sat cross-legged on the bed, careful not to squash any hidden parts of Maya. 'Well, everyone has bad days. It's war. Can't get all depressed about it, can we?'

Maya cocked her head, nearly displacing a cushion. 'Can't we? It's war.'

'Blah, blah.' Sierra kicked at Maya, and she grumbled. Sierra didn't like to baby anyone, and knew Maya appreciated that better than pity anyway. 'I've been bored out of my mind, as per usual. Any good gossip from your little trip?'

Maya chewed the inside of her cheek, mulling it over for a little while. 'There is something I want to tell you, but it has to stay between us. I don't even want Teddy or Arden to know. Can you swear?'

Not for anyone else, she wouldn't. But Sierra trusted Maya enough to keep her secrets. 'I swear,' she said, though she didn't hide her concern.

Maya lowered her voice. 'I thought of a way to stop Lire.'

'You—' Sierra tamped down the excitement growing in her chest. They'd had too many losses and their chances were too low to let herself fall under the false hope of an idea. 'Tell me what it is.'

'A trap.'

'A trap?'

'I'll tip her off about something she can't resist. Something we have that she wants.'

'She isn't a mouse,' Sierra said. 'I doubt she'd want our cheese, and anyway, how could we entrap her?'

'She won't be in the trap for long, because we'll be killing her.'

'*True.*' Sierra shivered with enthusiasm. 'I suppose that can be done. Can't be much harder than killing Muse. And I've been itching for another fairy murder.'

Sitting around Bearra these past months was bad enough, but waiting for Lire's next attack was torturous. General Isla wanted to bring the fairy to them, but this idea to truly entice and trap her was so *tangible.*

Still, Sierra wondered if she'd have competition for the kill. So many people wanted revenge on the fairy that she might have to fight her own allies first before she ripped those sparkling wings to shreds. Sierra *might* let everyone take turns slowly slicing Lire up, but she wanted the final blow.

Maya finally smiled – if only a small amount. 'I knew I could rely on you.'

'Any time, gorgeous.' Sierra narrowed her eyes. 'Well, what's your idea for a tempting object Lire won't be able to resist? Something to do with iron, so we can weaken and trap her? You know they call her the fairy of wisdom for a reason. She'll be hard to convince.'

'Pshh. Lire isn't as smart as she's made the world believe. In the end, her ego always gets her. It will this time as well. We just have to get word to her about the object.'

'Which is . . .?' Sierra pushed again.

Maya stayed quiet for a while, then finally whispered, 'A book.'

♡ ♠ 🎴 ♠ ♡

Sierra stalked back to her room with her head held high – within days or weeks, she'd be slaughtering Lire, ending the war, and saving everyone in the world. *And* those beyond.

Oh, that huge, world-shattering revelation didn't much bother Sierra. She had the people she loved here, and she had a purpose here. Why should she care where their world came from, or about anyone outside it? Why was everyone in such a *fluster*?

With the excitement of a forthcoming kill racing through her veins, Sierra burst into her and Arden's room. He was in bed, reading. Reading! At a time like this!

Arden offered her a smile, his eyes brightening, and carefully placed a bookmark between the pages of the cloth-bound *tome*. What was it, a thousand pages?

Sierra gave him the updates from her talk with Maya – except for their secret plan, of course – as she hopped beside him on the bed, stretching out her legs. She was achy and irritable. She longed to turn into the swan and fly, and fly. Get out all her burning energy and burst back into her human body refreshed and new.

She settled for massaging her feet.

'I had a quick talk with Ebony,' said Arden. 'She barely had time to give me this book – I guess she thought I'd like it – before she and Levi raced off to the ship to—'

'Understood. At least she's well enough for that.' *So am I.* Sierra slid the book off the sheets and sat it on the floor. She turned to Arden and glanced down at his shirt, then at his lips, then back again, until he finally got the idea and pulled the shirt over his head. Sierra grappled it out of his hands and tossed it across the room.

'Am I just a body to you, Sierra?' he teased. He took her hands, and ran her fingers along his abs.

'Of course not,' she replied, the heat under her fingertips making her shiver. 'It isn't just the body I like. It's how you use it.'

He rolled his eyes, black as midnight, and she let him swish her onto her back, arms pinned at her sides, with him on top. She gasped – only for effect – and he leaned down to her ear and whispered, 'Like this?'

She pulled herself up with the little strength left in her weakening core and kissed him softly. 'I love you, Captain Arden,' she hummed. She kissed him again, and he exhaled heavily as she pulled back to add, 'Do I tell you that enough?'

He leaned back in, speaking into her mouth. 'You *show* me.'

Sierra moved in again, but pulled back, struck by thoughts of Maya's plan. 'Do you really think Lire can be killed?'

'We know all too well that fairies can be killed.' He shifted, clasping his hands disappointedly.

Sierra had successfully killed the mood. She liked scheming about murder, but she cursed those thoughts for hitting her now. Usually she could ignore her mind, but she felt an incessant need to air her concerns – while remaining cautious not to reveal what Maya wanted kept between them.

She crossed her legs as he moved from atop her. 'Yes, but Muse was an idiot. Lire isn't. She's more powerful, and she has more followers, more fairies to back her up. She's always a step ahead. What if it isn't possible?'

He frowned, a hand on her cheek. 'Does it matter if it's possible? We're going to win or die. We've always known that. There isn't a third option.'

Sierra felt suddenly small, 'What if I don't want to die?'

Was there a third option they hadn't considered yet? She thought again of the swan. What if a curse like hers could be the loophole to Lire's demise? Maya had her plan, but Sierra decided to think on a scheme of her own.

I want that kill.

⊹ ♡ ⊹ ♣ 🎎 ♣ ⊹ ♡ ⊹

The day had come. Tension rose in Sierra's heart as her veins pumped blood with an unfamiliar ferocity. She stood at the bow of the *Neptune*, just outside Bearra, on guard waiting for the moment to arrive.

Arden was by her side, gazing at the canals, while the others – Wren, Ebony and Levi – leaned over the balustrade for better views. Maya and Teddy held hands at the shore next to Maya's father and Prima, careful not to be seen from their position. Even Dawn and Relia had descended from the castle to keep their royal eyes on the event.

The setting sun washed the canals with pink and gold, echoing off the clear water and painting the kingdom's brick walls and twists of vines. In the crook of a canal, a white-sand shoreline reminiscent of Grace's Waters, bathed in the light of dozens of candles carefully placed along the ground, stood Lark.

Facing his beloved.

Arden squeezed Sierra's hand. They were a hundred or so metres back but could see the scene well. 'Is he about to do it?' Arden asked no one in particular, bouncing on the balls of his feet.

'Shh.' Wren waved her hand in front of him. 'We might miss something!'

'Because we can hear from here?' teased Levi.

'Still!'

Sierra grinned, returning her eyes to the picturesque beach. Briar's silky, floor-length dress of baby pink flowed in the light breeze, her light-brown hair curled and dancing as she giggled at something Lark said. He was dressed-up too, in a fine suit made by the royals' tailor.

It hadn't mattered how much he badgered his friends for ideas. He'd come up with the entire plan himself, down to the viewing spots across the canals that hid their friends and family. He hadn't let anyone else touch the candles, lighting and placing them all himself, and only told Briar to dress nicely for a *special date*.

The only thing he hadn't done himself was the array of flowers. Dawn sent for blooms from across the world, arranged in delicate rainbows around the couple. More bouquets were hidden on the *Neptune*, so the onlookers could drown the couple in flowers once the *yes* was spoken.

Briar cupped her hand over her mouth, seeming to sense the big moment, and on cue Lark dropped to one knee. Sierra's well-trained eyes could see his hands trembling over the small leather box he held – made by Briar's father, of course.

Lark spoke words none of them could hear, but a glint of light showed the glimmer of tears in his eyes. Briar dropped to her knees to be on his level, cupping his hands and nodding along.

The box opened to reveal a shimmering pink gemstone so bright it almost absorbed the sunset around them. Sierra had already seen – and approved of – the ring. The gold piece had emeralds laid around the rosy centre, like an opening flower, and the metal looped over itself to create an intricate, vine-like band.

Dawn had presented dozens of rings from her own collection and the royals' treasury, but the one Lark chose wasn't offered or bought, but stolen. One of Opal's favourites. This ring was sitting on her jewellery stand when the pirates finally entered her old room and sorted through her things – a task that crushed each of their hearts afresh, but proved fruitful.

Sierra and the others all knew Opal would be honoured for one of her favourite pieces of jewellery to sit on Briar's finger.

The young woman's head dropped, and she laid her forehead over their clasped hands, over the ring box, as her back shook with cries of joy. Lark tilted his head, concerned, but she threw her arms over him, bowling him into the sand. Their overwhelming emotions turned to laughter.

She kissed and kissed him – Sierra wondered if she had any idea yet that there was an audience – and Lark gripped the ring box with one hand while holding her with the other.

Finally they pulled apart, and with a shouted, 'Yes!' the ring was placed on her finger. Lark waved to the onlookers.

'Let's go!' said Wren, gathering bouquets and sprinting down from the *Neptune*. Petals flew in her wake.

Sierra wasn't sure if it was just her imagination, but were the ship's sails flapping almost excitedly, despite there only being a low breeze? Grinning, she grabbed some flowers of her own and followed Wren, Arden right behind her.

They met the couple on the shoreline, careful of the candles. When Wren laid her eyes on her brother's face, splotchy from crying, she threw her flowers to the ground and jumped into his arms, squealing.

He picked her up and spun her around. 'She said yes! She said yes!' the siblings chanted, laughing as they kicked up sand.

Maya, Prima, and their father hugged Briar. She showed them the ring with a fierce blush across her cheeks.

Sierra and Arden glanced at each other, then at Levi and Ebony, who nodded back. It was time to turn this celebration into a party. The four of them launched at Lark, picking him up by his limbs.

'Stop— Wait!' he screamed, but they kept dragging him until their feet splashed in the canal.

'One! Two! Three!' they said between his cries of, 'No! No! No!'

They tossed him into the water. The red-haired Musan splashed, and when he rose, he fumed, his suit stuck to his arms and legs. Briar gasped from the shore. Maya and her father smirked and followed suit, pushing the girl into the canal beside her fiancé.

Brair looked ready to murder her sister at first, but she and Lark gave up and laughed wildly. The rest of the party joined them in the canal, clothes being tossed to the side as they splashed and danced.

Sierra felt layers of stress slipping away as she turned weightless, spinning through the water.

Arden, beaming, pulled her to his body, meeting her as she broke through the surface. Sierra pressed her forehead to his, both of them giggling as they kissed softly. She took a long moment to look right into his eyes as the sun dropped below the horizon, the black in his irises unchanging as the world turned from gold to blue.

Then she smelled something sweet. A feast had appeared on the shore, a long table of fruits and cakes and pastries arranged like artwork. Dawn and Relia sat nearby, the queen's head resting on her partner's shoulder as the two smiled tiredly.

One by one, the group made their way back to the sand to dry off and eat dinner.

Sierra gazed at her friends and felt a resolute truth harden in her soul: there was too much worth living for to let any of these people die.

Chapter
Twenty-Two

For probably the hundredth time this past hour, I wonder what on earth I'm doing on an evening walk with Maya Nova. She's part of Dawn's inner circle, but I'm not sure I've ever spoken a word to her before today – let alone been in the same room as her for more than five minutes.

She runs her fingers through a bush, picking a leaf and tearing it between her fingers. 'I thought you might not have seen this part of the kingdom yet.'

The Bearran girl, with her short light-brown hair and harsh little face that looks angry even when she isn't, insisted on taking me out, alone – and yes, I was sceptical – to *show me around Bearra*.

I said yes because everyone has such high respect for her. From the fearsome Sierra to Lire's son himself. It's clear she's the key to Dawn's circle. Much as they claim to have accepted me, we're hardly friends. So, despite it feeling like a possible risk to my life, I know taking a chance on Maya could help me be truly respected by Bearra.

Besides, I don't resent the distraction. Things aren't going well for me. I kissed the one person I was supposed to *not* be romantic with, I'm still not sure if I can trust my mother, and the world is on the brink of collapse.

She wants to get to know me, see what she makes of me. And I'm grateful for the opportunity, the hand being held out.

Unfortunately, except for pointing at some highlights of the area – a canal here, a big house there, nothing too interesting – and offering a few facts, Maya has not shown herself to be a very talkative person. I want to talk politics with her, or talk about the war, but neither of those seem suitable for a light stroll.

I *have* to turn this awkwardness around.

'You . . . like . . . uh . . .' I start, flailing for something, anything we might have in common. My cheeks flush even hotter than the warm evening air.

She glances at me, bites her lip, then bursts into laughter. 'I am trying *so* hard to be nice, and it's far too difficult. What are we doing?'

Her change in demeanour bursts the bubble of tension. I exhale. 'I wish I knew.'

'Honestly, I don't have any patience for politics,' she says, still walking, moving us from a darker alley onto a brick road lined with firelit lamps.

The stars dampen in the lamplight, but there's less still light pollution here than in the Ice Empire. Bearra displays all the same stars but with even more majesty – one of the few things I like about this kingdom.

Maya continues, 'From what I hear, politics is what you're brilliant at. But I just . . . can't make myself care about it in the slightest. Why can't everyone, I don't know, not be stupid? We wouldn't need leaders if people pulled themselves together.'

I can certainly respect that. 'So you like doing, not scheming.'

She smiles. 'You understand.'

'I do, though I'm the opposite. I've always had a knack for leadership, so I don't mind managing people.' I shrug. 'That, paired with a scary amount of ambition, has led me where I am today. I love politics. The schemes, the debates, doing what I can to improve lives.'

Maya kicks at a stone in our path. 'I see it now.'

'What?' I ask, glancing around at a patch of houses with white bricks and terracotta roofs. They look exactly the same as the rest of Bearra.

She chuckles. 'I see why I like you. I knew there was something. It's the ambition. You'll stop at nothing to get what you want.'

I cock my head. 'Of course.'

'And, General Isla, *that* is what makes you one of us.'

A strange thrill flutters in my chest. Acceptance. She sees my dedication not as a flaw, not as something undesirable, something that makes me crazy, but as a positive – as something that draws me to the Bearrans.

'Oh,' I stutter. 'Thank you.'

'Just trying to butter up the future queen of the world,' she says with a teasing smile.

Ah. I understand her popularity now. I like her, too.

Maya stops in front of a large house. It has huge windows for a Bearran property, and its front garden is an eclectic mix of cacti and newly-planted bushes. Behind the house rises the vine-protected wall of Bearra.

I stand beside her, sucking in my lips. 'Great bricks,' I mutter, unsure what we've stopped here for but trying to be polite.

'This was my aunt's house,' Maya explains. 'My sister lives here with her husband now. They're having a baby.'

'I thought your sister just got engaged? To the pirate?'

'My *eldest* sister.' She gestures to the house. 'You know, the reason all of this started – or, at least, part of the reason it's still going – is because I was doing everything I could to stop her getting married.'

'Oh?' I reply. She didn't seem the type, but Maya must have a big ego to believe she's *that* important in all this.

'I won't bore you with the whole story. I'm sure I'll write it all down someday, when I feel like I can talk about it.' A shadow moves past a curtained window. 'I didn't want my family to be apart. I felt like if Prima got married, she'd be abandoning us. We were so poor. Close to starving. So I went to find a crown that could lift us out of poverty. Then, even if she did get married, it'd be because she wanted to, not for financial reasons.'

Maya lets out a short laugh. 'Turned out that crown was being hunted by Lire as well, because it would've given her even more power. I destroyed it, and Lire killed my aunt. I didn't even know Olivia. I didn't get to. But Lire made sure I never would. Then her war cost me my mother as well.'

I don't know what to say. I certainly don't have any words that would make her feel better.

'You're here,' she says, 'because you want to save this world. A world you want to take for your own. Which is fine. We'll find a way to keep everyone happy if we win. But you don't understand the *real* fight, not really, because you don't have a personal vendetta against the fairies.'

Maya's brows arch from grieving to vengeful. It nearly makes me shiver. *Is she going to kill me out here?*

She says, 'Lire has hurt us all. Me and my family, Sierra and her friends, Teddy, Dawn, Relia. There won't be any forgiving, any kindness. I don't mind stooping to her level if it means making her pay for everything she's done to us.'

My veins turn cold. 'I might not have faced Lire, but I'm with you. She's a monster I want gone, too.'

A shadow appears at our feet, and I spin around. Across the street a deep darkness beckons amongst a set of leafy trees. 'A monster, hmm?' offers a voice, husky and feminine.

Maya and I share an alarmed look. *Do we need to run?* I try to ask with my eyes.

'Don't leave me waiting,' the voice hums. 'I don't have all night, and we need to talk.'

We don't move, and the voice seems to groan. The darkness lifts slightly, revealing two enormous eyes within the trees. I nearly lose all the food I've consumed this week, but Maya perks up.

'K—' she starts.

A shadow of magic silences her. '*Come,*' the voice says.

Maya nods to me, and even with the hairs on my arms raised, I follow her into the shadows, where the eyes reveal themselves as . . . attached to a pair of giant moth wings, which are attached to . . .

Kara. The fairy of death and darkness. I gulp. Her appearance is like an echo, sallow and shadowed, half-alive but bursting with power. I know so much about her younger, human self that I feel as if I know her, but the fairy before me is not the witch she was centuries ago.

No, this is the being Imperial children have nightmares about.

So many questions, sitting on the tip of my tongue, edge their way back into my throat as her dark figure looms over me, those terrifying fake eyes watching me with disdain.

I haven't had the pleasure of meeting her, but she knows Candace. We are, or were, allies. Maybe that will gain me some of the fairy's favour. Or it'll make her hate me more. Apparently it wasn't Maya I should've been worried about killing me tonight.

'Nice to see you again,' Maya says, placing her hands in her pockets. 'I'm not sure why fairies keep wanting to attack out of nowhere or meet us in the shadows. We'd be perfectly happy to set up a meeting in a nice, well-furnished and fashionably-lit room in the castle. But, greetings, I suppose.'

Kara waves a hand. 'You know I don't care for all that nonsense, my dear Maya, and nor do you. That's why I wanted to speak to you alone.'

'Fair.' Maya shrugs, then glances at me and back at the fairy. 'Do you want me to—'

'General Isla can stay. It's both of you I want.'

'Good timing,' I mutter, then swallow hard. 'I mean, certainly, I can talk.'

Kara shrugs, copying Maya, and the small gesture reminds me the fairy is, somewhere deep down, human. 'I take it you read my journal,' she says, and the slight illusion of safety drops.

My stomach falls to my feet – no, metres deep into the ground, buried in the dark where it can panic out of sight. Unfortunately, I can't hide the rest of my trembling self. 'Journal?' I whisper.

She laughs, the sound deep but friendly. 'You aren't in trouble. I left it for you. You needed the truth.'

I raise my eyes to meet hers – her real eyes, not the ones on her wings, my stomach crawling its way back up. 'You . . . planted . . . the . . .'

Maya lifts a brow. 'You planted your diary so we'd find out about Lire's real plan?'

Kara nods.

'Because . . . you want to help us?' Maya says, hopefully.

I'm glad she's carrying the conversation, because I'm still wrapping my head around my discovery of the journal not being a very lucky coincidence. It felt so much my own, a special piece of my world, out there, just for me.

Knowing it was all a ploy of Kara's has taken something away from me. What if she *did* fabricate the entire thing to trick us? We know most of it is true, because Candace confirmed it, but what if Kara isn't the victim she portrayed herself as?

'Yes,' says Kara. 'I believe Isla is the key to stopping Lire.'

'Because I'm from out there,' I finish. Candace said I'm the key to Lire's plan – that because I'm from the outer world, I can undo the enchantment. But how does that mean I can *stop* her?

Maya turns to me very slowly. 'You're from the other world?'

'The walls of ice are not impenetrable,' Kara says. 'Things slip through the cracks. Not usually people, but a child small enough to break past the magic and strong enough to survive in the cold . . .'

'How long have you known?' I demand. 'I've been searching for my family for years. No one had any answers. Candace lied to me. And Rhiannon knew, too. She goaded me about it even though she wouldn't tell me. So, what, can you all sense it?' My fists clench. 'And why didn't anyone want me to know? Know about *my* life?'

'Simple.' Kara tilts her head. 'Knowing would give you too much power. Your imperviousness to magic makes you different to anyone else. You're like walking iron, except you don't repel magic either. You could be the perfect warrior against a fairy. Or you could help her reopen this world. That's why Candace kept you hidden. And why no other fairy who has discovered your existence has ever shared that knowledge.'

Maya whispers, mostly to herself, '*She* can defeat *Lire*?' Her eyes dart back and forth, as if she's already formulating a scheme.

The shadows press in on me further, the weight of a responsibility I never asked for – not the kind I ever wanted, at least. Trees rustle and the trickling of water in a nearby creek takes my focus as I try to centre myself.

'Why are you here now?' I ask Kara, squeezing my toes to help me regain my composure. I put on my icy Imperial mask and stare her down. I'm a general, not a lost child. She needs to know that. 'What benefit does this visit have to either of us?'

The fairy's wings dip. I may be thundering within, but she's no longer the source of my fear. Instead I see the version of her Maya must. A gentle being tasked with a terrible role. I read her journal entries. I *know* her.

Kara was never evil. Lire was the one that made her a monster.

'I want you to know you can trust me,' she says. 'I resent Lire more than anyone else, and I want her gone. There's little I can do to help without risking my people – you saw how Lire made an example of Amora – but when the time comes, I'll be on your side.'

She gazes at me intently. 'This fight has always been more mine than yours, little Imperial. No humans should have been dragged into it in the first place.' I might be imagining it, but I swear the eyes on her wings darken. 'It was always Lire and me. This is all my fault. And I— I'm sorry.'

I falter, wordless. *Sorry.*

Maya, still a few steps behind, mutters, 'I've got to read this diary.'

Kara's eyes remain on mine. 'When two people love each other as deeply as Lire and I did, devastation is inevitable. It's just unfortunate that our destruction took so many others along with it.'

'That's melodramatic, especially for you,' says Maya. 'Not all love ends badly.'

'You know it does, Maya Nova.' The fairy's nonchalant aura falters. 'Has Lire's child not caused you anguish? That boy might be broken beyond repair. Has your love for him not pushed you into darker waters than you ever imagined entering? You were meant to be a bookmaker, and now you have the world on your shoulders. Your aunt, your mother – is the loss of love not devastation, even when it isn't war?'

Maya fumes. 'How d—'

I step between them. 'That's enough, Kara. Just because you failed doesn't mean we will. If you're sorry about this, if you want us to fight with you, making us feel bad won't help anyone. Fairy of death or not.'

Kara rubs her forehead, the gesture human and tired. 'Quite right. My apologies.'

'You say we can trust you,' I press her. 'How can we be sure?' I don't mention Amora has already let us down. The details are still too hazy.

'I gifted you a piece of my soul, Isla, and you protected it. I trust *you*. I'm able to overlook you creating an alliance with Bearra behind my back. Those political plays mean little in the grand scheme of what we're facing. And Maya – you know I've always favoured you.'

'Well thank you,' she mumbles.

Kara shakes her head. 'My chosen girls. There's nothing you need to entrust me with except for your hope. Hope that when Lire tries to reopen this world, I'll resist. I couldn't stop the devastation she caused last time, but now, with you and your friends, with all *your* power, I believe we can win.'

'I trust you,' Maya says, and the fairy gives her a small smile. Maya turns to me. 'Even if Kara can be cruel, she doesn't lie.'

I cross my arms, thinking it over. She wants hope – delusion – to be our strength. If we think we can win, maybe we will. Could that be enough?

'*I'm* the key to Lire winning,' I tell her, 'or the key to her failure. Whether you're with us or not, I'll do everything I can to protect the people in this world and the people outside of it.' I try to soften. 'I saw your heart, Kara, when I read your journal. I believe you're a good person, and I'll be grateful for your help. But I won't be counting on it. Whether or not this is ultimately between the two of you, and whether or not you're sorry humans have been collateral damage, we're here now. It's our business, our world, and we're going to save ourselves.'

Kara sighs, but her gaze is surprisingly prideful. 'It's a good thing Candace found you. You make the perfect Imperial.'

CHAPTER TWENTY-THREE

I get the news in the midst of scheming, in the midst of hope. It comes when I least expect it.

My knees hit the floor, the weight of it crushing me, pressing me down, drowning me in a haze of denial that threatens to break me.

'I know, sugar, I know,' says Candace. 'But this was the most likely possibility. We made that choice when we left.'

I shake my head. *The Ice Empire has fallen.*

Other empires, kingdoms, cities, *they* fell. Other worlds could end. But the Ice Empire is – was – unstoppable.

My home. My creation. It was supposed to be immortal. Yet all it took to take it down was one fairy and two royals who were too afraid to stand up to her.

A thousand years of strength, gone, because the Imperials *surrendered.*

'So should I not care?' I say to Candace, who sits on my vanity chair, a painful guilt across her face. 'If you want me to be the icy general who sees armies instead of people, castles instead of homes – I can't. That's the empire you raised me to fight for, and now it's all under Lire's control.'

'She hasn't destroyed anything or anyone. Not yet. It was a peaceful negotiation. There's still time to win this war and take our empire back.'

'She's destroyed our pride, Candace.' I stand, make my way to the window, wiping away tears.

Candace breathes deeply. 'Pride is not the most important thing.'

I spin to look her in the eyes. 'Isn't it? Then why did you raise me that way?'

My hands tremor with anger. It's finally happened. I lost everything. And it's *her* fault. Right now, it can only be her fault.

'I am your general, or I am your daughter. You don't get to pick and choose which, or when. What gave you the right to raise me to lead your armies just to patronise me when it suits you?'

'*Isla,*' she says. She takes a long moment as I heave with nothing more to say. 'You are not *my* general. You are a leader of your own accord, and I do not own you. But you are my daughter, blood or otherwise, whether you like it or not.'

Huffing, I turn back around. What does she know?

'I've made a lot of mistakes,' she says, 'and I've already apologised. My biggest regret is not allowing you to have a real life. My biggest regret is for too long seeing you as a prodigy instead of a young woman. You know how difficult it is to set apart goals and politics from your personal life. It isn't easy to be the false fairy and have a teenage daughter.'

'Oh, poor you,' I snap. Before today, I had no idea how furious I was, but the pain of the Ice Empire's surrender brings it all to the surface. Resentment boils freshly under my skin, bubbling and seething. 'You kidnapped a child for your own benefit and now that child has feelings? Must be awful.'

'Has feelings?' She stands, sweeping her strawberry-blonde hair over her shoulders like she does when she means business, and now I know I'm in trouble. 'Don't act as if I'm simply ignoring your emotions. I didn't even know you were in love, and suddenly you were engaged! How do you think that makes a mother feel? You hated Zeus for years, and now you're together. What am I to make of that? I can't ask you anything, and you don't tell me anything!'

'We aren't *engaged*,' I hiss back. 'We said that to show our unity to the empire so they wouldn't fall prey to Lire – and it didn't work anyway.'

She leans back. 'You pretended to love him for the Ice Empire?'

My voice softens. 'I don't hate him. I care for him a lot, and he's one of my closest friends. But no, we were never truly together.'

At least, I don't think so. She doesn't need to know about the rest of the drama between us.

Fairies, I'm turning into a Bearran, with all these trivial problems.

'You had me fooled,' she whispers, and then she does something that shocks me so deeply I freeze on the spot. She *cries*. She moves to sit on the end of my bed and her head drops into her hands, her shoulders convulsing as she lets out deep sobs.

'Mother?' I whisper.

'You're right. You're right. I'm so sorry, sugar,' she says, her voice breaking on each vowel. 'I have been so terrible to you. I have no excuse. Of course you can't trust me. Of course I've made you hate me.'

Tears fill my eyes for the second time in the last few minutes. 'Please, I couldn't hate you. But I've spent my entire life so confused, driven by one goal because if I didn't have that, I'd be lost entirely. I don't want to make you cry. I just want you to understand.'

'I do, I *do*.' She rubs her eyes. 'For years I've feared I raised you terribly. I feared I'd taught you to be so cold that you were trapped in your own mind, unable to get help. I saw you suffering, but I was so afraid of admitting my own faults to talk to you honestly. I took you and I ruined you, Isla. You are such a good girl. You deserved so much better than me, and you still do. You deserved your real life, out there. Your real mother.'

'Candace . . .' I shake my head, my gut pulling me back to the floor. I cross my legs and run my fingers over the grit of the tiles. 'I'm grateful to you for raising me. I always have been. No, you didn't do it perfectly. You could be so selfish, and you didn't always have the best intentions. You've lied, and made me feel like I can't trust you, and it's really, really hurt me.'

I kneel in front of her. 'But you didn't take me, and you didn't ruin me. You saved me and you made me strong. Please – please stop making yourself upset about it. For me, your apology is enough. Knowing you see my pain is enough.'

She slides onto the floor and pulls my head to her chest, and I release a deep sigh.

How long have I needed this? To be honest, to scream, to cry, to be held by the only parent I have?

'I'm going to do better,' she whispers into my hair. 'I'm going to be the family you deserve. You don't have to forgive me right away. You don't have to trust me right away. But I'm going to be here for you no matter how you feel. Even if you hate me, I'll be your mum.'

I nod, and we sit there for a long while as she strokes my head, until eventually I fall asleep in her arms. When I finally open my eyes, we've moved onto the bed, but she's still right next to me, a hand on my back. I sit up and rub my eyes.

'Shh,' Candace says. 'You rest as long as you need to.'

'No, Mum, it's okay,' I reply, but I could sleep for a week, a hundred years even. I don't know what the Bearrans were complaining about. It's like a heavy weight has been lifted from my shoulders, replaced with a pressing need to rest the muscles.

Candace moves her hand back into her lap, her face still blotchy, and smiles warmly. 'Zeus and Elm came by. I told them about the empire, but I didn't let them wake you.'

'Are they okay?'

'They're both as devastated as you are. But we all have hope.'

I drop my head into my hands. 'What are we going to do? What about my soldiers? What about our home? What about—'

She places her palms either side of my head and looks me in the eyes. 'Let me handle things.'

I let myself sink into her comfort. Today, at least, I might get to be a child.

◦♡◦ ▲ 🎩 ▲ ◦♡◦

There's a clarity in my mind I haven't felt in years. My emotional release with Candace has exhausted me, but it's freed me. With a renewed hope in myself, my mother, and our power, I *know* we can win this war.

We've never failed at anything. I'm sharper than ever. More confident.

The morning after our talk, we're ever closer to calling Lire in. Getting her here to destroy her.

We've lost the empire. But not the war.

I wander down to the basement room they've given Elm to work in, and I pull open the door to reveal a puff of steam filled with— *Is that glitter?* I fan the air in front of my face to find they aren't alone.

A tall young man dressed in sky-blue silk is showing Elm a ream of fabric, in which Elm is surprisingly interested. 'Consider *this*.' He's a city person, if his demeanour tells me anything. He points to a toy sailboat about the size of a hat. 'You could use this old cotton for the sails, but imagine if you used a more aerodynamic material. It would go faster, it would look far better, and . . .'

He trails off as Elm taps it with a glowing orange finger, and with a sparkle of magic, the sailboat floats through the air, the sail rippling as if it were in real wind. Elm smiles. 'I think my magic has it covered, though a different colour *would* make it stand out.'

'Hm,' intones the city boy. 'Rely on magic if you like, but the form itself would be stronger if better materials were used.'

'Then I might have to give it a try.'

He tilts his head. 'You should.'

I'm about to retreat from the room and let them have their strangely charged moment when a large presence, which I know intimately to be Zeus, bumps me from behind. He bounds into the makeshift workshop with a, 'Hello!'

I grunt at Zeus, who apologises quickly and puts his arms over mine to steady me. It makes my heart go uncomfortably warm.

Elm and the city boy raise their brows, watching the two of us. 'Hello,' says Elm, suspiciously. The boy glances at Elm, questioning, and they explain, 'My friends. General Isla and Prince Zeus.'

I clear my throat. 'Good afternoon. Nice to meet you.' I give Elm a long look.

'Right,' they say. 'This is Gus. He came back with the queen's friends, uh, Teddy and Maya, or whoever . . .'

Gus waves, his satin outfit billowing and *almost* catching fire on a nearby exposed flame. He startles as Elm pulls his sleeve out of the way. Then Elm ushers him out the door with a rushed goodbye.

'Oh—' Gus stutters. 'See you soon! I'll bring those fabrics!'

The door slams behind him.

Elm flashes us a pained grin, flushed. 'Hello, cupcakes.'

'You seem to be having a good time in Bearra,' Zeus says, leaning against the wall and playing with— *Is that stick on fire?*

I tear it out of his hands, smothering the flame. 'Elm, I need to talk to you.'

'But *I* wanted to talk to you,' Zeus says with a pout.

Elm glances between us. 'Do I need to start making appointments?'

'I got here first.' I cross my arms.

'You didn't come together?'

Zeus and I share a look and blurt at once, 'No!'

We've been avoiding each other again, since . . . Since we kissed and admitted we love each other and then I rejected him anyway. Which is awfully awkward. *Fairies.*

'Candace told me you both heard about the empire falling,' I say, and a heaviness falls over the workshop.

I *had* come here to seek comfort from my best friend after my ordeal with Candace, but I suppose it's fine if Zeus hears about it too. He's seen me broken up about it all enough – unless, is it crossing a line, now? Wasn't it always? I *don't know.*

Still, I mumble, 'I was really upset, of course, and Candace and I ended up fighting, and then all of these feelings came out, and—'

'Oh no.' Zeus cringes.

'No, it was actually . . . good. We needed it. I think she understands me more now. I feel better.'

Elm nods, *I-told-you-so*-esque. 'Well done. But remember you don't have to be okay overnight. We're dealing with a lot.'

'What about *my* parents,' says Zeus, and Elm gives him a sympathetic look. 'Handing over the city to Lire. Disgusting. You know, it's really hard for me—'

'I'm first,' I snap, and Elm glances back to me, Zeus huffing offendedly. 'I called her "Mum" for maybe the first time ever, and I cried, and I fell asleep in her arms. I felt like a child – but a *real* child this time. Like I knew exactly where I belonged, and I was safe.'

'I'm really proud of you,' says Elm, shuffling over and taking my hand. 'Really, I knew the two of you could work things out. Candace struggles to show it, but she really loves you. She *is* your mother.'

Zeus sulks. 'My mother handed over our empire to our enemy. And now I bet Lire is sleeping in *my* nice bed in *my* nice room in *my* nice castle, waving down at *my* people and wearing *my* nice furs—'

'We'll stop her,' says Elm, taking Zeus's hand too, and he visibly relaxes. 'So, the two of you, have you gotten to the bottom of . . .'

'I just think,' I say, 'that if we weren't in the middle of a war, Candace and I could really fix things between us. I know everything she's hidden from me now, and we're closer than we've ever been, because there's nothing to keep us at arm's length. You know?'

'Right, I suppose you've been distracted,' says Elm. 'But can we clarify, after the other day, when you two—'

Zeus moans. 'In my bed! Lire! Or even worse, one of her lowly soldiers. Imagine!'

'Yes, and we'll win the war, and you'll both be absolutely fine, and none of these problems will be problems anymore,' says Elm. 'But I do think you need to talk about—'

'It's like a weight lifted off my shoulders.' I smile.

'It's like my very soul has been violated,' Zeus cries.

'I don't have to always keep a mask on around my mother anymore.'

'I don't even have a home to go back to! None of us do! Even if our city stays intact through the war and Lire and her people leave, it'll always have their germs all over it!'

'Oh, and you should've seen Candace's face when I told her the engagement was a sh—'

The door bursts open. Gus, Maya, and Sierra fall through.

'*Fairies!*' Maya yelps, righting herself by leaning on Sierra, who picks up Gus by the collar and pulls him upright. The door is nearly off its hinges. 'This castle is in worse disrepair than I thought.'

Elm's eye twitches. '*Yes?* How can I help you?'

Sierra bites her lip, Gus flushes, and Maya stares back wide-eyed. 'Oh,' Maya says slowly, searching for an answer. 'See, I wanted to talk to Gus, and Teddy said Gus had come down here, so I was on my way, and Sierra was roaming around, so I bumped into her and she joined me. Then we found Gus, and that's when we heard you all bickering behind the door, so we were pressed against the wood trying to listen in – *fairies*, you're insufferable, though I mean no offense, of course – and then right when I was about to burst in anyway, because you were all being so irritating, the door fell right from under us. *Crash.*'

'And we are so sorry to hear about the Ice Empire,' Sierra adds.

Whiplashed, I raise a brow. 'You are?'

She puffs her cheeks. 'No, I don't really care.'

'Well—'

I'm cut off by a burst of orange, like someone's opened black curtains to full sun. A deafening silence makes my ears ring, and everyone squints through the light to see what happened and why no one can make a sound.

Elm holds up a finger, Adellan magic swirling around it. The usually patient and faraway toymaker is an earthquake on fire. *Fairies.*

But still – I *was* here first!

'Finally, peace,' they whisper. 'You are all the most self-centred, frustrating— No. I won't start insulting people. I just need you all to shut up.'

They take a few deep breaths, and I follow the movement of their chest, matching mine to theirs. It's a trick I learned many years ago; that if I match my breaths to Elm's, I'll always calm down to their much more stable level.

Maya looks to me for help, and I shrug. *We're safe.* Elm's just at their wit's end. Aren't we all?

'Let's talk about *me.*' Elm waves, and their flying sailboat soars over to us. They hold it gently, stroking the fabric, which Gus is observing with astute attention. Elm shushes him, despite the silence. 'Isla,' they say, 'you've asked me for years if I'd help you make weapons using my ideas. You told me that if I did, the empire could be so much stronger.'

I nod. I never wanted it for Elm – not something they hated the idea of so much. But how could I not have at least asked?

Zeus grips my hand from behind, and I let out a soundless gasp before embracing his coolness and stepping back into his embrace. He's worried about Elm. We both are, because if they're saying what I think they're saying, going against their values like this, they must be truly afraid.

'Well, the empire has fallen,' says Elm, their expression dark. 'The war is dire enough that I can't do nothing. I won't make any weapon that's too dangerous. I don't want anyone to die. But if my skills will help save us, the Imperial toymaker is at your service. That's all I wanted to say, if you can all take care of your own problems from here and leave me to do my job?'

I nod again, a lump in my throat. I should be thrilled, knowing the advantage this gives us. Their skills could turn the war around. But my Elm would never do this, and my heart breaks for this lovely person who has only ever wanted to bring people joy.

As the sound returns, and I whisper a thank you, Zeus pulls Elm into an all-encompassing hug.

While they're distracted I turn and flee the room, eyes burning. Because I know, now, that this is the end. That no matter what happens between now and our final battle with Lire, no one will be unscathed, and nothing will be the same. Elm's choice is an omen of chaos.

Whether our world is reopened or not, there will be a wave of destruction.

Whether this world becomes mine, or falls into the hands of another, I'll pay a heavy price.

And whether we live or die, there will be sacrifice.

CHAPTER
TWENTY-FOUR

At the sparkling triarue gates of Bearra, I'm a rock. Steady and unbreakable. My head is in sharp focus, my limbs stretched and poised. We leaders and our friends, the pirates and our people, are lined up in clear form. Under my orders. The way I trained them.

My world. My war.

This is what I'm made for, and I'm not afraid.

Before me, flanking the entrance to the vine-smothered kingdom, stand hundreds of my soldiers – those who've stayed by my side, and many who travelled from the empire to stand with me after the royals surrendered.

Only hours ago, Maya sent the call, delivered with Teddy's magic: *Come and get us. Today.*

Lire didn't hesitate. Beyond my military, with a sprawling army of their own, three fairies float ten metres off the ground, their wings beating and their bodies ringed with sparkling, terrifying magic. Dragon-like Rhiannon, rainbow-winged Amora, and in the centre, the one we're all vying to kill: Lire.

Her wings are almost clear in the bright blue sky, their lilac tint and pointed tips gently swaying like a ship's sails in light wind, her blonde hair billowing over her shoulders. Her cold eyes stare us down with unwavering surety.

My spine tingles. I clench my fists. Take in the scene, analyse all I can. My army can hold down the kingdom, especially with their iron weapons. Lire's soldiers may be powerful, but they're untrained. Theirs is an army formed in chaos and thirst. They're nothing compared to the power of the Ice Empire.

As for the Bearrans lining up behind us to protect their home, their numbers have dwindled from previous fights, and they've spent over a year hungry. As much as the pirates and my soldiers have tried to train them, even armed them with magic and iron, these people are walking into a fight they may not survive.

Not unless the most powerful among us can save the rest – and I believe we can. Bearra has bested Lire twice; their bravery alone is far stronger than the greed of their enemies.

We have great powers: Candace, Teddy, Arden, Relia.

The pirates killed Muse.

Elm's weapons are poised for destruction.

And, of course, there's *me*. Bearra hasn't seen me fight yet, and I'm ready to show them why I lead armies.

Lire calls out over the plain, her voice blaring with enchantment. 'How adorable that you've prepared for a fight. However, dear Bearrans, I'm not here for you. I'm here to use *my* triarue and *my* castle to bring this all to an end. This is my world. You can surrender now, or I'll wipe you out.' She checks her nails. 'Regardless, this world will be unrecognisable by the time I'm done, so it would be easier to simply let me kill you all now.'

I try not to let it show, but some of my resolve crumbles as I try to run through the logistics of her claim. We knew she'd be attempting to reconnect the two worlds at *some* point, but right now?

She wants to put us all down and complete a massive enchantment in one blow.

'Well we're going to—' Maya yells back, but quickly realises Lire won't be able to hear from across the battlefield. Teddy dutifully produces a glowing orb of the same magic as his mother's, and Maya screams so loud, with such amplification, my ears nearly bleed. 'You'll die when I kill you, Lire!'

The fairy mock-shivers, and counts on her fingertips. 'One, two. Aunt, mother . . . I look forward to wiping out the entire Nova family, little Maya. But my darling Teddy is next.'

Maya staunches forward but Sierra holds her back. Meanwhile, Teddy stares at his mother, unshaken but pale.

Dawn and I share a glance and step forward together. With her at my side, I feel *powerful.* The effect of her blessings is strong, extending to those around her in waves of confidence.

I'm the greatest leader of the Ice Empire and she's the world's last queen. Together we're the face of humanity in what might be our generation's most pivotal moment.

'This is *your* final chance, Lire,' says Dawn. The usually ballgown-wearing princess is dressed in sturdy pants and a tight shirt, ready for a fight. The only signal she's the queen is the layer of iron necklaces on her chest – inlaid with diamonds. None of her kingdom's famous triarue.

'I am willing to negotiate peace,' Dawn continues. 'We can find a way to continue this world as it has happily run for centuries.'

'Or,' I add, staring Lire down, 'you can fight us. But no matter who wins, you *will* be hurt. You won't make it through this unscathed, and your followers will take the brunt of the losses. Think wisely about whether you're prepared for what you're planning.'

'Because as far as we're concerned,' Maya kindly finishes, with a pointed look at Amora, 'you're all already *dead.*'

Even from here I can see the fresh shame in the fairy of love's pretty face. Yet the fairies are so ethereal, so divinely beautiful, it's near impossible to imagine them fighting us.

Their territories saw them as beloved, benevolent beings. And how easy it would be to fall into that trap, to follow these greater powers, to feel safe even if we weren't free.

Unfortunately, I've always had a problem with giving up control.

'How *terrifying.*' Lire claps, her airy lilac wings shimmering. 'But I'm not interested in backing down. It's time to get what I came for.'

Her magic builds into a deep magenta, swallowing the air around her. Soldiers on both sides stumble with uncertainty. Rhiannon and

Amora's magic joins Lire's, crimson and blush pooling from their hands, their feet, their wings – a kaleidoscope of swirling fuchsia.

Enchanting and dooming.

My heart beats ferociously and I nearly call for our people to duck for cover – but the fairies aren't aiming this flowing power at us. They're aiming for the walls. Heads turn as the magic seeps up and over the vines, choking every vein of emerald.

'They're destroying our defences!' shouts Dawn, and her people's eyes flick to her. But she looks to me. *Do we begin, or do we wait for them to attack first?*

I'm itching to signal my army. The vines are rotting, turning brown – beneath them the brick walls crackle with loud creaks and the sound of rockfalls. An avalanche. It smells – it *stinks* like rotting vegetables, left for weeks, years.

No. I'm not waiting for the fight to come to us.

We'll wipe out their soldiers first. Then we'll take care of the fairies.

I nod to Dawn. 'Let's move.'

She echoes me, shouting to her people and mine. 'Go! Bearra remains ours! This world remains ours! *Protect it!*

The echo of crumbling walls elicits screams from around the barrier. 'Now!' I urge our people into battle before they're crushed. They charge towards Lire's army, tripping over their own feet as the crashing vines and bricks shake the ground.

Screams. Screams.

Then: *slash.*

Metal meets metal and magic meets magic.

I cover my eyes from the sunlight and observe for a few moments as people whirlwind around me. Analyse their strategies. Their numbers. More than us. *Not enough.* Not while the fairies are too busy with the walls to help them.

Army first, fairies second.

'Hello,' Sierra sing-songs, bumping my shoulder. Her silky black hair flows down her back, her fists clenched. The chaos in her eyes is tempered by a deep sense of control in her body. She says with utter calm, 'Why are we missing out on all the fun? Let's *go.*'

'You read my mind.' I grin, and together we *run*. I unsheathe my sword and the screams around me go silent, the battle narrowing as I meet my first foes. I cut past my army, past the Bearrans, and right into the storms of Lire's soldiers.

Magic users try to attack me with red power. But they're pathetic, and *I'm* immune. I skip through the glow, emerging on the other side like a dragon, breathing the scarlet magic like it's flame. I slice three throats in one swish. Wide eyes turn blank before me.

'*Very* good,' Sierra says, holding a soldier by the throat while she watches me. The soldier kicks their feet. 'I'm impressed, General.'

A wave of pink magic washes over me, and I take a stab in the dark, driving into it with my sword. There's the telltale squelch of metal landing in a stomach and dust kicks up and glitters in the air, replacing the pink magic. The soldier appears, convulsing, and drops to the dry ground.

I glance back at Sierra. 'It's what I do,' I say with a satisfying ease over my mind, body and soul.

My army battles around me in perfect form, while Bearra's people fumble with their iron and magic. They still take down more of Lire's warriors than I'd expect.

The fairies, for now, are still distracted – but with a final *crash*, the walls turn to dust.

Our people are all out in the open, far from the walls enough to not get hurt. Those who can't fight were evacuated to Darraport yesterday. Though we'll try to save the kingdom, our main goal isn't to protect the architecture – it's to stop Lire. So, disregarding the damage to the walls, I urge our people on.

'It's what *we* do.' Sierra flicks her wrist with a harsh, perfectly-angled snap, and her dangling soldier stops kicking. She shakes herself like a snake shedding its skin as the body falls. 'I needed that. Killing is so warming to the soul.'

She spins, kicking a few people in the head before turning back to me. 'Remind me to take you out on the *Neptune* sometime. I'll give you a ride to the Ice Empire, and we can destroy *so many people* along the way.'

'Oh!' I reply, gutting an enemy before I get a chance to even see their face. They drop in a grunting heap. 'Sure, one day!'

We spot a Bearran soldier struggling under three of Lire's, and hop over corpses to help her. Sierra ducks and swishes her long legs under the enemies, knocking them down. I take care of them with quick stabs to the heart.

The Bearran soldier, panting, gratefully nods to us and races back into the heat of the fighting.

I don't enjoy killing, not like Sierra, but there *is* something methodical and satisfying about the crunch of ribs, about knowing you're making progress removing one foe at a time from the battlefield.

Sierra stretches her arms. 'I'm very serious. I know so many good bars in—'

Her excited expression drops along with her arms. She's looking out into the distance, startled, at six white figures speeding towards us like wraiths. Although they're running, their footsteps are so light, their white hair flowing behind them, they could be floating. Flying.

I'm so mesmerised that I nearly miss the soldier about to swing a sword and chop Sierra's head off from behind. Even she misses them. I use my heavy boot to kick them to the ground and stamp on their chest until they pass out.

'You know who they are?' I ask, taking Sierra by the arm to shake her from her daze.

Her face hardens. 'My sisters.'

'Um.' I gulp. 'The Reeds? The Reed sisters are here?'

'What did I just say?' she snaps, and I jolt back.

'Sierra, why? Why would they be here?'

'You know what this means.' She looks me dead in the eyes. 'Grace has chosen Lire's side, and they've come to fight alongside the fairies.'

Shuffle. I stamp on a foot and pull my sword over my head and into a shoulder, a spurt of blood covering the ground as a soldier falls.

'You can fight them,' I say. 'Can't you?'

She cocks her head, a little of that chaotic gaze returning. 'Of course. I just didn't think it would be today.'

'And . . . What if they're here to help us?' I pant as I strangle another enemy between my arm and my ribs. 'Can you be sure Grace has sided with Lire?'

Sierra pouts, stamping her foot in time with a punch to a magic user's face. 'I suppose they *might* be here to help us.' The soldier reels and swings back, yellow in their palm, so Sierra yanks them towards her and trips them over her feet. 'But can't you let me dream?'

'Huh?' The enemy I'm holding clunks to the ground in their flimsy armour.

'I really want to kill them. And if they're on our side, how can I do that?'

The six women are fast approaching; we have only a few minutes until they change the tide.

A few minutes we can't waste. I jump into a few smaller spats and break apart enemies from my soldiers, surprising them when they can't use their magic against me. *Cut. Slash. Stab.*

I unleash all my training against them. All the parts of myself I love and all the parts of myself I hate. The perfect soldier. The perfect general. An outsider immune to magic.

All this work, even though once the fairies change their focus from the destruction of the kingdom to the destruction of *us*, exhausting myself on their human army might prove useless.

Zeus, Ebony and Levi reach us, bloody and heaving. 'The Reeds,' Levi hyperventilates. 'They're here!'

'I noticed,' Sierra says, licking her lips.

'Right. And we didn't ask Dawn about the alliance they came to us about, did we . . .'

I twitch. 'Excuse me?'

'Well . . .'

'An alliance with Grace? You just *didn't bring it up?*'

'I didn't feel like it! They can't be trusted.' Sierra waves away the judgement steaming off me and asks her friends, 'Where's Arden?'

Ebony points east, where the pirate captain is next to Teddy and Relia, demolishing dozens of soldiers at a time with magic. Their tornado of bright colour makes me wish I could stop and watch.

Sierra looks him up and down, even from where we are a few hundred metres away. 'The others?'

I twitch. Again. The pirates might have lost us a fairy for an ally, and all they can focus on is their friends. '*Seriously,*' I moan, only to be ignored.

Levi smiles. 'Lark is probably *kissing* his *fiancé.*'

'Wren is probably killing,' Ebony adds, wiping blood from her hairline and inspecting it. 'Wouldn't worry about it.'

Zeus shoulders up to me. He doesn't take my hand, but his heavy breaths beside me are reinvigorating. I turn and whisper, 'You okay?'

'Never better,' he replies. 'You know how great at fighting I am.'

I don't. But he does look very good in the silver armour over his chest, with a white shield in one hand and a beautiful decorative sword in the other. He's more here for show, for morale, than actual battling.

And I'm . . . grateful. Because it's working. Our people look to him with admiration, like how the Bearrans look to Dawn. As if they're deities of our own.

Then a sudden dread comes over me *because* Zeus is here. In the middle of a battle. Protectiveness surges through me. I can't let him get hurt. He still has a bad arm from when he broke it falling from the sky. He has barely any training. He . . .

He taps me on the forehead. 'Too much going on in there, darling. Your people need you out here.'

'Right.' I exhale. *He can take care of himself.* I want to say more. *Sorry*, to start with.

Everything instantly becomes clear. Knowing now I could lose him at any second, I can't understand why I ever turned him down. For my own pride? What was I thinking?

And I almost allow all those unsaid words to spill into the chaos when—

'Cygnet,' sneers one of the Reed sisters, hurtling to a stop before us. She has pearlescent skin and fully-black, creepy eyes. They all do. *Swans.*

'My dear blood relatives,' Sierra replies. 'You made it. After the let down last time we met, I've been looking forward to this.'

'Still not here to kill you,' one of them says, flexing her fingers.

Sierra rolls her head back. 'Still?'

'Wait,' Zeus says. 'Does that mean . . .'

'You're on our side?' I finish.

'Unfortunately,' says the oldest-looking one. 'This battle is about the world, and Grace's Waters are in the world, are they not? We've come to fight for our home and people.'

Something in me brightens. 'Grace – you're saying she didn't side with Lire? She's with us?' Which means Lire might not be able to make her enchantment. Which means we may have a better chance at making it through today without the world ending.

She stares at me blankly. 'Do you see the fairy of justice here, Imperial?'

The brightness dims.

'You defected,' Sierra says. I'd have thought she'd be teasing them delightedly, but even she's balking at the weight of it.

'Grace told us Lire's plan,' a younger Reed says. 'She felt powerless to stop it. She promised us a place with her in the new world and we refused. Our duty isn't only to the fairy. And it certainly isn't to Lire.'

Slash.

The eerie Reeds might have momentarily scared back our foes, giving us a quiet moment, but Lire's soldiers are congregating at the edge of the battle. They're circling, collecting into wolf-like packs.

I need to jump into the fight before it gets me first.

'Reeds,' I say, turning to the six swans. 'If you want to help, the fairies aren't going to fly quietly much longer. We need you on the ground so we can face Lire.'

'Understood,' says the eldest.

They start to move, but Sierra calls out, 'Wait!'

The six stop, glaring at her fiercely.

'I had this big reveal planned, but now's as good a time as—'

Sierra's mouth falls open, gasps pushing through from the silver sticking out the front of her chest. I stumble back.

They came so fast.

The soldier has already disappeared into the crowd. Too scared. A coward.

Stabbed her and ran.

Blood pools down Sierra's front, down to her feet.

CHAPTER TWENTY-FIVE

Ebony flies to her side, trying to hold the flowing scarlet in, but Sierra ushers her away. Even her sisters appear upset at first – until I realise their grimaces are anger that someone took their kill. One of the Reeds races off, chasing down the killer.

The killer.

We've lost Sierra Reed.

'No,' Sierra rasps, watching her sister ghost into the battle. 'I wanted you *all* to see this.' She grins with all her blood-coated teeth showing.

'What?' someone says. I can't tell who.

And then . . .

Sierra Reed is *gone.*

There's a flash of navy blue, and a black swan soars into the air.

I shake my head, gripping Zeus. 'Uh . . .'

A death omen with a wide wingspan swoops and circles above. She squawks, arcing her neck to make sure we're all watching.

Levi *laughs*. Wags a finger appreciatively. 'She really had me for a second! That stab couldn't have come at a better time.'

'She— She got the curse back?' Zeus asks. Someone sneaks up behind the prince and I block their blast of red magic, quickly putting them out of their misery with a knock to the head.

'Ah!' Zeus gapes at me and I shrug.

'Apparently,' Levi says. 'She must've gotten Arden to do it. Guess she wanted to surprise us.'

Ebony's eyes narrow, ready to kill someone. She obviously didn't appreciate the prank. On cue, she slashes through a charging enemy's dominant arm and they tumble, screaming.

The Reed sisters are already gone, their youngest forgotten as they slice through Lire's soldiers. Sierra is pecking out eyes and tearing at throats. A perfect fighter in either form.

My attention is caught by a scream that rings different from the rest. Near the gates, Maya Nova is pointing at the black swan and jumping with excitement. 'We're *back*!'

But I'm not so thrilled about all these swans. They're two new cards drawn that I didn't expect, and it's distracting me. I have to remember what's most important.

'The fairies,' I utter. Surprises are the sort of thing I have to deal with, have to be prepared for at any moment. I've trained myself to focus better than this. 'We have to face the fairies before . . .'

Zeus looks up the same time I do. They're no longer in the air.

'Follow me,' I tell him, and I race towards the gates.

In the distance, Teddy, Arden, and Relia are locked in a cloud of their magic as they try to keep the fairies back. The three deities are on the ground, their soldiers surrounding them, trying to keep Bearrans and Imperials at bay.

I resist the urge to break into the fights happening around me as I charge towards them. *The real battle is with Lire.* I need to lead, not let myself be distracted with petty fights along the way. Even if it means I can't save everyone.

Shaking off the guilt, I reach the once grand gates, now replaced by shattered triarue littered across the ground. I sidestep it like I would sharp glass.

The kingdom already looks so different. No battles have made it within yet, but to see it from this angle without the intimidating walls and vines is . . .

It makes me feel like Bearra is already lost, like Amora's Territory. Like the Ice Empire.

A *boom* cracks the sound barrier and I nearly lose my footing. Grace and Candace shoot into view like a meteor, grappling each other as they crash through the sky. Rainbows pollute the air; their magic pours out of them, leaving an echo in their wake.

I shiver. I *wondered* when my mother would show up.

Zeus pauses, like he wants to do something, but I pull him forward. We all have our role here. I can't halt – not even for Candace. Every person here can handle themselves.

I reach the cloud of blue, purple, red, and pink, and analyse the scene. The fairies laugh with pleasure, watching our most powerful like they're nothing but mice. Lire, Amora, and Rhiannon are predators. Not lions, but snakes, beautiful and agile.

'Get her!' screams Maya, side-by-side with a Reed sister as she grapples with a soldier of Lire's. She lifts an iron knife and covers her head while the Reed snaps their enemy's neck. '*Teddy, get her!*'

But he's overcome by his mother's magic. There's no physical fighting between them, no brute violence. It's three on three for enchantment. Even if Candace managed to get out of her battle with Grace and help, we still wouldn't have enough power to face three fairies.

The colours pool like water flooding our feet, like smoke choking the air. It's clear our side is losing. They're trying to create a shield, unable to attack and relying only on defence. But the fairies are pushing back and back and back.

Arden is unfocused, squeezing his eyes as his power ebbs. He tries another tactic and goads, 'We killed Muse with one iron sword! You won't outlast the armies we have now!'

He doesn't believe that. I can see it in his eyes. The way they search above every few moments to keep sight of the black swan.

Teddy and Relia face the fairies, glowing twins of red hair and purple magic. They're mesmerising, but they're losing.

We're losing.

This battle might be over too easily. Before Lire has even attempted to reopen our world. *What do I do? How can I stop this?*

I scratch at the nicks on my skin, an itch all over my body, the only thing I can control.

Lire laughs at Arden. 'I'm not concerned. You'll pay for taking Muse from me.' She sends magic their way in a tidal wave, and they push back once more.

Arden stumbles, his body pulsing with blue.

'Do your worst!' shouts Relia. 'You haven't defeated us yet!'

'Do you think brute power is all I have?' Lire cocks her head. She isn't expending much energy at all. She's toying with them. 'You know I came with smarter plans than that.'

Teddy and Relia are already faltering, but now Arden is barely standing. One more wave, and he'll—

Sierra falls out of the sky, turning human and yanking him out of the fray. He scrambles after her; he knows he's overpowered.

She might have just saved his life. But the two don't stop – they jump back into battle, fighting side-by-side in a perfect dance only they know.

The others still try to hold Lire, Rhiannon, and Amora back, but the lilac coming from Lire swallows any power they have. Without Arden, they've lost any chance. Their magic . . . It's returning home to its mother.

That engulfing lilac turns their lighter magic darker, darker, until that darkness is seeping *back* into them.

Teddy and Relia take hands, trying to push her more fiercely, but it's useless. Lire's magic is Lire's magic, not theirs but a gift. It's obeying her as its master.

Maya runs to help, but she touches Teddy and the magic jolts her. She shudders and falls back. Sierra runs into the clouds of magic and pulls her out even as Maya fights to run back to Teddy, cradling her impacted hand.

'*Enough*,' Sierra growls at her, and Maya falters into stillness.

Teddy and Relia's arms drop to their sides, their faces going blank as the dark purple magic runs up through their pale bodies, their veins glowing until it reaches their eyes. Magenta shimmers from where their irises should be, pools in their mouths.

Maya and Dawn scream for their lovers but it's no use. They can't do anything.

Lire is killing them.

The lilac twins step forward, one foot in front of the other, mechanical as they return to their maker.

Lire *isn't* killing them. She's *possessed* them. Which means they're no longer in control of their magic or themselves.

No longer on our side.

I go to run in and block the magic – attempt to save the most powerful of us so we still have a chance – but a strong hand holds me in place.

'Don't even think about it,' says Zeus.

'But I could—'

His grip on me tightens. 'If you've ever thought about obeying your prince,' he says, 'now's the time to try.'

'No. Zeus, you can't tell me what to do.' I struggle against his strength. 'You don't have that right.'

'Don't I?' He gives me a dark look. 'I'm a royal, and you work for my army, Isla.'

I go still. 'Well soon, I'll be a royal too. And if you try to tell me what to do *then*—'

'You. What?' He lets go of me. Oh, no. What have I done? Why on earth would I say that? 'Isla?'

I cover my mouth with my hands and mumble, '*Fairies.* I mean, well, I love you. If you'll still have me as your princess. I was going to wait for a better time—'

He pulls me to him and . . . kisses . . . me.

My body weakens, possessed as much as Teddy and Relia, maybe worse. This is extremely inappropriate. So why don't I care?

I lean into his touch, kissing him back, my lips already sore from hits to the face. *I don't care. I don't care.*

He breaks first, pushing back a loose strand of hair from my braid. 'I knew it.'

Wait. Have I lost my mind? I'm in *battle.*

But by the time I turn back to the magic, it's too late for me to run in. Zeus got what he wanted. Teddy and Relia have already walked into the fairies' glow, standing and facing us with lilac simmering around themselves.

Lire has stripped us of our greatest powers and added them to her own arsenal.

'Like my new trick?' she says. 'Not my favourite tactic. It isn't honourable to take the will of another. But this is what you've forced me to do.'

The battlefield's attention is drawn to new magic lighting the skies. Lire grins, and I could swear she's looking right at me as she does.

Adella and Kara have appeared on each end of the horizon, east and west. A bright sun and a dark moon. My legs shake. I hoped they wouldn't show. At least then, Lire wouldn't be able to use them for her enchantment.

Now the fairies are all here, and as it appears, they've all chosen Lire. The coven is reunited. Ready to make all the same mistakes.

Even after a thousand years, they can't live in a world without each other.

'Isla, it's time,' says Zeus. 'We need Elm's help.' He's trembling, mouth open as he watches Relia with deep fear. His best friend is gone. All her light, lovely energy turned to a blank slate.

I have to play my final card.

Breathing through the stifling heat, I reach into my back pocket and pull out the enchanted flare Elm gave me. *Just for emergencies.* But we knew – we knew it would come to this.

My fingers threaten to freeze. I make myself tap the sequence Elm taught me. I toss the flare as high as I can.

Bright Adellan orange forms a second sun. The fighting lulls. Even the fairies' heads turn. The flare elicits a deafening screech as it rises and rises, a signal to my best friend.

It's time to bring out their weapons.

Fire lights up behind the castle, arcing towards us. The ground trembles, and I grip Zeus to stable myself.

Roar.

Dragons with flaming Adellan magic fly from the ruins of the ballroom. Three of them, their bodies made of brown leather, blue silk, and shining metal. Soaring. Built to take our enemies out of the air.

Elm had days. *Days.* Yes, they had help, but I never expected their creation to be so . . .

I gape at the creatures. As incredible as any of Elm's others, but with so much more majesty and ferocity.

Lire cackles. 'You still think this is a fairy tale? You think you can defeat me with mythical creatures?'

Rhiannon watches them warily as they come close, circling as they find their targets. The dragons may not be real, but they know who their enemies are. The war fairy can sense the threat. So can Amora. She nearly stumbles when one of the dragons bares its teeth.

They aren't iron, not with that much enchantment, but the fairies might be shocked enough not to realise it yet. All the dragons need to do is weaken the fairies – then one of us can use an iron weapon to get them in the heart.

Teddy and Relia are still blank-faced. Amora shifts on her feet, trying to step towards Teddy then reeling back when Lire catches her. If she ever wanted to help us, it's too late now.

I use the distraction of the dragons to observe the battlefield. The fighting has slowed, but people are still ravaging each other all across outer Bearra. Even in the waterways, fights splash through the shallows as soldiers attempt to drown each other.

There are fewer screams now, and there are more of us standing than them. On the human side, we're winning. Like I knew we would. If the fairies weren't here, even if it were only one or two, we'd have won this war with ease.

But *all* the fairies are here, and these enchanted dragons are our final hope.

Crash.

Wings of leather meet those of red scales as Rhiannon soars and attacks one of the dragons head-on. They tumble over each other, soaring up and down as the people below them scurry away. Screeches. Roars. Leather and scales zip through the air like arrows as the dragon and fairy tear at each other.

It seems the entire world has stopped to watch, everything stilled.

The dragons don't have as much magic as a fairy, but they're violent machines in their own right. Rhiannon is already tiring – the dragons aren't.

Lire stands, nonchalant, with her hands folded neatly in front of her. Amora cowers, a shameful sight, with Teddy and Relia before her still as statues.

Where are Kara and Adella? They were on the horizon not long ago. And Candace, Grace . . .

Slam.

The second dragon screams into the fray. Rhiannon's giant wings beat, fending off their sharpened teeth. Her magic billows in smoke around her.

It's fire. Fire. Fire.

The dragons are sturdy enough to withstand it. Rhiannon is a fairy of battle, but how could she have ever imagined facing something like this?

Lire grinds her teeth. Is she going to help?

And where is the third dragon?

Glancing around, I steady myself as the vertigo of searching the skies threatens to topple me. There's a cut on my arm, I realise. I'm losing blood. Not enough to worry about yet. But I'm weakened.

Elm's dragons are all we have – they, at least, can make good on our promise to not let the fairies get through this unscathed even if they win.

Adrenaline, stay with me.

A horrific tear echoes across the plains; Rhiannon's wing, ripped in half by the dragon's teeth. I stumble. She's nearly falling, magic barely keeping her in the air. The dragons clasp her between their large paws as they scratch and slash at her, whipping her from side to side like dogs with a rope.

I almost want to help her – it's such an awful sight.

Then I find the third dragon: circling the castle, where blue, black, and orange magic stream through the windows of the old, crumbled ballroom.

'The real fight isn't out here,' I say.

Zeus's eyes zip to me, his gaze drawn from the horror above. 'What?'

I breathe, and shivers run across my exposed skin, my neck prickling. 'This is a distraction. We need to get the others.'

'Isla, what are you saying?' There's a cut on his lip, blood smeared across his cheek. Will it scar, I wonder? Will even he be changed by this war?

'The *enchantment*,' I explain, taking his hands. 'The other fairies are inside preparing to put the worlds back together. Lire is only playing with us here to keep us out of the way.'

Lire narrows her eyes at me. She knows I know.

'We have to get back to the castle.'

'And abandon our people out here?' Zeus asks.

I nod, albeit guiltily. 'It's them or the world.'

Tear.

Rhiannon's torn wing drops to the dirt ground with a savage crash. Screams blaze through the landscape as flashes of red rip through the sky.

I squint through the light to see above – a dragon with Rhiannon's torso between its teeth, the fairy flopping, exhausted, between them. Her right wing unbalances her, tilting her to the ground where the other lays crumpled.

Silence falls over Bearra. Rhiannon is as good as dead, as long as no one tries to save her before someone can—

The arrow that lodges into Rhiannon's chest can almost be heard whistling through the air.

The fairy goes utterly still. Her heart and back ooze scarlet blood and magic. The dragons hold her in the air, displaying the dead fairy to her sisters, to every soldier. Droplets of red fall, blood raining on the battlefield.

Hands on my thighs, I follow the trail of the arrow to a young woman atop the rubble of the walls. Bow in her hands. *Wren.*

She had her iron arrow ready. She timed her shot perfectly. She didn't miss. A true warrior, and *of course* she is, trained by Sierra and Ebony.

Someone sighs. I spin to find Lire clapping slowly. Something isn't right. We've killed another fairy, but there's a darkness clouding the scene, a looming dread that tells us we haven't gotten closer to winning.

I realise why when I search for the queen. Dawn is missing. Maya. They've both left the battle, taking their confidence with them.

Are they already in the castle? Did they realise this is a distraction too? Are they safe?

Lire's twins step forward, their magic storming around their feet. Amora has her eyes closed, her wings low. And Lire – she's never looked happier. Rhiannon is *dead.* Why isn't she upset? Furious?

The red fairy's magic, every last flicker, streams into the air. It takes the dragons with it. Their enchantment is overpowered as they burst into flame, thudding to the ground as soldiers sprint from the landing zone.

And the magic. It goes *straight to the castle.* To the enchantment. Like it *knows.*

Lire smiles. Directly at me, perfect teeth bared and glowing. She speaks under her breath, but everyone can hear her. 'Naïve child of the outer world. Did you really think I hadn't prepared for every possibility?' She cackles. 'Thank you for getting my most reckless sister out of the way. Rhiannon may have been powerful, but I did *not* want to babysit any longer. Much easier to have her magic for myself.'

She ascends, those ethereal wings beating like there's no blood at her feet, no battle raging at all. Rhiannon's magic surges towards her, and she consumes it as easily as water.

'General Isla,' says Lire. 'Prince Zeus. Any of the rest of Dawn's *circle.* You'll all come with me to the castle now. I want you to watch with your eyes wide open as you lose everything you've fought so pathetically for.'

CHAPTER TWENTY-SIX

It's worse than I imagined. That circular rainbow of light peaking white in the centre – just like Kara described in her journal – strikes like sunrays through the ruins of the ballroom.

Five fairies. Dawn and Maya still nowhere to be seen. The pirates circled up with Zeus and I behind our guards, Teddy and Relia, as we're forced to watch on through a glittering purple barrier. Candace crumpled in a far corner behind a barrier of her own.

Soon the enchantment will be ready to reconnect the worlds. And I don't like my chances of making it out alive once Lire's used me as her key.

Only I can give her everything she wants. Only I can take it all away. But *how*?

I keep my hand in Zeus's, standing in front of him. I squint against the blinding magic and the sunlight streaming through the ceiling – caved in from the last fight in here.

My skull pounds. On our walk up to the ballroom, we came quietly, followed Lire's orders. But she still very kindly knocked me on the back of the head with a surprisingly corporeal wing when she passed by.

I'm fine. I needed to get here either way – and though I didn't like it being on her terms, at least I'm now in the eye of the storm.

We need to be with Lire, with her enchantment. We need to wait and see if we can catch her in a moment of weakness. We were never going to win on the battlefield against all these fairies.

There must be a hundred thousand schemes going through everyone's minds right now. *Have we lost? What are we going to do?*

My mind, though, is silent. I'm dizzy and I can't think of a single option. The fairies have complete control. Even Kara, who promised me she'd try to help us, seems to have defected to Lire's side just as Amora did.

In the end, they showed they don't care about us.

They'll follow their leader because it's the only option the stubborn, ancient beings can think to take. They're all too scared of the power of the coven to go against it; they saw what happened to Kara the first time.

Surely *someone* has an idea, some last minute, last-ditch, ridiculously Bearran move. Isn't that their trademark? Unconventional. Messy. Reckless.

Not like me. And that's what we need, because, I suppose . . . I've failed.

Something in my heart snaps. I drop Zeus's hand, and my body moves on its own, slumping to a section of wall that's still half-standing. My feet step over upturned tiles. My back meets the brick. My eyelids drop as my palms clench over my ears.

General Isla, a fraud.

I go to my own little world, because I don't belong here, and I don't deserve the one I was born in either.

I couldn't save us.

Both worlds could be doomed.

Maybe Candace should've left me in the snow.

How did I truly think I could beat fairies? Lire has had centuries to plan, has always been two steps ahead. Her only weakness is her own ego – and even that can't be used against her in her now savage attempts to destroy us. She doesn't care about her image anymore. She doesn't care if she looks like a monster, a coward, a hysteric. She'll simply remake herself in the next world and start again with new devotees.

All our secret weapons have been drawn. My immunity to magic couldn't save us. Sierra's returned curse couldn't either. Nor Elm's dragons. Nor Kara's promise. Nor Amora's love.

Lire was always going to win. In the end, no matter how powerful we try to be, we're only mortal.

But . . . so was she, once, and she *doesn't* hold all the cards.

My eyes tear open, and Teddy is staring right at me, his empty gaze baring into my soul. Almost as if it's Lire looking through those eyes instead of him. Because of course she's keeping a close watch on me – she needs me alive to use me.

She needs me.

I'm the key.

I stamp up to Teddy, the two of us on either side of the purple shield of magic. Zeus gives me a wide berth, and I'm grateful for the space he's allowing me to think.

The others remain in their own internal battles. Arden and Sierra in each other's arms. Ebony and Levi side-by-side. But the Musan siblings still aren't here; even Wren hasn't shown up since shooting Rhiannon.

So no one stops me when I demand, right in Teddy's face, 'Tell Lire I want to talk.' I stare into his brown eyes and know that the bubbly, sweet boy everyone talks about isn't home. I can only hope he's not gone forever.

Wherever Maya and Dawn are, *they* should be here trying to save their sweethearts.

Lire – from twenty metres away where she's pulsing lilac into the growing rainbow of her enchantment – turns her head to me.

I do have bargaining power here.

She could find a way to force me to do whatever she needs. Throw me right into the white-hot centre of the magic. But I have time to get under her skin. If I talk to her, politician to politician, I could try to make a deal. My help for saving the lives of my friends.

The fairy won't agree, but I could buy us enough time for a real plan.

Lire doesn't come my way. She gestures me forward with a bent finger. Teddy steps aside, and I pass through the barrier of magic. Of course, it was never going to stop me.

'Isla,' Sierra warns, but I walk steadily away.

Unless Lire wants to fight me with her fists, she can't hurt me. And I imagine that fight as I approach her: wrapping my hands around her slender neck, squeezing until she collapses. It would feel good, but it wouldn't kill her. I'd need iron for that.

She already took all our weapons.

I face the lilac fairy with my hands at my sides. 'My mother,' I say. Candace is still wrapped in the corner, staring at me with gut-wrenching worry. Grace must have really beat her down. 'You'll show some honour by allowing her to stand with the others, rather than be tossed to the side.'

Lire continues working on her enchantment, barely giving me a glance. 'I'm simply keeping her tucked away so I can use her magic later.'

'You need me more than you need her,' I say, deadpan, 'so I'd think about who you want to use more.'

She turns her head, laughing. 'Bargaining? When you've already lost. Useless human.'

'Okay.' I shrug.

Her jaw hardens. 'Excuse me?'

'*Okay* – if I'm useless, I'll go and have Sierra kick the life out of me. Then no one gets what they want.'

The fairy huffs. '*What* do you want?'

Already, Relia is walking to Candace to bring her to the others. Zeus can check on her, much as they'll both hate that, but it's enough to take one problem off my mind. Relia waves away the magic around Candace and hauls her to her feet.

I try not to show my relief. 'Immunity,' I say. 'I want you to go back to your old world, and leave us to ours. You stop destroying everything, killing everyone, and I won't put up a fight. I'll even *help* you. I'll let you use the enchantment to portal yourself and the fairies out, and we'll keep our world.'

A raspy voice whispers in my ear, nearly making me jump. *There's something she doesn't want you to know.*

Kara? I turn to look at her, glimpsing her lips moving even as she pretends to focus on the enchantment. Quickly, I plant my eyes back on Lire so she doesn't realise what's happening.

You go into the enchantment of your own will, says Kara, and it's your choice. You decide whether to open or close it. You can keep this world safe. But if you go in and you lock that door, you can never return. You'll be stuck on the outside.

Lire is shaking her head at my request, and it gives me barely a moment to process Kara's secret words. My heart races so loudly I can barely hear my thoughts over its thunder.

I don't know that I can trust Kara, but she's the fairy I know best. I read her journal. I know how painful it is for her to be here now. She's only here because she believes she has no choice.

Kara and Lire haven't looked each other in the eyes once.

Kara has given me the answer I need. I *could* stop this. But even if I jump into that magic right now and close our world back up, that doesn't mean Lire's war will be over. She'll still be here to harm this world, and someday another child is going to slip through the borders. She'll get another key, and the cycle will continue.

'If I were you,' I say to Lire, her thick magic clouding my vision, 'I'd be taking me more seriously. I'm the only person in this room you can't touch, and the only person in this room you need. You even let Rhiannon die for you – but you'll keep me alive.'

More Lilac magic blows like steam out of her pinched nose. 'Only until I'm done using you.'

I scramble for conversation. 'What about Rhiannon and Muse? I thought you needed all the fairies' magic to do this.'

She returns to focusing on her enchantment, mesmerised by the glow. 'Their power is within me already. I *didn't* need them. I called their magic to me and it obeyed.'

The enchantment isn't open yet – it needs me in there first. But already, things are falling out of the sparks of rainbow: little toys, books, forks and spoons, just like in the borders. This power is only going to cause more damage, whether or not Lire's plan works.

'Yes, General.' Lire notes my fear. 'If it's opened, there will be incredible destruction. And if it isn't opened, there will be just as much. All that power has to go somewhere.'

Unless I can close it down from the inside.

'Do you have any more begging to do,' she teases, 'or may I return to my work?'

I *wish* I had more begging to do, but I'm fresh out of ideas. I turn to Zeus, searching for inspiration – when Maya and Dawn crash through the ballroom doors.

Fairies! My heart skips a beat. They command everyone's attention, and a new wave of nausea enters my gut.

Why are they back? Why now? And what's the reason for the heavy leather-bound book clutched in Maya's arms?

I trust them. I do. But their fiery gazes do little to inspire me.

Instinctively I move in front of Lire – I know their history enough to know the fairy *really* wants Maya dead.

Her wings poke into my periphery. 'You made me a promise, Maya Nova,' she says. 'Give me my prize.'

I spin back to the fairy. *Promise? Prize?*

She sends me a knowing, victorious look. 'Poor General Isla. You think you're some sort of chosen one. But you aren't *that* important to me. You're not all I'm here for.'

'What—' I look to Maya, but her expression gives me nothing. 'What is that book?'

Even Candace has gotten to her feet, my friends at the edge of their magical cage peering at us. The other fairies stare around with thinly veiled curiosity, attention to the enchantment waning.

Goosebumps run down my arms. This isn't right. This isn't part of the plan. This isn't—

I shake my head. If Maya knows what she's doing, and I have a feeling she does, I have to relinquish control.

'You don't need to pretend,' Maya says to me, stepping forward slowly, approaching Lire like she's a wild animal. 'You know this is Kara's diary.'

No. No it isn't. I'm not sure what to do, but I look at Kara, and she says nothing, stares blankly. Doesn't even whisper to me.

So I do it. I relinquish control. 'Maya, whatever you're thinking, do not give that diary to Lire. She can't know the secrets written inside.'

Or . . . *something*, I suppose? I can only hope I'm not getting in her way.

Maya disregards me. 'Lire. If I give you this book, do you accept my terms? Our lives spared in exchange for this information?'

The fairy's hands twitch beside me. She wants it terribly. Why? What does she think she'll find in there? What power does she think she'll gain?

I catch her eyes darting to Kara, her dark fairy.

Oh. It's nothing to do with power, or the end of the world. Kara has no schemes hidden away in the journal, but that isn't what Lire wants.

Lire *loved* Kara. They were inseparable, and that's why Kara's betrayal hurt Lire so terribly. She's desperate for Kara's inner thoughts. She wants Kara's vulnerability so badly she'd give anything for it. Even hundreds of years since they fell apart.

Kara. She is the one weakness Lire has left.

There's nothing that can distract Lire from her plans to take both worlds back – except the chance to finally, truly *win* against Kara. To open up her guarded, dark mind and see what's inside. To see if Kara ever really loved her.

I already let Maya read the real journal. But I don't understand – if this isn't it, what is she hoping to achieve? Lire will realise it's fake within minutes. Maya can make a good book, but it can't be that convincing of a duplicate.

Lire nods, starved. Maya moves to hand the book over, but I stop her. The fairy is unpredictable. I don't want Maya near her unless she has to be.

'Let me,' I tell her, and she hands it to me. The journal is heavy in my hands. Heavier than I expected. I try to glean any part of a hidden plan within it, but sense nothing. I face the fairy. 'Lire, I've read this. You might not want to know—'

She snatches it from me. Her skirts balloon around her as she drops to a crouch, sitting with the book in her lap. She carefully opens the first page, heaving, and I watch over her. I read the beautiful writing Maya copied from the real diary – the hand uncannily the same.

Real entries blend with made-up pages as Lire's pace accelerates from opening the believably-old paper slowly and cautiously to furiously tearing through the book.

Kara watches her with sad eyes. The other fairies move to her side, having lost interest in the slightly diminishing enchantment that still leaves rainbows cast on their faces. 'Lire,' Kara says softly. 'It was so long ago. Can we not move forward? I'm here with you now, aren't I?'

'Hush, monster,' Lire breathes. The pages further into the book are stuck together, and Lire licks her fingers to pry open each one, skimming the words. 'This is my last victory before my new world is born. The end to a story that has haunted me for centuries.'

Everyone watches on in horror, like witnessing a wolf tear apart a rabbit with its teeth, blood everywhere as we powerlessly stand by, unable to stop it. Unable to look away. No one seems sure what to do with themselves.

We didn't expect this.

How can a *book* have paralysed the fairy so deeply, put such a halt in her plans?

I try to think. Maya has brought us more time. Can I use it? Or does she already have a plan? She isn't moving, though. There's no secret she's trying to tell me or the others. If she has weapons hidden, she isn't making use of them while the fairy is down.

Lire licks her fingers again to turn to the next page, and the next. Her eyes water, and I wonder if she's crying. But she's too frantic for that, too excited. Everything she's ever wanted is finally coming together.

And instead of watching fearfully, Maya looks at the fairy with a smug little grin on her face, arms crossed. Dawn, beside her, looks equally as unbothered by the ordeal, even with the enchantment above us threatening the lives of everyone in the world.

They have to have a plan.

Lire clears her throat, then shudders. *Is* she crying? But that's not—

She sniffles, rubbing her eyes, then continues flipping through the pages. The fairy starts coughing, rubbing her eyes more.

I take a few steps back. A shiver tickles the back of my neck. Something is wrong here, and I don't know what it is, but it's so obvious now I can almost touch it.

One more page, and as Lire tears the sticky edges apart, a cloud of dust puffs out of the book. She chokes on it, tries to wave away the particles, but even as they settle her eyes are red and watering.

She's hacking like there's something lodged in her throat.

Her wide, bloodshot eyes shoot up to Maya. 'Wha—' she starts, but she doubles over in a fit of coughs.

'Oh, Lire!' says Maya, finally reanimated, like she's just woken up in the middle of a party. 'One thing I forgot to tell you. I inlaid the pages with ground iron . . .' She offers a big, sarcastic shrug. 'You poor, naïve little fairy.'

The pages are smoking now as Lire's magic fights the iron dust still lifting. She clutches her throat, pushing the book away from her. It steams across the floor. Lilac magic pulses through her body, an inner glow on her neck and chest as her being tries to reject the metal.

But it's in her lungs, her blood.

The other fairies watch mutely. In awe. Shock. Devastation, even. But everyone is so still. No one knows what move to make.

Surely someone here has an iron sword? Someone must have *something* we can finish the job with. Otherwise what's this all for?

The magical barrier Teddy and Relia put up against the others lowers as Lire's hold on her children ebbs. They're still controlled, but the power is weak. Are they fighting back, trapped in their own minds?

'T-Teddy— Relia—' The fairy tries to call to them, her back retching up and down as her face touches the broken tiles. 'Stop her— Someone— Adella, Amora— *Kill them*. I want Maya and Dawn d-d . . .'

The fairies ignore her. She's lost the two sisters who were truly on her side. The others are only here because they saw no other choice. Why would they help her now? The coven is broken. Their leader is weak. They bet on the wrong team.

Teddy and Relia step forward, their hands circled with Lire's magic. The control in their eyes is lessening, and they shake their heads, but it's still too powerful.

'If y-you let me die,' the fairy chokes out, 'you won't get them back. My magic won't die with m-me. They'll remain dead inside.'

With a laugh, Maya says, 'Did you think we wouldn't know you'd stoop that low? Did you think after all of this we wouldn't know how to bring them back if you tried to take them for yourself again?'

She moves to Teddy tenderly – not a care in the world about the dangerous magic he holds, ready to kill her – and pulls him into a kiss. A burst of purple sparks out from them, and when Maya pulls back, Teddy's face is once more full of expression.

I stare at them with my jaw on the tiles. How is this *real?*

'Um . . .' Teddy starts. 'That was nice, thank you. But why are we kiss—' He catches the glowing enchantment and shuts his mouth.

Dawn places a gentle hand on the back of Relia's neck. 'How many times have we been here?' she says, pulling her lover into a kiss of their own. The same sparks, the same beautiful spill of power. 'When has a kiss of love ever not worked, Lire? *You* taught me about their power to break enchantments. You invented the rule.'

Lire is now convulsing on the floor, an insect taking its last breaths, poisoned, scared, and alone. But I can't feel sorry for her – not after all she's done. In fact, she deserves much worse than the mercy of letting her die before everyone gets their chance to take their revenge.

Something bursts past Teddy and Relia's melting barrier – Sierra in the air, the black swan beating its wings.

I shuffle backwards, out of her way. *What's she thinking?* She has waves of magic waving around her as she rises. From her wings, rings of bright blue magic blow, pouring out of every feather as she slows and points them at Lire.

It's happening so quickly I'm not sure where or who I am for a second. I'm in the air, and I'm the book, and I'm the fairy, and then I realise I'm on my knees, so I scurry back to Zeus.

There's nothing I can do. My body tingles with the need to join the fight.

Trust Sierra Reed.

The fairy weeping on the floor doesn't see the immense amount of magic coming. Not from the swan. Not from Arden. Not from Teddy and Relia, my mother, and Amora and Adella and Grace, who can't know what Sierra is doing but add their power anyway, a storm engulfing Lire.

Everyone in this room wants to be free of her control.

Everyone except Kara, who simply watches on, heartbreak in her gaze.

Magic flickers, forming a globe around the lilac fairy as she screams. And *screams.* Deathly screams of hatred, or revenge, of terrible loss. Of knowing she has no one and nothing.

And when the magic begins to subside, her purple wings fade with every flutter. They lose their visibility, their realness, until there's barely anything there. Until the low back of her dress reveals nothing but skin.

Her hair and skin dull. She turns sallow and paper thin, her dress hanging lankly on her body as hundreds of years of her madness descend upon her at once.

I cup a hand over my mouth. Sierra had two curses planned for today. She brought back the swan. And she cursed the fairy to become human.

Maya jumps atop Lire and a gasp shocks through the room. Before anyone can say otherwise, the Bearran stabs the mortal fairy right in the heart.

My vision blurs.

What . . . ? What?

Maya heaves, blood spurting on her face as she carves the knife in deeper. 'I win, fairy,' she hisses, Lire fighting for breath beneath her. '*I. Win.*'

So she *did* have an iron weapon concealed on her; she just waited for the exact right moment. It didn't even need to be iron, not with the fairy turned mortal. But she had a plan. Maya Nova saved us.

Of course she did. She told me herself she set this entire war in motion. I should have believed her.

Kara hurries to Lire, shooing Maya away, the knife left in Lire's chest. Maya obeys, falling back to Teddy. Her job done.

He places an arm over her, his jaw set. The boy can't tear his eyes from his dying mother, but he's clearly in pain. Lire's magic tries to go to him, next in line for all that power, but he ushers it away and it seeps back into the ground. Towards the triarue below the castle.

We all take a step back, holding our collective breath as we watch an unkillable immortal die.

Muse. Rhiannon. Lire. All the constants of the world shift once more.

Kara turns Lire around and holds her in her lap. 'I'm sorry,' Kara whispers. 'I'm so sorry this is what became of us.'

Lire meets her eyes, no longer able to speak. There is so much loss and heartache in her gaze, so many years of utter loneliness in a chase for something she could never truly achieve.

Wheezing, she puts her hand around the hilt of the knife, awing at the blood. With a shuddering heave, she pulls it out. Any last tendrils of magic leave in the flow of red that pours from the wound, staining her once-perfect dress.

Lire turns the blade in her weak hands. With a strength and speed I didn't know she still possessed she— she—

She stabs Kara through the chest.

Kara flinches and folds, gasping before pulling out the knife and tossing it to the floor. 'What have you—'

Scarlet bleeds across the broken tiles, seeping into cracks, into the earth beneath, as Lire's life returns to the world it created. Kara's magic follows, a dark snake, a shadow.

Always Lire's shadow, so of course one couldn't live without the other.

With clasping hands and teary eyes, Kara's wings fall over the two as they die in each other's arms. The moth's eyes protect them even in death.

CHAPTER TWENTY-SEVEN

Amora, Adella, Grace. The remaining fairies stand gobsmacked and uncertain, three of seven.

More than half our deities are dead.

Adella tries to run, but the third dragon appears from behind the walls, landing before her with a thud and baring its teeth. The golden fairy reels back, screeching.

'No!' I yell at the creature, made of Adella's own magic. Its maw smokes with threatened fire. '*Down.*'

Elm, Gus, Lark, and Wren crawl out from behind it. So *that's* where the Musans were. Protecting Elm and Gus while they took care of our enchanted weapons.

'Don't kill me!' Adella begs, but the dragon, obeying my order as its general, has crouched into submission.

Grace and Amora exchange a look. 'They aren't going to kill you,' says Grace. 'But they might consider it if you act a fool.'

Adella shudders.

Elm sidles up to me. 'Lire's magic was dripping down into the mines,' they explain. 'We came up to see, well . . .'

'If the world ended?' suggests Maya, scratching at a forming bruise on her neck while smiling at my friend. 'You're just in time, because it didn't.'

Not *yet.* I give Elm a grateful look, but the enchantment still swirls around us. A foolish part of me hoped it would die with Lire, but it's as if her unmoored power has only fed it more with her dying breaths, making that rainbow above us even brighter, more violent in its white-centred whirlpool.

I can close it. But I can never come back.

Kara's warning haunts me, because . . . we've won. Haven't we? So why does it feel like the threat is getting bigger, calling me to finish the fight?

Relia stares at her hands – Zeus too, since he's had a huge arm around her since she became un-possessed. 'It's sapping my magic,' she says from the prince's armpit. Wispy clouds of lilac float from her and into the Lire's enchantment.

Dawn takes her hand. 'We need to close it. Now.'

The ground tremors and I crouch to steady myself. *Fairies.* The enchantment can't work fully unless I unlock it, but it's certainly trying. Nudging at our world, taking our magic and, based on the impact we just felt, pulling down the walls of ice. This place is crashing, and it doesn't matter that Lire is dead.

The colours swirling above and around us are no longer beautiful. This rainbow isn't a signal of passing rain. It's the threat of an even greater storm. A storm only I can protect us from.

The enchantment is hungry. Everyone with magic has colour falling off them in waves – Teddy, Sierra, Arden, the fairies. Even Dawn, with all her blessings, seems to be confused and wavering at the edges of her being, that magic simmering around and out of her.

I nearly lose my footing as the ground rumbles again. Buildings *crash* as they collapse in the distance.

Sierra demands, 'How do we fix this? Any ideas? Fairies?'

Amora steps forward, shoulders drooped. 'It can't be stopped.' Her rainbow wings are dulling to grey, so much of her magic now consumed by the enchantment. 'It will only grow.'

Maya sends a glare her way. 'We don't want to hear from you, traitor.'

'Sweetheart, I didn't *want* to—'

'But you did,' says Teddy, dark rings around his eyes.

The passion fairy's lips twitch, but she meets his gaze. '*Please* understand. Lire destroyed my city and threatened to kill me too. She had my people in her estate, under her control. What did you want me to do? Yell and scream and get everyone killed? I acted as her friend to save us.' Her fingers clasp pleadingly. 'There was nothing more I could do than remain by her side until someone could save me. Which you *did.* And I'll be forever indebted to you, Teddy, so why will you not let me help you now?'

Teddy and Maya share a glance. 'We'll discuss it later,' says Maya. 'Once the rest of this is sorted out. But I don't want to hear any more from you right now, Amora.'

I bristle. That kind of harshness is to be expected from Maya Nova, but somehow I sympathise with the fairy. We're all surviving in our own ways. We've all done things that have hurt others, even when trying our best to do good.

Candace massages her bruised collarbone. Was I too harsh on her? I'm so far past resentment now that I feel guilty for ever pushing her away.

'Mum,' I call her over, and gesture for Zeus and Elm to follow. I need to speak with them privately before I do what I have to. Before I close the enchantment and leave them forever.

We move out of the ballroom and into a long corridor. It takes a while to see properly after the brightness of the rainbow, and I nearly rub my eyes before remembering my hands are covered in blood, dirt, and grime.

Zeus sticks next to me, our arms pressed together. *Fairies,* I wish I'd never fallen in love with him. It makes this sacrifice even harder to make.

In the ballroom, the others are discussing what they're going to do about the enchantment. What they're going to do now the war is over. They don't know I'm going to fix it. But I need time to come to terms with this myself before they all try to weigh in.

'What's wrong, sugar?' asks Candace. Her green dress is torn all over, her arms and legs covered in scratches. My mind flashes with the memory of her beaten down by Grace, crumpled in the corner of the ballroom like an old, forgotten doll. Even all her magic, all her strength, wasn't enough to keep her from harm.

How can I leave her?

I try to swallow the lump in my throat. 'Kara told me I can close the enchantment,' I explain. 'I'm the key. I can unlock it, or, I suppose, lock it back up.' At once, Candace, Zeus, and Elm untense with relief. I quickly add, bursting their bubble before I lose my nerve, 'But once I close it, I'll be stuck on the outside.'

'Excuse me?' Candace says with a scoff. 'No. We'll close it another way.'

'Or we could just leave it open.' Elm suggests, their big brown eyes so childlike yet so tired. 'Why not? Lire trapped us here against our will. We could reopen this world to the old one, like it's meant to be.'

'We can't.' I cross my arms. I won't be swayed, not even by those doe-eyes. 'I want to protect the world we have. We don't know what's out there, how dangerous it is, if they'd accept our return. We can't risk the millions of people here on an unknown place. In Kara's journal, she said users of magic were condemned, even killed. If we bring magic back to a world like that, what could happen to our people? People like *you*,' I say pointedly to Candace and Elm. 'Besides, I need to close it before it causes more damage.'

Candace huffs. 'The *only* way I'd let you do that is if I come with you.'

'Mum, no.' My voice cracks. 'This world needs you to command it. With half the fairies dead, magic all over the place . . . You need to be here to protect our people. To bring back the empire.'

'Then *I'm* coming,' says Elm, but there's a tremor in their hands.

I tilt my head. 'Snow angel, I will always want you by my side, but this world needs you too. You can help rebuild. You can give our people hope. And you're too wonderful for me to risk out there.'

'But what about all you've worked for?' Candace pleads. 'You finally won, sugar. You can't give it up now.' She pauses. 'Please.' She says it like a question; she knows I won't change my mind.

The back of my nose stings and I cover my eyes for a moment. 'I know. But if I can save all these people, my sacrifice will be worth it. I'll be giving my power up, but it'll allow the world to go on without me. Protected by *you.*'

She wipes her eyes. There's another obvious reason the decision is already made. It's a chance for me to go home, to really find out who I am.

Zeus has been quiet this whole time, biting his lower lip, so I meet his eyes. 'I'm so sorry,' I tell him. 'I do love you, but I have to take care of my – *our* – people. I'll miss you so much, Zeus—'

'Absolutely not.' He stares at me with the most serious expression I've ever seen on him, and for a second I'm taken aback. My stomach twists with heat. 'They're not going,' he says, 'but I am.'

'*Zeus*—'

'This world can survive without me. But I can't survive without you, Isla. Besides, you're not going into all of that unknown without protection.'

I want to roll my eyes, make him shake off his bravado, but this isn't ego. He's being so genuine it hurts.

'Listen,' I try to explain. 'Everything we've fought over all these years, I'm handing to you. You won't have to compete with me anymore. You don't have to compromise and make me your princess. I'm giving up all we ever wanted. It's all yours.'

'*You* are what I want. You're more to me than this small world. We'll find new horizons to make our own, wherever we end up. Together.'

'Don't,' says Elm. Tears spill on their cheeks. 'Stop it. You can't both leave me. You can't. I'll find a way to stop the enchantment. You know I can do it. I'll—'

'You won't be alone,' Zeus says. 'The Bearrans will take care of you. Relia will love you, I know it. You're going to be safe, and so are we, and it's going to be absolutely detestably awful, but we can live with it.'

I pull Elm into a hug, burying my face in their soft, warm shoulder. '*Please,*' they whisper.

Zeus gives us a long moment before hauling Elm into a hug of their own, and I nearly pull them apart. 'Zeus,' I groan. 'I appreciate the offer, but you are *not* coming with me.'

Because how could I possibly allow him to fall into the same trap I have? Give everything up for me? What if he gets there and hates it, and grows to resent me, and—

Candace takes my hand and pulls me to her, while Zeus pouts at me with his chin atop Elm's head. 'Sugar,' my mother says, 'he's going with you. You have to let him. Even if it's more for my sake than yours. I couldn't live knowing you were out there alone.'

She dabs my eyes, and I notice even more bruises on her face.

I can't bear it. I can't bear to leave her. And Elm. My family. I *can't.*

'Let me tell you this before you go.' Candace sniffles. She tucks a strand of hair behind my ear. 'Thank you, thank you endlessly, for letting me be your mother. If you ever find your real family, tell them I'm so grateful for my time with their baby. Tell them they created the most wonderful, strong woman in the world.'

'No,' I cry. 'Mum, you made me who I am. You're my real family. Please don't say—'

She runs her hand up and down my arm. 'I know you won't forget me, Isla. Whenever you feel scared out there, whenever you feel alone, or lost, remember I'll be thinking of you every second. Remember we'll always be together. And you'll always be okay.'

I hold my hand over my mouth, my fingers slick with tears. 'I— I'll miss you so much.' I let her hug me, her arms securing me tightly for the last time.

I'm a little girl again, and she's cleaning up a knee grazed after running through the city, and she's teaching me to fight with a blunted sword, and she's singing me to sleep after a nightmare.

'Come on,' she says.

Zeus squeezes my hand, and I know Candace is right. I do need him. He has to come with me.

Finally, I have to let him in. Fully. Entirely. Because I don't need his power, his protection. But I do need his love.

I wipe my nose with my jacket sleeve, and we return to the ballroom, much to the confusion of the others. The enchantment has grown further, a sun stretching in every direction, auroras of every colour emanating around it.

A masterpiece I have to destroy.

Zeus hurries to say goodbye to the others. He makes a belated apology to Sierra for abandoning her a lifetime ago. He nearly bowls over Levi, scrubbing his hair. Shakes Dawn's hand. And while there are tears all round, Relia is the one who falls to her knees.

He gives her a hug so consuming she disappears for a few moments. Her cries echo in the ballroom, louder than the whooshing of objects falling from the enchantment, the tremors in the ground. Dawn has to help her up so Zeus can leave.

My heart breaks anew for him, because he's doing this for me. Giving up his world, his best friends. Yet as selfish as it is, I need him more than they do. I'm *happy* he's coming with me.

Rather than say goodbye to the others, I stay with Candace and Elm. I don't want or need to explain myself to anyone else. I'll miss these people, their drama, their banter. This tragedy and comedy of a kingdom. But I'm not caught in that web anymore. Not Bearra's, not the Ice Empire's, not the fairies'.

I'm free.

The remaining fairies look upon us with trepidation. Would they come with us, if I gave them the choice to return to their original home?

I don't make any offers. This is their world, and they need to help piece it back together now. That's their consequence for helping Lire.

Zeus rejoins me, taking my hand firmly. 'We're going to be okay out there,' he says, not a doubt in his voice. 'Who says we can't create a new empire, my princess?'

I allow myself the slightest hint of a smile. I'll be leaving a lot behind, but there is so much out there for me to discover, to conquer. So many people I can help. My birth family to find.

Maybe this is what I've been chasing my entire life – I just didn't know it before. Maybe I have gotten my happy ending.

I kiss my mother on both cheeks, then cup Elm's face and tell them they're going to be okay. My heart races and aches at the same time. I want to stop time, sit in this moment with them, have treats from the empire one last time, play in Elm's workshop, sit by the fire with my mother.

Instead I lift my chin and channel the immovability of a mountain, holding back the sobs that want to retch through me. If I'm going to leave this world, I'm going to leave it strong.

Zeus is crying too, blowing kisses to his friends. But he's so good – so good to give it all up with me. He doesn't hesitate. He follows my steps.

Dawn mouths, *thank you,* while Maya gives me a reassuring nod, and I know I'm doing the right thing. I can relinquish control of this world, because I'm leaving it in the best hands.

Zeus and I step through the growing aura as the ground trembles again, hand in hand. We don't stumble.

I'm going to save this world.

My skin prickles and my body shivers, but the enchantment can't hurt me. Because this is what I was made for. The orphan, the general, the key.

In the white light I can't see Elm and Candace anymore, and suddenly Zeus disappears as well. We're entirely swallowed up. My world and my life already so far behind me.

I don't know where we're going. Who we'll be when we get there.

My arms curl around Zeus's neck, his coolness always there, even when I can't see it. He'll be my home now.

When I pull him into a kiss, it's even brighter than all this light. More magical than all the enchantment billowing around us.

White turns to black.

EPILOGUE

HERE AND NOW…

The laughs of the baby woke Maya Nova far too early, but she could never hold her frustration – not when it came to her niece. She raced downstairs to join Prima, Matthew, and Livvy, pulling the little girl out of her crib as her parents teased her.

Maya kissed the baby's little pink cheeks. 'Your mummy and daddy are just awful,' she cooed. 'Aunty Maya is here now. I'm your favourite. Remember?' She blew a raspberry on Livvy's belly, eliciting more little giggles.

Whenever Maya felt exhausted from all she'd been through, she only had to look at Livvy, and then out at the beautiful, enchanted world the bubbly baby was growing up in. Maya would know, then, that everything had been worth it.

And not just for Livvy, but for Prima, so she could enjoy motherhood in a safe place, in a real home. They all deserved peace and happiness.

Despite all they'd lost, there was still so much to delight in.

Teddy was already knocking at the door with a tray of breakfast from the castle – as he did every morning. Though he and Maya didn't live together, that often didn't keep the pair apart.

In fact, between her friends and family, no one was ever alone for long. It would be dinner in the castle one night, lunch by the canal the next day.

Dawn and Relia remained in the castle with Teddy, and while the pirates often visited, they could be anywhere in the world on the *Neptune*. Briar, Lark, and Wren took residence in Aunt Olivia's house with Maya's father, and Maya had moved into her old family home with Prima, Matthew, and the baby. Gus and Elm went to the Ice Empire to help Candace, and as for Isla and Zeus, Maya could only hope they were alive and well.

In short, there was always *someone* around. Someone who needed help with something, or who wanted to explore a market, read together, garden, or sew or—

Maybe it would be nice for Maya to have a day to herself.

She and Teddy were looking for a small place of their own, but they weren't ready to be tied down. They wanted to travel. Sierra and her crew had been gone months now, only the occasional note sent back detailing their adventures. Maya longed to join her. Wind in her hair, mysteries and stories on every horizon.

But they were going to wait a little while. Spend time with Livvy, help Dawn and Relia rebuild Bearra. The walls were down, and Darraport and Naroport were using the freshly reopened canals to bring in trade. Bearra was returning to the sparkling, rich kingdom it was a century ago.

Maya swung open the front door and went to kiss Teddy's blushy cheeks as he came inside – but she feigned and kissed the top of the silver tray instead. 'Strawberries?'

He laughed. 'And raspberries, and blueberries . . .'

She took the tray and pecked him on the lips. 'You're incredible.'

'I like to think so. But these came from the chefs, who washed them in the kitchens, where they were delivered by a very lovely fruitmonger, who brought them all the way from Adella's Territory, where the farmers grew them . . .'

She placed the tray on the kitchen bench and popped a strawberry between her teeth. 'Mhm. Then they're all incredible too,' she mumbled over the mouthful. Biting down, all the wonders of the world exploded over her tongue. *Thank the fairies*, or better, thank *herself*.

This was her world more than theirs now.

Teddy grinned at her widely, so much adoration in those chocolate eyes. This over-the-top romance would have been a little sickening to Maya once, but now she grinned right back. She was so giddy. Someone as loving as *him* cared for *her* with all his heart.

As a pair, they were doing so much better. Healing themselves after all they'd been through. Healing their relationship. Talking. Talking so much, every day, getting it all out in the open.

And Maya was content. More than she ever thought she could be, more than she thought she'd be once, with the crown. Because this wasn't a cover up, a bandage over a broken limb. This was real joy, from the inside out.

Her friends were safe. Her family was happy.

She had an entire world to enjoy. And it wouldn't be simple or easy, not ever, but she was filled to the brim with excitement.

Maya slung her arms over Teddy's shoulders, bringing him down for a long kiss that made her heart burst with love. Such a real, true, genuine love that it could break any curse, save any world.

·♡· ♠ 🎩 ♠ ·♡·

Maya tied her shoelaces, packed her bag, and checked her map one last time. The world had changed, and with Teddy by her side, her friends awaiting her, and endless miles of journeys ahead, Maya planned on getting completely, utterly lost.

The End

Acknowledgements

Woken Kingdom has been a huge part of the last three years of my life, and become such an integral part of my identity that ending the series, letting it go with this finale, feels like a relief, a huge achievement, and a massive loss. I haven't figured out yet how to say goodbye to this world I've lived in so long, and these characters that feel like family to me – especially when their voices are talking over each other in my head, telling me how to write my own story.

I hope you're feeling similarly bittersweet, having read the final pages and finished this journey with me. I hope you gained something from this series: maybe you learned to let yourself soften from Maya; perhaps you came to terms with your anger through Sierra; or Relia might have taught you patience and self-love. Each Woken Kingdom main character had a stubbornness they needed to ease, or a lack of faith in themselves and others they needed to heal.

Isla is no exception. She follows this pattern of healing (spoiler alert, these books are just about me, in the end), learning that true strength comes when you learn to love yourself and others. You can hide and hide behind the power you mask yourself with – money, intelligence, creativity, brute strength, skill – but there is so much joy in discovering your truest self. Woken Kingdom has taught me that, and I'll always be in gratitude to each of these characters, who have taught me so much about myself.

So, let's do the acknowledging and talk about the people who have helped me create my fairytale.

I sometimes wish I had editors who take one look at my work and say, 'This is a masterpiece, don't change a thing,' but I'm very grateful to have a brilliant team who are honest and intelligent. Pauline Menchavez, Ellyssa Paik, and Lizzie Augustine are creative geniuses with eagle eyes. Not every author gets to have such a wonderful publishing family – especially when self-publishing – and I'm well aware I'm very, very lucky the universe sent these three to me.

Haylee Buswell has created yet another cover of my dreams, and the most adorable interior designs. I also have to once again thank my late grandfather Robert Ixer for the cover art. This one is my favourite.

To my family and friends, and especially to my writer friends from near and far, thank you endlessly for supporting me. Sometimes I forget to feel proud of what I've created, and having people across the globe cheer me on and help me advocate for myself and my books is absolutely unreal.

So, with a warm but broken heart, this is my goodbye to Woken Kingdom. Thank you Maya, Sierra, Relia, Isla, and everyone else. The boys I fell in love with as I wrote them, the villains I loathed even though I created them, every side character I tried to remember, and of course the magical, ethereal fairies.

I'm never going to stop writing and publishing books, but my debut series years are over. Does it get easier from here, or harder? Only time will tell.

Thank you, thank you, thank you.

With all my love,
Princess Poppy.

Follow @PoppysVintageBooks on Instagram and TikTok for Woken Kingdom content, and sign up to the Poppy's Pages mailing list for sneak peeks at upcoming stories!

poppyspagesediting.com/newsletter-sign-up

About the Author

Poppy Rose Solomon's YA novels reflect the traumas and lessons she experienced as a teenager, and she loves creating 'unlikable' characters who learn to heal themselves. Evoking inspiration and escapism is the goal of her storytelling. From her home in Tasmania, she freelances as a YA editor and coach through her business Poppy's Pages, and runs the Writing YA With Poppy podcast. Woken Kingdom is her first series, with plenty more to come.